JENNIFER ARMINTROUT

Blood Ties Book One: The Turning

"Every character is drawn in vivid detail,
driving the action from point to point
in a way that never lets up."
— *The Eternal Night*

"[Armintrout's] use of description
varies between chilling, beautiful,
and disturbing...[a] unique take on vampires."
— *The Romance Readers Connection*

Blood Ties Book Two: Possession

"Armintrout continues her Blood Ties series
with style and verve, taking the reader
to a completely convincing but alien world where
anything can—and does—happen."
— *Romantic Times BOOKreviews*
[four-star review]

"The relationships between the characters
are complicated and layered in ways that
many authors don't bother with."
— *Vampire Genre*

Blood Ties Book Three: *Ashes to Ashes*

Blood Ties Book Four: *All Souls' Night*

JENNIFER ARMINTROUT

QUEENE OF LIGHT

A LIGHTWORLD/DARKWORLD NOVEL

MIRA®

ISBN-13: 978-0-7783-2662-5

QUEENE OF LIGHT

www.MIRABooks.com

Printed in U.S.A.

To me, this book symbolizes a beautiful flower that grew out of the rotting rib cage of a murder victim abandoned in a shallow grave. Thank you to everyone who made that weekend such a horrible experience and forced me to retreat into a fantasy world where a sewer full of monsters offered more hospitable company than yours.

Nice people and objects that made this book possible were the Friday Night Mudslingers, my supportive family, Diet Coke, and Emmy Rossum's *Inside Out* album.

One

In the Darkworld, the filth made it difficult to fly. Faery wings were far too gossamer and fragile to withstand the moisture that dripped from the murky blackness overhead or the clinging grime that coated everything, even sentient things, that dared cross over the Darkworld border.

Ayla knelt in the mire, searching the mucky concrete ground for signs of her quarry. She'd had no problem tracking the Werewolf this far. The foolish creature did not even realize it was being followed, and her wings, not delicately made but leathery flaps of nearly Human skin, thick boned and heavy against her back, had given her the speed to keep up with him as he rampaged through the depths of the Darkworld. But they had made her too conspicuous. As she tracked the Wolf, something tracked her.

She heard it, lurking behind her. Whatever followed had wings, feathered, if she guessed correctly from the rustling that echoed through the tunnel like tiny thunder. Perhaps it thought she wouldn't hear it. Or couldn't.

The chill that raced up her spine had little to do with the gusts of cold air that blew through the tunnels. She knew the beast that followed her. She'd heard it spoken of in hushed tones in the Assassins' Guild training rooms. It was a Death Angel.

The stories were too numerous to sort fact from fiction. Some claimed an Angel had the powers of the Vanished Gods. Some dismissed them as no more powerful than a Faery or Elf. And some insisted that to look upon one was death to any creature, mortal or Fae. Once, not long after Ayla had begun her formal Guild training, an Assassin was lost. His body was recovered, impaled upon his own sword, wings ripped from his back. She'd seen him, though Garret, her mentor, had tried to shield her. The marks on the Faery's ashen flesh indicated he had not been cut, but torn, as if by large, clawed hands. The killing blow had come as a mercy.

Whatever the Death Angels were, they did not look kindly upon other immortal creatures.

The blood pounded in her veins as she forced

herself to focus on resuming the trail of her Wolf. Pursued or not, she had an assignment to carry out. Until the Death Angel struck, she would ignore his presence.

Closing her eyes, Ayla called up the training she'd received. She reached out with her sightless senses. She could not smell the Wolf, not above the stench of the sewer. She could not hear it. The irritated buzz of her antennae, an involuntary reaction to the tension vibrating through her body, coupled with the rustling of the Death Angel's wings in the shadows behind her, drowned out all other noise. She reached her hands out, feeling blindly across the pocked concrete of the tunnel wall. Deep gouges scored the surface, filled with fading rage. Her fingers brushed the residual energy and her mind lit up with a flare of red. The Wolf had passed this way.

Rising to her feet slowly, she traced the walls with her hands. Here was a splash of blood, blossoming with a neon-bright flare of pain behind her closed eyelids. Innocent, simple blood. There would be a body.

In a crouch, she moved through the tunnel, her arms low to the ground, trailing through the congealed filth there. Something dripped farther down the tunnel. It was audible, like a drop falling from a spigot to a full bucket. There was water ahead.

Dirty water, no doubt contaminated by waste from the Human world above, and the Wolf's victim would be there, as well; the despair and fear of its last moments tainted the air.

She followed the trail of blood and pain, the water rising to her knees, then to her waist. Something brushed her bare skin below the leather of her vest, and her eyes flew open. Floating beside her, split neck to groin, the empty skin of a rat. The Wolf had come this way to feed.

Summoning energy from her chest, she directed it into a ball in her palm. The orb flared bright, and she tossed it above her head to illuminate the space. To her left, another tunnel led deeper into the Darkworld. Another opened ahead of her. In the yolk of the three tunnels, hundreds of eviscerated rats bobbed in the stinking tide.

Rats. My life is forfeit for the sake of rats.

Wading through the sewage, she made her way to a low ledge. Another body waited there. The Werewolf, already twisted and stiff in death, caught between his Wolf and Human states. The grinning rictus of his Human mouth below his half-transformed snout gave testimony to the poison that had killed him before she could, and would have killed the rats if he'd not gotten to them first.

It was said among the Assassins of the Lightworld that Death Angels wait in the shadows for the souls of mortal creatures. The one that had followed the Wolf's trail behind her would not be pleased to find her there when he came to claim his prize.

She spun to face the Death Angel, caught sight of it in her rapidly fading light. Paper-white skin stretched over a hard, muscular body that could have been Human but for the claws at its hands and feet. It hung upside down, somehow gripping the smooth ceiling of the tunnel, its eyes sightless black mirrors that reflected her terrified face. It hissed, spreading its wings, and sprang for her.

Gulping as much of the fetid air as her lungs could hold, Ayla dove into the water. The echo of the creature's body disturbing the surface rippled around her, urging her to swim faster, but her wings twisted in the currents, slowing her and sending shocks of pain through her bones. She propelled herself upward and broke into the air gasping.

In a moment, the creature had her, his claws twisting in her loosened braid. He jerked her head back, growling a warning in a harsh, guttural language. He disentangled his claws from her hair and gripped her shoulder in one massive fist, his other hand raised to strike.

The moment his palm fell on her bare shoulder, she saw the change come over him. Red tentacles of energy climbed like ivy over his fingers, gaining his wrist, twining around his thick, muscled forearm. His hand spasmed and flexed on her arm but he was unable to let go, tied to her by the insidious red veins.

That was another rumor she'd heard about Death Angels. Though they craved mortal souls, the touch of a creature with mortal blood was bitter poison.

With a gasp of disbelief and satisfaction, she raised her eyes to the face of the Death Angel. His eyes, occluded with blood, fixed on her as the veins crept up his neck, covering his face.

"I am half Human," she said with a cruel laugh of relief. Whether the creature understood her or not, she did not care. He opened his mouth and screamed, his voice twisting from a fierce, spectral cry to a Human wail of pain and horror. Ayla's heart thundered in her chest and she closed her eyes, dragging air into her painfully constricted lungs. In her mind she saw the tree of her life force, its roots anchoring her feet, its branches reaching into her arms and head. Great, round sparks of energy raced to the Angel's touch, where her life force pulsed angry red. The pace of the moving energy quickened with her heartbeat, growing impossibly rapid, building and swelling within her until she could no longer withstand the assault.

She wrenched her shoulder free and staggered back, slipping to her knees in the water, sputtering as the foulness invaded her mouth.

The Death Angel stood as if frozen in place, twisting in agony. The stark red faded into his preternaturally white skin. His bloody, empty eyes washed with white, then a dot of color pierced their center. Mortal eyes, mortal color. A mortal body. Ayla clambered to her feet and stared in shock, the rush of her blood and energy still filling her ears. All at once it stopped, and the Death Angel collapsed, disappearing below the water.

In the still of the tunnel, Ayla listened for any other presence. Only the gentle lapping of the water against the curved walls of the tunnel could be heard, no fearsome rustling of wings. Would another Death Angel come for him, now that he was to die a mortal death?

He burst up through the water with a pitiable cry, arms flailing. Ayla screamed, jumping immediately to an attack stance, twin blades drawn. She relaxed when the now-mortal creature dragged himself from the water with shaking arms to collapse on the ledge. His chest heaved with each jerky breath of his newborn lungs, and his limbs trembled with exhaustion. He was no immediate threat.

Curiosity overcame Ayla's training, which dictated she should kill the Darkling where he lay. How many Assassins had the chance to survey their prey this closely? How many had the chance to destroy a Death Angel? Her weapons still at the ready, still poised to carry her into legend with the kill, she moved closer.

The Angel lay on his back, his ebony feathered wings folded beneath him. His hair, impossibly long, lay matted and wet on the cement, dipping into the water. The fierce muscle structure that had made him so strong remained, but his body twitched, sapped of strength.

It seemed wrong, cowardly to kill him in such a state.

An Assassin knows no honor. An Assassin knows no pity. An Assassin is no judge to bestow mercy, but the executioner of those who have already been sentenced, those Darklings who shun the truth of Light. The geis, seared into her brain through hours of endless repetition, burned her anew, and she lifted her knives to deliver the killing blow. His eyes slid open, flickered over her hands and the weapons she held.

With a deep breath and a whispered prayer, Ayla closed her eyes. "Badb, Macha, Nemain, guide my hand that you might collect your trophy sooner than later."

He made no noise as her daggers fell. If he had,

perhaps she would have been able to finish the job. But when she opened her eyes, saw the flashing blades poised to pierce his throat and sever his spine, saw his face impassive…

Her hands opened and the knives clattered to the ledge. She did not retrieve them. Let him have something to defend himself from the creatures that would come for him, the ones who would not kill him as quickly as she would have, if she had been mindful of the geis. She had never broken an oath in her life, but no power on Earth or in the long dissipated Astral Realms could turn her head to look on him again or stop her as she waded into the tunnel that had brought her there.

He cried out then, when she was out of sight, but it was not to her. Probably to his One God, begging for help. But there had never been a God or Goddess in the Underground. Ayla knew she alone heard his prayer, and it haunted her all the way to the Lightworld.

Two

~∽◦◦∽~

Malachi never understood why they fell. Mortals were so bland and pink and fleshy. So uninteresting when compared to the glory of Heaven. Why fall, just to become one of them and whither and die, growing old with each breath?

As he did now.

After the foolish Humans had split the veil with their love of chants and regressions and crystal energies, after Hell and Heaven flooded onto Earth like a great, hopeless tidal wave, after the mortals had banished the creatures they once revered to the Underground, then he understood why an Angel might be tempted to fall. Unending existence became torture when separated from the Creator. Resentment of the Humans they were meant to protect crept into them, infecting them like parasites, coiling and twisting into their minds, the way it had during the first great fall. It thrived here in the Dark, beneath the Humans. Men had once raised their eyes to the heavens. Now, they needed only to look through a sewer grate to find the dying remains of God.

Malachi cried out again, though he knew the Lord could not hear him. It seemed almost comical now, to his bitter, Human mind, that in the confusion the Almighty could have slipped away and been lost. But the connection he'd felt, the connection any of them had felt, had vanished into thin air the same day the Afterworld merged with the world of the mortals.

They'd carried on without him. After all, they were merely servants. They had no free will. If any other course of action had crossed their mind, they would have fallen instantly. But it had not, and would not. They collected the souls of the departed, storing them in the Aether Globe until God returned to claim them. One by one, they began to fall, more as of late. Malachi had puzzled over that, continued to. His fall had been accidental, but there was no reward he could imagine that would tempt him to this pain voluntarily. Blood rushed beneath his skin. Bones and muscle ached. He had never ached before. Without wanting to and with no way to stop it he died more every moment.

Time. He'd never had a concept of it before. With nothing but eternity to measure it by, it had never meant anything at all.

Somewhere in the tunnels, they moved toward him. He expected them. He'd seen so many fall, during the first war over Lucifer's petty jealousy and since, he knew what he would endure. Soon enough, he heard the rustle of wings in the darkness, and then the darkness was no more. When the Angelic Host assembled, it was a sight to dazzle a mortal's eyes. They gazed at him dispassionately. He thought he knew what they felt and realized they felt nothing. Now that he was Human, or something like it, he knew true emotion. It hurt. He envied them.

Warm, golden light surrounded him, and he climbed to his knees, looking to the source. Above him, the circle of light receded to a single point of sheer brilliance. He lowered his gaze, closed his eyes, but the light had already marked his vision. Red spots swam behind his eyelids.

"Broken One," a voice intoned sternly, and then, softer, "Malachi."

When he opened his eyes, he saw two pale feet before him, bare as they peeked from below a robe of pure golden light. Azrael, Angel of Death. Fitting it would be him.

Malachi reached with trembling hands to lift the

hem of the Archangel's garment. He kissed it, balled it in his fists. It felt like cloth under his fingers, though he knew it was an illusion, immaterial, and he wouldn't have been able to touch it in his old form.

"Rise, Malachi," Azrael commanded, and Malachi did. Still, he could not look at the face of this creature he'd so recently been. He could not see that face, so beautiful and genderless, full of understanding and compassion, but no mercy. Never mercy.

"You have fallen." The voice was the same. Comforting without promising.

"It was an accident." The words seemed so inadequate in the face of the charge. "I would never have fallen through choice."

Azrael reached for him, lifting his hands, and Malachi did look at his face then. The Archangel's face displayed only mild interest as he unwound a flame-red strand from Malachi's fingers. "You touched a mortal."

"I did not know it was mortal. It had the appearance of an immortal from the Lightworld. I thought to kill it." He flinched at his own explanation. There was no reason to have touched her, no directive from the Creator to kill the ones that were not like them. He had made the choice to fall, and for such a foolish whim.

"The affairs of the denizens of this Underground, mortal or immortal, are not our concern." Azrael's sad, kind smile reflected the truth. "You have chosen. And you have fallen."

The faces of the Host assembled around them faded. The light grew dimmer. Azrael stepped back.

"No!" Malachi looked desperately at each one, sickened to know it was the last time and certain there was some way to make them understand. "It was not my choice. I had no will of my own! Even now, my will is that of the Creator!"

The light around him flared again, and he fell to his knees, knowing what would come. Flashing whips of gold lashed his wings, his back. He'd watched this so many times, wondering why they all cried out as their wings were pierced and torn, certain that mortal pain could not be so unbearable. He'd been wrong. The agony of it stole the breath from his lungs. His fragile mortal hands clenched against the rough stone beneath him, splintering his fingernails and tearing them loose from his flesh. He screamed, not to pray to his absent God, but to release the fearful pressure in his chest, to lessen some of the pain.

And then, the spectral lashes were gone. Alone in the darkness, Malachi collapsed, unable to support his body enough to prevent crushing his ruined wings. He turned his hot face to press his cheek to the cool ledge. Sticky red oozed slowly across the stone, feathering into the thirsty pores to create a dark, wet stain.

This would kill him. The pain, the blood, the desperation. No being, mortal or immortal, could withstand such suffering. He closed his eyes, resigned and a bit relieved to know it would not be long now. He waited hopefully for the flutter of wings and the Angel who would return him to Aether. It seemed ages passed, and still they did not come. The searing pain dulled to an agonizing throb, and the wetness at his back congealed. He wondered if it was a sign of imminent death. Many of the souls he'd claimed had been victims of gruesome violence. They had not bled in torrents as he had. But it seemed to take so long.

At every noise, be it a drip of water or the click of vermin's claws against the ledge beside him, he startled, sure it was time. His hopes soared, then crashed, and with each repetition the anticipation and disappointment magnified. He remained alone, stranded in his mortal prison, stranded on an island in a seemingly endless sea of filth. If he had the strength, he could find his way to Aether, the place in the Darkworld that the Death Angels had claimed as their fortress. But the halls would be empty to him. Another Angel would not show him their face until the moment of his death. And he did not have the strength. He would wait, for help or for death, it did not matter which.

Finally something did come along. Slogging through the fetid water, whistling a simple tune that echoed almost sinisterly off the stark walls. A light shone, not the holy white of death. Yellow, mechanical, dirty and dank as everything in this Underground. It bobbed with the movement of its bearer, and as it moved closer, Malachi saw the shape of a man, painfully thin, hair curled from the damp, wearing an odd contraption to keep the water from his garments. He waded to the ledge, took off his strange hat with the light atop it and held it away when Malachi lifted his arm to shade his eyes.

"Holy shit." The man sniffed, wiped his nose on his forearm. He looked up and down the tunnel, as if guilty of some crime he'd not yet committed. "What the hell are you?"

Too fatigued, too ambivalent to bother answering, Malachi looked away.

"Right. Okay." The hat clattered against the ledge, and the man muttered as he seemed to be looking for something. Malachi did not care, as long as he left him to die in peace, and soon.

The sting of something piercing his arm caught him by surprise. He looked from the syringe in the man's hand to the slightly apologetic expression on his face.

"Listen, buddy, this is really for the best," he said, wiping the needle on his shirt before returning it to a pocket. Malachi's vision faded. His stomach churned. And then he knew no more.

Three

The training room of the Assassins' Guild was deserted. No one would come to practice or spar at this hour, which was exactly why Ayla had retreated there. The night guard, a retired Assassin, grumbled when she'd roused him to open the door, but she'd not apologized. She needed time to meditate on her failure in the Darkworld, time to formulate the answers to the questions she knew she would face. A more intelligent Assassin would think of a quick lie to cover such shame, but Ayla had no talent for lies. She became tangled in and tripped over even the most simple falsehoods.

No, she would probe the root of what had gone wrong, find that answer for herself before Garret or, Gods help her, the Guild Master, sought it and she looked a fool.

Or an incompetent Assassin, which she assured herself she was not. Beneath the high cement pillars of the training room she moved across the rough floor, wielding a simple wooden staff as she moved through her forms. She would start with the easiest weapons and move to the most demanding, working all night if she had to in order to punish herself for her ineptitude and prove she was better than the weakness she'd displayed in dealing with the Darkling.

The Darkling. How was it that now, when he was almost certainly dead, victim of some insidious predator of the Darkworld, he haunted her? Her shoulder still ached from his punishing hold. She would find a healer in the morning, not Guild employed so there would be no questions. She would find time to slip away to the Strip before she was required to report to the Guild Master.

She closed her eyes, spinning the staff from hand to hand, reveling in the bite of it against her palms. It had been five years since she'd entered Guild training and first used the clumsy, cumbersome weapon. Her hands had blistered and bled, but she'd endured. Now, her calluses had faded, pampered by the leather grips of her more elegant daggers.

She was pampered. That was the root of the problem. She'd lost touch with what it was like to be an Assassin for the Queene of the Faery Quarter. Perhaps she should use a staff more often, to toughen herself up.

No, it was not just her fighting. It was her lack of opportunity to fight. Every morning she would wait hopefully on her bunk until Garret came, somber-faced and shaking his head. The Queene did not fancy Humans, he'd explained once, and Ayla should not expect many assignments to pass her way. It was whispered that Cedric, the Guild Master, was one of Mabb's many consorts and would bend to her every whim, even if that whim prejudiced him against the Assassins in his charge.

It was with the Guild Master's smug face in mind that Ayla whirled through the bow staff forms. But as always, she could not remain angry at him. Her rage was irrational, turning instead to Garret, her mentor. He should defend her. He should demand that his sister lift the ban against Ayla, however it may have come to pass, and procure her better and more frequent assignments. It was his responsibility, after all, and she was his only charge.

No, Garret was far more content to let Mabb do as she pleased, coddling her and venerating her as if she were a Goddess rather than a mere ruler. As he wished to coddle Ayla, turning her from a hardened Assassin into a soft and willing mate.

Judging from the way she'd faltered tonight, his strategy was effective.

As if called by her venomous thoughts, Garret strode through the arched double doors. The night watchman called something after him, certainly not complimentary, but it was swallowed up by the clanging shut of the doors and Garret's heavy boots thudding across the floors. For a moment, Ayla expected anger and had to rearrange his sharp features in her mind to resemble the anguish painted on his face.

"When did you return? I have been ill with worry!" His robes flapped behind him as he hurried to her side.

In the guise of fixing her braid, Ayla quickly unbound her hair, letting it fall over the mark on her crushed shoulder like a flame-colored veil. "I have only just returned."

It was then he became angry, his brow creasing below the antennae that flattened against his dark curls like the ears of a maddened cat. "And you did not come straight to me? You have been gone two days longer than the assignment called for—"

"I was to abandon the trail?" she interjected, setting one end of the staff against the ground as she drew herself up straighter.

"You were to follow the instructions I gave you!" He grabbed her by the arms, dangerously close to the place where the Darkling had left his mark.

She did not fear him, though she feared his discovery of her bruises and the questions they would provoke. Glaring at him with her coldest expression, the one she'd practiced on countless victims as they'd begged her for mercy, she bit out, "I must finish my exercises."

His expression softened and he released her. She knew it pained him to show anger. It made him unattractive. "I apologize. I am merely fatigued. Mabb sent a squadron out to search for you, but they were unable to penetrate the Darkworld border. I feared you were lost."

She turned away, dragging the staff to the weapons rack. Mabb's troops could have easily breached the border of the Darkworld. Unlike the heavily guarded entrances to the Lightworld, the tunnels leading into their enemies' territory were defenseless. But she would not risk threatening the denizens of the Darkworld with her troops, possibly starting a war. Certainly not over Ayla, who Mabb strongly disliked.

Ayla reached for a broadsword, though her muscles screamed from overuse and her brain begged for sleep. More training, more time to think, that was what she needed.

"Ayla, please," Garret soothed, his footsteps

indicating his approach. "You are tired. We can train tomorrow, but now I would like you to sleep. Stay with me tonight. I can take you to Sanctuary in the morning."

Sanctuary. The word held such a sweet promise of rest and spiritual calm. She could meditate at Sanctuary, bathe in the pools, be renewed.

Be free of the memory of the Darkling.

The very thought of him steeled her resolve to keep working. "I will go to Sanctuary in the morning. Alone." *As I will sleep alone tonight,* she added silently.

Garret gave a heavy sigh. "As you wish it."

She watched him as he left, his slender form disguised by his voluminous Guild robes. His wings lay at his back, transparent as water, swirled with gossamer color like oil polluting a puddle. He was much admired by the ladies at Court, as Ayla had seen on the occasions when she'd gone to the Palace to make her reports. To have the attention of the Queene's brother was an envious thing, and Ayla appreciated her position even if she would not accept his love. It was no secret that her Human father had won her place in the Guild in a gambling house on the Strip, but that Garret had chosen to tutor her, that was a touch of luck she could never count on again. She was grateful to him. Most students and mentors were assigned unless prior arrangements were made, and Ayla had been in no position to buy a better one.

"But when I saw you in the assembly," Garret often told her, "I knew I had to be near you, if only as your mentor."

She did owe him her gratitude, but she found it difficult to parlay that debt into a lifetime bound to him. And she knew what was whispered about her. That she was proud, that she did not know how unrealistic her expectations were. It was not as if one could aspire higher than an heir to the kingdom. That the kingdom, indeed, their entire plane of being, no longer existed did not matter. Nor did their immortality. Mabb could rule for eternity, so long as she was not harmed. It seemed unlikely that the Queene would fall to injury or illness with her retinue of guards and healers. Still, for a half-breed like Ayla, a match with Garret was more than she should ever have hoped for, and she knew it.

So did Garret, and that was some of the problem.

Why could she not simply accept his affections for her own gain? She did not like living in the barracks, constantly guarding her possessions from the Pixies and Tricksters that shared the quarters. Of course, she would not have to worry about her meager possessions if she went to live with Garret in his home outside the Palace. She would have possessions worth guarding. A fine rug instead of the coarse, cold cement of the tunnels beneath her feet. Food and rich wine that she didn't have to fight for, stolen from the Human world above, where things were clean and worth stealing. There weren't many luxuries Underground, but Garret would give her anything he could, simply because he wished to.

She worked through defense with the broadsword, waiting until she was certain Garret had left the Guild compound. It was nearly morning by the time she stumbled from the training room. Soon, it would be the Human noon hour, and the sun that Ayla had never seen would be directly over the surface of the Earth, spilling light into the grates and gutters, illuminating the Underground with secondhand dawn.

Ayla had not been born yet when the Humans had destroyed the Astral and Etheric planes. Garret had been there, and like all of the Fae who had fought in the wars against the Humans, remembered it well, though nearly three hundred years had passed. He sang songs of it at times, strumming his harp with a look of regret so keen it seemed woven into the enchantment of the music itself. There had been a spiritual war amongst the Humans, one side wielding their sacrificial God like a sword against "nonbelievers." Like a pendulum swinging, Human society embraced this way of life, then rejected it. It was during the last shift that the boundaries between what they believed to be real and the lands of their dreams and nightmares were severed.

Garret spoke with disgust about the behavior of the Humans who'd claimed their practices were a revival of the old ways, marketing crystals and oracles and glossy books claiming to hold the secrets to powerful magics. "Some claimed to be Druids," he'd scoffed once, when he'd used his pipe a bit too much. "Druids. I walked with Amergin. He gave me this harp. The fools, if they had any idea of what it meant to be a true Druid…ah, but half of them don't even eat animals. They believe it is too cruel."

But it hadn't mattered. With the followers of the One God calling on him in prayer for even the most mundane situations and the pretenders invoking spirits and attempting to force their consciousness onto the Astral plane, the veil rent. The Gods "Seemed to disappear as mist into the air," as Garret described it, and the creatures the Humans had long thought of as myth had spilled onto Earth with no hope of ever leaving. They were welcomed at first, celebrated even. But when they did not show themselves to be the helpful sprites consumed with admiration for the Human race that the mortals expected, they turned on them.

It was said the war began when the Fae races drove the Humans Underground, though the story that existed outside the Lightworld was that the Humans had fled below the Earth of their own volition. They abandoned their world for the caverns they had hewn from the dirt, tunnels for sanitation and great vehicles that shook the ground as they traveled on rails. The Humans drilled passages to connect them and create the great cities of the Underground.

As more Humans fled the world above, a mortal rose as leader among his people. Uttering his name was forbidden in the Lightworld, but Ayla had not always lived there. In her childhood on the Strip, the neutral zone between the borders of Dark and Light, she'd heard him spoken of. Madaku Jah, the Prophet. Or the Traitor, depending who told the tales. No matter if he was reviled or praised, he'd raised an army against the creatures above them and forced them into the very Underground they'd made the mortals endure.

Now, the tides shifted again. Only a fool would ignore the signs. Another battle brewed, but this one was not against the Humans, the common enemy of the Light and Dark worlds. This war would be fought in the Underground. The grim thought haunted Ayla as she shuffled to the barracks, her body on the verge of collapse.

Inside, only the Pixies had begun to rouse. They always rose early, desperate for what little sunlight they could get.

One of them stopped her with a wide grin. "Ayla, you look terrible. Come with us to Sanctuary."

"Of course I look terrible. I have been training all night. Now I need rest, while I can still have it."

"Suit yourself." The Pixie flashed another winning smile. Any creature with a drop of mortal blood would look terrible in comparison to the Fae races, preternaturally young and strong. And they had gotten rest. They had not been plagued with thoughts of a newly mortal creature lying helpless in the Darkworld.

Neither had she, she scolded herself. There was no reason to think on the creature. Not to pity him. That had been her first mistake. Not to revel in her victory, obviously. All she needed to think of was a good enough reason for her failure.

So, why then, did she fight for sleep on her hard bunk, ignoring the sounds of the other Assassins as they rose, unable to chase away the memory of the Darkling's voice and anguished face?

Four

~~~
‿‿‿
~~~

Malachi opened his eyes to a strange, mechanical whirring and a pressing weight on his back as he lay on his stomach. He remembered the man in the tunnel, the one who had stabbed him and drugged him, the shock and horror as he realized he would be defenseless against whatever would come.

Panic seized him, and it was an emotion he did not like. In fact, he did not like any of the emotions he had experienced thus far. He jerked up, bracing his hands beneath him, the bite of cold metal meeting his hands where his flesh had not warmed it.

"Don't move, I'm almost done." The command was most calm, considering the man had abducted him.

Malachi swallowed, his newly mortal throat as dry as parchment. "I am thirsty."

"Sorry, nothing to drink during surgery. It's unsanitary," the man responded. A flare of something passed Malachi's face, and when he peered over the rolled edge of the table he saw the withering remains of those addictive tubes of paper the mortals in the Underground despaired of finding regularly enough to feed their habit.

Mortals lived in the Underground for two reasons. They sympathized with the denizens of the Underground, or they had been banished from the Human world for practicing magics. But the man's reason for being there did not concern Malachi so much as what he was doing. "Surgery? I do not understand."

"Of course you don't." Another burst of whirring, accompanied by an acrid scent that Malachi recognized as burned flesh, punctuated the man's words. "Your kind are ethereal. You never need patching up, or at least you're not supposed to. But you, my friend…you were in bad shape when I found you."

Though the man's words were strange, his meaning was clear. Malachi cursed him silently and rested against the table once more. "You should have left me to die."

"It was tempting. I haven't ever gotten my hands on a pair of these beauties. Promise me if you kick

off before I do, you won't mind me keeping them?"
Another burst of whirring, then, "Okay, all done."

The man jumped down from the table—it must
have been his knee causing the pressure, Malachi
decided—and helped him to sit up. Malachi
teetered under the weight of his wings. They'd
been too heavy from the moment he'd turned
mortal, but they were lopsided and unwieldy now.
"What have you done to me?"

"Saved your life. And your wings." The man
touched one of them, and Malachi hissed involun-
tarily at the pain. "Well, they're gonna be tender for
a while."

"Who are you? Why are you doing this?"
Malachi moved to stand, but his weakened limbs
would not support him. Light danced before his
eyes, leaving the room darker with each starburst,
and he fell onto the table again, bending the tips
of his wings beneath him.

"No, no, don't go passing out. You're too big for
me to catch if you fall." The man steadied him, then
held out one blood-crusted hand. "Name's Keller.
And I'm doing this because I hate to see perfectly
healthy folk go down for things that are easily
fixed. You would have bled to death out there.
Don't let me tell you how to live, but I'd much
rather live a life that's worth something than die
alone in the Sewer District. Place is a hellhole."

"Where am I?" His vision cleared, Malachi surveyed the room. Pipes made a grid of the low ceiling, and the Human had used them to hang too-bright electric lights that gave off a terrible fizzing sound. He'd covered the walls in a wide, wire mesh fence, forming crude walls around their space. Everywhere were boxes and steel cabinets, and tables strewn with mechanical parts and tools.

"You're in my shop," Keller said with forced pride. "In the Sewer District. But hey, the rent's cheap, and at least I found a dry place. You wouldn't believe some of the hovels around here— they have to sleep in hammocks to stay out of the muck."

Malachi said nothing. He'd seen many homes in the Darkworld. Creatures mortal and immortal fought to survive in the harshest half of the Underground, and their ingenuity knew no bounds. Keller's humble shop seemed a palace in comparison to some Darkworld dwellings, and his numerous boxes indicated he had some way of earning material possessions.

"I outfitted you with some lightweight aluminum I won in a card game. I heard it came from an airplane." Keller tapped one of the sore spots on Malachi's wing, and the resultant clang distracted Malachi from the pain. When the man faced him,

Malachi saw one arm was completely missing from the elbow. In its place, an intricate system of metal and wires imitated the severed body part. In fact, the man's head seemed to be fitted with metal, as well, a long, curved piece of shiny steel that scooped around his ear. Keller scratched at the metal fragment in his skull with the false hand, and sparks jumped from the contact. "So, now you know why I'm not living the life fantastic up on the surface."

"Yes." There was nothing else to say. The man was clearly a Bio-mech, a creature who believed the Human body an appliance with replaceable components that could outlast the ravages of time. It was not as the Lord intended, as evidenced by the high number of souls the Death Angels claimed from experiments gone awry.

"Yeah, well, I saved your life, so go to hell," Keller snapped, and only then did Malachi realize he'd been staring.

"I did not ask for your pity. I prayed for death, and this is how I am repaid?" Malachi shook his head. The motion seemed oddly natural. "I am not meant to be here."

"I can always put you back." Keller sounded… insulted? Malachi had such a difficult time putting the word to the tone of voice.

"You are not pleased." He could not summon up

more empathy for the man's reaction. Malachi's only concern was for his mortal body, and the death that had been stolen from him.

"I'm a little pissed, yeah. I did save your life." Keller turned to one of his worktables, moving some equipment there. "That's worth something, whether you believe it or not." After a long pause, he tossed something heavy onto the table with a clatter. "What were you doing in that tunnel?"

Malachi did not wish to discuss the details of the past hours with this man. It horrified him enough to know it himself. But the thought of not speaking made the ache of sorrow expand in his chest, and the only relief came from releasing the words he did not want to say. "I have fallen."

"Didn't the fall happen a long time ago? Like, in bible times?" Despite his questions, the Human seemed genuinely impressed.

"The first time. But Angels continue to fall." Malachi closed his eyes. "It was an accident."

Keller's voice came from a great distance. "Well, ain't that a bitch. One minute you're immortal and the next you're…not."

When Malachi opened his eyes, the room spun. He listed to the side, felt as though he might slip from the table. With a shout of alarm, Keller raced to his side. "Lie down, lie down," the Human ordered. He peered into Malachi's face with an expression of worry. "I've got to get you something to eat. Then we're going to the Strip."

"Why?" The word sounded hollow from Malachi's parched lips.

"Because you need a healer." Keller moved away, and Malachi could not follow him with his eyes. They were too sore, too set on closing.

"Here, eat this." The Human shoved a chunk of bread into Malachi's hands. "It isn't much, but I don't keep supplies on hand for entertaining company."

Malachi struggled to lean up on his elbows. The experience of eating was strange. The coarse, grainy bread made his mouth drier. It tasted horrible, but he could not stop stuffing more and more of it into his mouth, desperate to fill the aching void inside him. He gagged, and Keller rushed to his side. "Whoa, slow down. Here, drink this."

Taking the cup offered him, Malachi swallowed the bread and gulped the water. Now, instead of empty, he felt uncomfortably tight, and he wished the Human had never offered him food.

Keller took the cup from him. "See, that's good clean water. You're lucky you found someone who's got connections."

"I am still thirsty." Malachi reached for the cup, and Keller held it away.

"Not right now. Sometimes, when people are starving, they consume so much so fast that they…" He waved a hand. "Well, you'll just cause yourself more trouble than you're in now."

Searing pain ripped down Malachi's torso, as if he'd been run through with a sword. "Where is…where is the healer?"

"On the Strip." Keller eyed him as though measuring him. "But you'll need some clothes."

"I do not wear clothes." As an Angel, any garments he had needed had manifested from pure energy. Material objects, especially coarse fabrics, were too unpleasant to tolerate.

"Yeah, well, you look a little more Human than you used to." Keller went to one of the cabinets and pulled out a box. "I won some clothes off a guy on a bar bet. He was shorter than you. Smaller all around. But there aren't too many Humans your size."

"Give me what you must, then take me to the healer." If he survived the journey, he would devise another way to die.

"So, how did this happen to you? I mean, how does one accidentally fall? It seems like something you'd have to do intentionally." Keller's voice was muffled by the box he'd buried his head in. Occasionally he cursed and tossed something over his shoulder.

The memories were clouded, but something flickered through Malachi's mind. A blaze of orange. Had there been flames? No. It had been…a Faery.

Rage burned his veins. Now this was an emotion he could grow to enjoy. It pulled the past few hours into sharp focus, gave him purpose. He could not seek death. Not when he could feel this anger grow in him, fuel him to seek out the Faery who had stolen his immortality and get the revenge due him. If mortals felt this exhilaration every time someone wronged them, perhaps he did envy them a bit after all.

"Hey, buddy?" Keller had been staring at him, Malachi had no idea how long.

But he did know what he would do next. "Take me to the healer."

Five

The Queene did not leave her chambers until long after sunup. It annoyed Garret to know the reason for his sister's laziness. It was either Cedric, Master of the Assassins' Guild, or Tristan, his Second-in-Command. It could even be Robin Goodfellow, that low-class Trickster, just because he amused her.

Disgusting, the way Mabb carried on. In her hunger for an heir, it seemed she would bed any attractive Fae that could charm her with pretty words. It was ridiculous, really, for an immortal ruler to worry about her lineage. Especially when she had a younger, more qualified brother who would gladly assume the throne should something happen to end her reign.

Gods forbid.

He waited in her personal drawing room, easily one of the most extravagantly decorated rooms in the Palace. No bare cement for Queene Mabb. She had real wood panels shielding her eyes from the rough sight, and thick grass grew to cushion her delicate footsteps. The furniture had been fashioned of real wood, intricately carved, and somehow she found fresh flowers to garland the round doors. The entire Palace was a wonder to behold, but only in Mabb's private rooms was there such sumptuous detail. Garret thought of his own dwelling outside the Palace, one room, large for the Underground but still minute compared to the Palace. And why was this not his? Because he had been born second.

He was welcome to live in the Palace, of course, if he wished to be subject to his sister's scrutiny. She had a keen insight and wielded it against her brother like a sword, but could she turn it on herself? *Of course not,* Garret thought bitterly, watching maids scurry to and fro with bowls of hot water and towels for her morning beauty rituals. The water had come from Sanctuary, no doubt, for Mabb found it inconvenient to leave the Palace and demanded the springs brought to her.

"Don't you make that face at us, Garret." Scota, a pretty maid with butterfly wings the color of saffron, clucked her tongue disapprovingly at him

Her tone was reproachful, but her dark eyes sparkled with mirth. "Your sister works hard and deserves a bit of pampering."

"Oh, I agree on that score. My only doubt lies in who exactly she has been working hard." He gave the maid a drowsy smile, knowing the effect it had on the low-class females of the Palace. Scota had lovely fair skin and yards of curling dark hair, but he would never consider someone of her station for more than a bit of sport. Still, it did not hurt to leave his options open, especially when he had not enjoyed such diversions with Ayla yet.

Scota blushed prettily and dipped her head, but Garret's mind now centered firmly on his student. Ayla. Low-class if ever an urchin was born. Half-Human, and how that tormented his dear, dear sister. But there was a wild sort of elegance to her, the way she moved as though she were meant to be a dancer, the way her hair snapped like red ribbons all around her. Of common birth, yes, but not so fragile as his dear, worthless sister. Ayla would give him heirs, and his sister would despair.

But it wasn't all to torment his sister. His affection for Ayla ran deep and true. Of all the Faeries at Court he could take as consort, it suited him that the only one he wanted was the one who would not have him. Oh, she would, and soon. He sensed her will bending like a reed under a stiff wind. Still, his prey would succumb only after a long and satisfying hunt.

Another maid exited the Queene's bedchambers and bobbed a small bow to him. "She will see you now, Your Grace."

"So soon?" He snapped, knowing this quivering servant was not to blame for the delay and not caring. Forcing down his anger, he fixed his most charming smile and strode into the Queene's bedchamber.

If the sitting room was extravagant, the Queene's bedchamber surpassed it. The floor here was marble, polished to a deep green shine. No other place in the Underground could boast such splendor. Mabb's bed sat on a dais, and curtains of sheer gauze were pulled back, displaying the mountains of rich fabric pillows and bolsters Mabb nested amongst. The tall, carved posts reached almost to the ceiling, where, in a marvel of Underground ingenuity, an illusion of the sky had been fashioned to disguise the broken tiles and pipes that had been there before. Mabb detested anything mortal, but she condescended to allow electricity for this one purpose, to keep a facsimile sun glowing down on her in the day and thousands of tiny, fake stars twinkling above her at night.

In the middle of all the disgusting excess, Mabb stood before a floor-length mirror held by one of

her maids while two others fussed over her appearance. Like a beautiful statue, she stood straight
and tall, her pale skin appearing even paler above
the lavender gossamer of her gown. As always,
her wings were bound and covered. Garret was
not certain he had ever seen her wings, even when
they were children. Mabb was such a beauty, there
could be no part of her that was less than fair, and
perhaps that was why she kept them covered.

One of the maids adjusted Mabb's sleeve and
Garret spied a pattern of flowers comprised of
amethyst and peridot. The stones practically sang
their outrage at being used for no real purpose
other than to decorate a spoiled Queene's
garments.

Mabb's gaze met her brother's in the mirror,
and her expression brightened by cool degrees.
She waved away the servant fussing over her hair,
so ice-blond as to appear white, and jerked her
sleeve from the other maid. They did not need a
verbal cue to dismiss them, and they scurried from
the room as Mabb turned to her brother. "Garret.
When I heard you waited for an audience this
morning you could not imagine my deep pleasure."

"I am sure I cannot." He had come to her prepared to charm, but now he could only snipe at her
like a petulant child. "I am sorry, I did not sleep
well."

"Did the patrols not return your errant student?" She punctuated the sentence by flicking a piece of nonexistent lint from her shoulder. "No matter, I am sure she will come back on her own."

"She did come back, no thanks to the patrols. But it was an upsetting experience I do not wish to repeat." He eyed the elaborate writing desk in the corner, piled high with sheaves of parchment bearing the Guild symbol and hoped Mabb's gaze would follow.

"Garret, would you really hold her back from her ambition for your own comfort?" A mothering tone colored Mabb's words.

It was meant to grate on him, Garret knew, not guide him. "We have discussed this before. When she is my mate—"

"She has not yet accepted you as her mate, has she? Nor have you declared her." Mabb waved a dismissive hand. "If you have only come here to argue with me—"

"I have not come here to argue. I have come to request your permission, as head of the royal family, to name Ayla my mate." If he could have frozen the moment in time, he would have chosen this one, when his sister's icy facade showed rare cracks, her mouth gaping open with shock and outrage.

Mabb sputtered a few times before she spoke

coherently. She pressed one long-fingered hand to her chest as if suffering mortal pangs. "She is a commoner."

"There are no rules in creating a royal match apart from a mate not being mortal, and Ayla is not." Garret had spent long hours poring over the Scroll of Succession and could quote whole passages against his sister if she brought the argument to such a point.

"She is half mortal!" Mabb raged, her face coloring an unhealthy pink. The slender antennae at the crown of her forehead buzzed and throbbed vibrant red, and she smoothed them down, her mortification at having lost her temper distracting her from her anger for the moment. "I am sorry, Garret, I forbid it."

"Ah." Garret shrugged, walking a wide circle around his sister. "Well, no matter. I will take it before the council. They have grown tired of your excesses, Mabb. They will read the laws of succession and find no fault with my match. They would not, even if I proposed mating with a Troll, such is their desire to rule against your wishes. Would you like that? A half Troll waiting for the throne of the Lightworld?"

Mabb whirled to face him, her fists clenched tight at her sides. "You would not dare! We are the only ones left of Mother's line! Only a Queene can ascend to the throne, and you would put that…that common whore in my place?"

Overcome by his rage, Garret slapped her. A bright red hand print glowed on her alabaster cheek, and flames of anger flared in her eyes. "How dare you strike me!"

"How dare you drive me to these ends!" He turned away before he would strike her again, for if he started to hit her now he might never stop. "Do you think I enjoy threatening you? Do you think I like speaking with any of the council? The only reason they would grant me this is because they wish to see our line disestablished! They want to rule the Lightworld, they want to rule the whole Underground. They will side with me only because it makes you appear weak. But if you do not acquiesce, if you do not allow me to have Ayla, you will bring it upon yourself!"

In the silence, so crashing after his outburst, Garret listened to his sister's muffled weeping. It sent a dagger through his heart. Curse her for making him so vulnerable with such poor playacting. But he knew his role well, and knew he would not achieve his ends if he did not participate in her disgusting performance. She had sunk to her knees on the cold, stone floor and he went to her, kneeling beside her to put his arms around her, ever the strong, supportive brother. "There now, I did not mean to be angry with you."

"I have done everything in my power to keep her

from you," Mabb wept against his shoulder. "So many times I have sent her on assignments knowing in my heart the task would be the death of her, and still she lives to take you from me. To take the throne from me."

It was not true, but Garret would not tell her so. Those assignments had gone to more qualified Assassins, and it was the Guild Master who had done it. Not out of malice for his Queene or from any pressing by Garret, but because the Assassins were his charge. It was his duty to keep them from harm, and he would not send an Assassin on a mission if he knew them to be unprepared for it. On Garret's end, he had kept Ayla woefully unqualified for the most dangerous assignments, but what he had failed to teach her she had learned on her own from watching the other students. That was, perhaps, her only flaw. She was a bit too intelligent. It was another quality he tried to tamp down in her. No sense in letting a common half-breed think above her natural capacity.

"Mabb, I will never be able to take the throne from you. You would have to die first, and that is something I would prevent with every last part of myself. I merely desire some of the happiness that has eluded me. Remember how Mother and Father were, how they loved each other?" Another lie. Their parents had barely spoken to each other. But

in the centuries since their death, Mabb had roman-
ticized the Sidhe Court. It helped that the rending
of the veil had destroyed any evidence of the bitter
feud between the former Queene and King.
Without anyone to correct her, Mabb had lost
herself in the love story she had constructed for
their parents, the grand tales she told of events at
Court that had never happened. Her subjects were
just as desperate as she, and if they could not have
happiness in the present, they were content to
rewrite history.

She sniffled against his sleeve and gripped his
arm, pulling it tighter around her. "Yes, I do. And
I wish you all the happiness in the world. But you
know me to be a selfish creature. I want to keep
you for my own happiness."

"You will never lose me." That was a sad truth.
No matter how he might try to escape her control,
only death would free Garret from his sister. He
cursed the immortality of the Fae. "I will always
be here for you."

"I will let you have your silly half-breed." Mabb
sat up, wiping her eyes. "But not tonight."

"Why not?" Garret demanded, then forced a
more neutral tone. If he angered her it would undo
all the painstaking work he had just done. "You
understand I am eager to tell her the joyous news."

Turned to stone once again, Mabb glided across

the room to the writing desk. She withdrew a sheet of parchment, sealed by her own hand and addressed to Ayla. "She has an assignment."

"Then I shall deliver it to her." He turned to go, eager to see what fresh torment his sister had laid upon his student—*no,* he thought, *my mate,* and that cheered him some—and how he might manage to avoid it.

"Deliver it to her, and then return to me." Mabb settled onto her bed, though she had only just risen from it. "And send in my healers. This argument has taken a grave toll on me. I so detest this family strife."

"I will return to you," he promised warily. "But I will take Ayla as my mate tonight. I have waited long enough."

Mabb laughed at this, a sound like crystals singing. "You assume she will have you."

"She will." Of that, he was more than certain. He hadn't spent the past five years grooming her to be his only to allow her to refuse him.

He tucked the assignment into his robes and left his sister to play the part of the invalid. In the antechamber he dispensed curt orders for Mabb's healers and ladies-in-waiting, then fled the stifling order of the Palace altogether. No space in the Underground was big enough for him now that his heart soared with joy for the victory he had won.

By morning, Ayla would be his mate, declared before the council and consummated in his bed. The anticipation spurred his steps faster on his way to the Assassins' Guild.

Six

Though Ayla did not get much sleep, what she did manage was deep, and she felt rested enough when she rose from her narrow bunk. It was far too late in the day for a trip to Sanctuary. If she went now, she would miss the chance to report before the Guild Master and pay for it later. She bathed in the cistern and scrubbed the blood and grime from her pants and vest. Sanctuary could wait, but her report could not.

Or her conversation with Garret. She'd decided on her course of action regarding her failure in the Darkworld, without the guidance of prayer. She would tell him the truth, or at least the brand she found it easiest to sell to him. She had been weak, foolish and not intending harm. He might rage a bit, but in the end he would forgive her and smooth things over both with the Guild Master and the Queene. It was not the most honorable way, asking Garret to excuse foibles she was certain she did not have, but perhaps her lie was for the best. It afforded her a fresh start. The promise she'd broken to the Guild and to herself would mend in time, through her actions and personal discipline.

This was the thought she intentionally circled through her mind as she headed to the Great Hall.

The Great Hall of the Assassins' Guild was crowded for this afternoon's assembly. Beneath the high-reaching cement columns that used to arch over the heads of Human travelers hurrying to their trains, Faeries, Elves, Orcs and Dwarves milled in their own clusters. Some sat on the rows of benches in the center of the room, waiting for their turn to report. Others were Guild Members and courtiers who had nothing to report but liked to listen to the grisly recounts to be "in the know." The best gossip came from the Guilds, or so Ayla had heard. Mabb had increased the number of assignments in the past days to combat the growing threat of the Darkworld forces infiltrating the Lightworld. There were rumors already of Darkworld Assassins stealing across the border and striking lone sentries. Retaliatory strikes were called for, though the Assassins often grumbled that the cycle would never cease. Ayla did not listen to such criticisms. Her place was to follow the Queene's orders, not question them.

Pushing through the larger-than-usual throng, Ayla caught sight of Garret's dark head. He spoke with another mentor, and appeared to be in high spirits. The Faery smiled and bowed to Garret, and he clapped him on the back with a wide grin. Ayla wondered what could have caused such joy in her mentor, then she spied the folded parchment in his hand and the Queene's seal upon it.

An assignment! Ayla's heart swelled. From Garret's apparent elation, it was an important one, as well. And why shouldn't he be pleased that his student finally received her due? The mentor who had been speaking with Garret noticed Ayla. He motioned toward her, catching Garret's attention. When he turned and spied her there, his smile grew even larger, if possible. "Ayla, I have wonderful news."

As he approached and the mentor withdrew, Ayla's mind wandered back to the reason she'd sought him out in the first place, and her heart sank. For a moment she wondered if she should take the new assignment and confess after, but no, she would then have to recant her report to the Guild Master and her credibility would be lessened. Before he could speak again, she blurted, "I did not fulfill my last assignment."

"What?" Garret grasped her arms, his face twisted in shock and anger. He collected himself and glanced over at a group of Faeries that stood near them, then guided her firmly to an alcove at the back of the hall. Though Ayla noticed no one watching their retreat, Garret kept a distracted eye on the assembly. "Ayla, you told me—"

"I know what I told you!" She lowered her voice, ashamed at herself for having raised it to her mentor. "There was another creature who got to him first. A Death Angel. I fled."

Garret sighed heavily, smoothing his antennae back. "Ayla, I have trained you far better than that. Were you wounded? Are you certain it was a Death Angel?"

She thought of the bruises marring her shoulder and thanked the Gods for the darkness of the alcove. "No, I was not wounded. And I know what I saw. It was a Death Angel."

Garret's face paled, white as Ayla imagined the moon would be. "Gods. Then the stories are true?"

She could do little more than nod in answer. This was a turn she did not imagine events to take. It had never occurred to her she might be the first Lightworlder to catch a glimpse of such a creature and live.

"You'll have to report this at once." Garret's face lit up, then fell again. "You didn't kill it?"

"I…I did something to him. I do not believe I killed him outright." Her guilty mind assailed her with the image of the Darkling lying on the ledge where she'd left him. "But he will not survive."

"I will take this information to Cedric privately. Do not make a report today." Garret reached for her, running his hands down her arms affectionately. "It would have been better if you were injured. But I do not think Cedric will rule that you've broken the geis, given the circumstances."

As he turned to leave her, she called after him. "You said you had news?"

"Yes." He tapped the parchment against his palm, seemingly unaware of it even being there. "But first I must speak with Cedric. Go to Sanctuary, use the time to calm yourself, then come to my home tonight. We will discuss it there."

With that, he strode away from her, leaving her disappointed and alone.

Seven

The true foulness of the Darkworld had never seemed so raw to Malachi as it did when he left the Bio-mech's workshop. When Keller swung open the thick, metal door and stepped down into the nearly waist-deep sewage, Malachi's mortal throat had closed on a gag.

"Listen, I know it doesn't seem real sanitary, but that's the price I pay for such roomy digs. Get your ass down here before something comes along and swallows me whole." Keller reached his hand up, and Malachi had little to do but accept it.

"Is that a danger?" The water was slightly less than cold as he eased into it. Cold would have been somehow better, cleaner. Something brushed Malachi's leg, and he repressed a shudder.

Keller studied him with interest, his grizzled

face working toward a smile. "With you around? Never. You're my insurance policy. Not a lot of Darklings are gonna mess with a guy who's traveling next to the Angel of Death."

"I am not the Angel of Death. I am merely—was merely—his servant." The man had begun to slog ahead of him, and Malachi struggled to keep up. It was a difficult thing to walk through water. His muscles ached after only a few steps. "I am pleased to provide you protection. You have been kind to me. I know Humans enjoy hearing that their actions are approved of."

"Yeah, we're real suckers for heartfelt expressions of gratitude." They had come to a fork in the tunnels. Keller flipped the light on his strange hat off and held a finger to his lips. "Okay, we've gotta go quiet through this part. I think we'll have less trouble down that way." He gestured to where the tunnel branched to the left. Water lay deep, and there seemed no end to it.

The other tunnel sloped upward quickly. Malachi could make out dry ground only a few feet from them. "Why not that way? You wear a contraption to keep you dry. I have nothing. I would prefer to take the drier path."

"For one, this is not a contraption. These are waders. They just look strange because I won them off a Rock Troll who wasn't all that good at cards.

Two, that way looks easier, but trust me, it's not."
Keller scratched the plate behind his ear with his
metal fingers, the sparks fizzing out before they
reached the water. "Easier in the Darkworld means
more dangerous. There'll be a tax, for one thing."

"A tax?" Malachi had traversed these tunnels
usually invisible to the denizens of the Darkworld.
He had never been charged a tax. Then, the creatures he had been visible to may not have been
brave enough to charge him.

"Yeah, a tax. For going the easy route. Hell,
even some of the not-so-easy routes are taxed. If
it's a mortal, they usually want money or smokes.
If it's a Bio-mech, like me, they want scrap metal
or spare body parts." Keller held up his mechanical arm. "But God help you if you meet up with an
Elf or a Succubus. What they want…" He punctuated his sentence with a shudder.

"Elf?" Malachi had not paid much attention to
the species of the Darkworld he'd not had to
collect. "I have never heard of Elf."

"Elves. Outcast Fae. They were dark-sided long
before they wound up down here. Nasty blue skin
and yellow eyes." Keller made a face. "They don't
like anyone. Barely get along with each other."

"This world is…" Malachi struggled for the
word in the Human language. The gift of tongues
continued to slowly wear away. "Strange."

"Strange to you? Imagine if you lived up there, where I'm from originally." Keller gestured to the ceiling of the tunnel. "And it's not like you haven't been here for a while."

"Too long." When had time become an issue to him? They slogged on, the water growing deeper, almost to the top of the Bio-mech's wading contraption. The tunnel around them changed shape, growing wider, and they followed it until Malachi saw a high ledge of dry ground beside their heads. "What is this place?"

"A subway?" Keller shrugged and leaned against the wall, reaching into his waders for the cigarettes he seemed to rely on more than food or drink. "I guess trains used to run under here before they cluttered up the Aboveground. That was before I was born. Are you doing a history on the Humans or what?"

"You are Human," Malachi snapped back. "And I am merely trying to acclimate myself to this existence."

"Correction, pal. I *was* Human. Now I can't show my face up there." The blue smoke from the Bio-mech's cigarette spiraled through a dim shaft of light from an overhead vent, and Keller's gaze followed it. "I could wear a hat. Gloves. Fuck them, they'd still get me." He chuckled, a bitter sound. "Did you ever have to go up there?"

"No." Only now it occurred to Malachi to question that. "I suppose we should have."

"Uh, yeah. There are quite a few more mortals up there than down here." He took another long draw off his cigarette. "Did any of you go up there?"

"No." Another "why" he would not have worried about before.

"Don't you think that's kind of…" Keller gestured with his metal hand. "Unfair?"

Malachi shook his head, and the movement felt strangely natural. "I do not decide what is fair or unfair. I merely carried out the will of God."

"And His will is to abandon those poor bastards up there?" The Bio-mech took another long draw off his cigarette. "Good thing I came down here, then."

"That is not what I meant. You have twisted my words." Malachi's hands fisted at his sides, hands that would never have thought of committing senseless violence before. But this mortal and his confusing questions sent sparks of doubt through his brain. His immortality may have been ripped from him, but he would not allow this perversion of God's work to take his last certainty from him.

"It's a logical argument, though, right? I mean, if you guys aren't up there doing what you do, who is? Does God have some other Angels making the rounds?"

"No. Only Death Angels collect souls." So, why did no Death Angel go above, where the bulk of the mortals in existence lived? What happened to those souls?

Keller looked pleased with himself. Pleased at having infuriated him? "That's what I'm talking about."

Malachi slogged away, his confusion and rage giving fuel to his sore legs.

"Hey, you can't do that," Keller called after him.

Malachi did not look back. "Yes, I can."

"No, you can't. See, if you go that way—"

"I will become lost without you? I will fall prey to some creature lurking in the depths?" He struggled through the water, which inhibited his movements like a length of rope around his thighs.

"Kind of," Keller called, but his voice held a troubling lack of concern. "But by all means, prove me wrong."

Malachi took two more steps, though tentatively. Humans had a way of speaking words that were entirely different from the meaning they wished to convey. Another few steps, and his confidence returned. Nothing loomed in the shadows ahead, nothing brushed past his legs below the surface. It was not so treacherous as the Human warned.

And then the ground slipped from under his

feet, and Malachi's world reduced to water. His eyes shut under their own power, stranding him in darkness. The filth clogged his nose, rushed into his ears. He could not breathe, nor could he hear above the rhythm of his flailing limbs as they cut though the water. Forcing open his eyes he spied silver-green orbs rising to the surface that seemed impossibly far above him. The air from his lungs, stolen by the water and carried away.

I will die here. The panic clawed in his chest. His lungs cried out for breath, watery or not, to ease the burning ache in them. He opened his mouth, choking in surprise when something clutched at the uncomfortable collar of his shirt, then at his neck, catching hair and some feathers bent from the currents. His head broke the surface and he gagged, coughing a geyser of filthy water from his lungs.

"Easy, easy," Keller repeated, grasping him under an arm with his metal one. The Human used his organic limb to pull them through the water, until Malachi got his footing and leaned against him for support. "I told you not to go that way."

"Yes, you are very wise." Why did he feel foolish? It was not as though the Human had given him explicit reasons why he should not have gone that way. If he had said, "Please, do not go that way or you will slip beneath the water and drown," certainly that would have been a more effective warning. He opened his mouth to tell him so when the Bio-mech pointed to steps rising from the water at the level of their heads.

"We're going up those," Keller said, holding his arms out from his sides as he sloshed through the water. "They go all the way up to the top, so good news, you won't have to fly me up there."

"I could not fly now. Not with wet wings," Malachi admitted grudgingly. "If I can fly at all."

"I don't see why you couldn't. I did a bang-up job on those puppies," the Human puffed as he gained dry ground. "Oh, damn it. Now look, I had to swim after you and now my smokes are all wet."

"Your legs will be wet, as well," Malachi pointed out, trying to be helpful. It appeared the Human wasn't interested in his brand of help, from the way he swore and kicked the waterproof contraption aside.

The area they'd ascended to was drier, though their feet and clothing left splashes that soaked into the concrete. The walls of this tunnel were decorated in stark tiles that might have been white beneath the forests of mildew growing on them. From beneath a dying mold colony, a warped paper image of a Human woman holding a piece of Human technology to her ear with a wide grin declared "per minute," the rest of the words swallowed by the layer of filth. Another set of stairs led up.

"Does that go to the surface?" How deep could the Humans have dug? Malachi had forgotten how long it had been since the rift spilled his kind onto Earth. Time had been circular to him as an immortal, an infinite loop. It must have been hundreds of years now.

"No, but we do get a little closer," Keller called, disappearing behind a column with his wading device folded over one arm. "In fact, we cross that bridge up there, take a turn and we're in a tunnel with surface vents."

"What are you doing? I thought I required the services of a healer." A drop of cold water dripped from one of the slimy stalactites hanging from the ceiling, and Malachi dodged it. "This place is foul and smells of decay."

"Then you should be right at home," Keller said with a small laugh. "I'm looking for a place to hide my waders. I don't want someone swiping them, but they're too heavy to carry."

"Hurry up, then." He wandered around some of the large, square columns with their crowns of mold, but he went cautiously, still shaken by his near drowning. "Tell me more of where we will go."

Keller gave a sigh with much suffering melded into it. "The Strip is a neutral zone between the Lightworld and the Darkworld. Stop me if I'm going too fast for you. It's a place where people from either side can go to do whatever seedy business they've got there, and a lot of unaligned types hole up there if they've been banished and don't have ties to either world. Lots of Gypsies and Bio-mechs stay there."

"Why not you?"

Keller heaved another sigh, this time too dramatic to believe. Why anyone would wish to make themselves appear so miserable, Malachi did not know. "Because I take a side. I don't like living down here. So I've got two choices. Do what I'm supposed to do as a loyal Human and stay the fuck out of it—which involves paying the god-awful high rent to live on the Strip—or pick a side keen on ending this whole mess. The Darkworld doesn't want to destroy the Human race—"

"And the Lightworld does." Malachi knew this well enough, from overhearing countless Dark-world assassination plots.

"And the rent is cheaper," Keller said. Whatever this rent was, mortals placed much importance on it. Then, the Bio-mech grinned and said, "Well, more like free."

"So, this Strip, I will not be harmed there?" Malachi asked, watching as Keller knelt and positioned the waders behind a loose tile.

He laughed and stood, wiping his hands against

each other as though he could clean the dirt and mold from them. "I never said you wouldn't be harmed. But you won't be persecuted for being a Darkworlder, either."

There was nothing but death and violence in the Underground. This Malachi knew well enough. But when he had been immortal and invisible to nearly all creatures, he had not given danger much thought. He did not think he even knew what a dangerous creature would look like. He had been concerned only with the mortals, and no matter their species they had never been a threat to him.

Was this how it would always be then? To fear that every step would bring him closer to his death? To lurk about in the dark as Keller did, mumbling and consuming the addictive smoke in an effort to simply keep from becoming insane?

"Hey, you coming?" Keller's voice echoed through the space, and Malachi startled. He had not been paying attention, and the Bio-mech had moved ahead without him.

He followed, unwilling to be left alone in the Darkworld, which now seemed much more intimidating than it ever had before.

Eight

❧━━⟨∞⟩━━❧

At the appointed hour, Ayla left Sanctuary for Garret's home outside the Palace walls. The only place in the Underground with living trees, Sanctuary was the gem of the Lightworld. So much so that it was under constant guard, lest an unworthy Darkworlder stepped on its sacred soil. Submerged in the crystalline waters of Sanctuary's springs, Ayla felt her Fae blood so deeply she could almost believe it was all that ran through her veins. That nothing so lowly as Human tainted her.

The effect did not last once she left the place. Her heart hung as heavy as the sword strapped to her back. She would not normally carry it, but Sar, a Pixie who slept at the end of the bed row, had been eyeing it a bit too covetously for her to be foolish enough to leave it. Besides, Garret might give her the assignment he'd received for her, and she might need it. It would give her a chance to evade his relentless questioning and wait until the situation with the Darkling faded from memory. If she told him, he would blame it on her Human blood, and shame her for it.

This doubt is Garret's doing, an inner voice scolded her, and she pushed it aside. Garret did openly disdain her Human half, but with good reason. Weren't Humans the enemy that had driven the Faeries to the Underground? Wasn't it a Human who'd wielded his sword against the Harpy Queen, cursing the Darkworld to chaos? Ayla thanked the Gods it was not Mabb who'd fallen in the battle. The lawlessness of the Darkworld would have been unbearable for the Faeries, who thrived on ritual and courtly manners.

Ayla passed by the Palace doors. As always, the corridor before them was crowded with Lightworlders, all waiting in their makeshift living quarters for their appointment to see the Queene. It was a difficult thing, for someone outside the Court to gain audience. More difficult still for someone not living or working in one of the Guilds. It was nearly impossible for any creature outside the Palace walls to gain Mabb's attention, and they traveled miles, sometimes for days through dangerous tunnels, to wait. Upon arrival, a guard would take their names and business, then mark out a plot of space with chalk on the breaking cement and ask the traveler to kindly wait for the next available audience. It was not as simple as it sounded. In her short five years living at Court, Ayla had seen countless pilgrims arrive begging a word with the Queene, yet none had ever been admitted. Some died waiting. More were born to take their place. When someone wished to speak with the Queene, they would wait forever.

Ayla kept her head high, her gaze straight ahead as she cut through the teeming throng. This was a journey Garret made every day, or so he'd told her. Ayla had heard rumors of secret passages from the Palace so that Mabb could travel unmolested to other areas of the Lightworld. It seemed unlikely that if such passages existed, Garret would be denied access to them, so Ayla did not believe his claim. No one would take such a depressing path if they were given another choice.

A baby cried somewhere, a babe no doubt not only born, but conceived in the line to see the Queene. *Do not waste your lives waiting to venerate such an idle monarch,* Ayla raged silently. *Mabb cares only for your praise and your coin.*

A hand closed around her ankle, nearly tripping her. She looked down, made the mistake of looking into the eyes of the unhappy wretch that had grabbed her.

"Please," the Faery rasped through a mouth missing many teeth. This was not a true Fae, but she must have had some Fae blood, no matter how watered the bloodline might be, to be a citizen of the Lightworld. "You have the mark of a Guild member. Can you take me to see the Queene?"

A chorus of voices raised up around Ayla as Fae creatures swarmed her. "What does she look like?" "Is she in good health?" "Will she be receiving us soon?" Then the voices shattered into panic as Mabb's guard cut a swath through them, clearing the way so that Ayla might escape.

How, she wondered, had Garret turned out so kind and generous when his sister was vain and spoiled? Were the roles of the Queene and the Male Heir so vastly different?

They must be, she decided as she passed through the Palace doors and into the common streets of the Lightworld. Stalls lined the tunnel leading to the Palace, all selling wares emblazoned with Mabb's image or name. Tired from your long journey through the Lightworld? Use Queene Mabb's Restorative Potion! Used signet rings! Gain an audience faster with documents stamped by Mabb's own seal!

Garret did not crave the kind of fame that Mabb

had encouraged. It was a shame that only a female heir could ascend to the throne. He would not have abided such folly.

But he had not lived a life with such restrictions as Mabb had, either. Mabb had not been free to pursue her own interests, as Garret had. And she had to keep her wings hidden, by some royal edict that her parents had passed long before they had died, long before the destruction of the Astral plane.

Turning from the main tunnel onto a slender byway, Ayla avoided further exposure to the Palace market. Garret made his home in a more quiet— and exclusive—part of the Lightworld, near enough to the Palace to be convenient, far enough to keep him away from the tourists and pilgrims. The tunnel widened slightly, ending in a long concrete staircase. Ayla opened her wings and drifted down, the weight of the sword dragging some of the grace from her flight. It was good to be in the open, away from the stifling rooms of the Palace. Though the training areas of the Guild had plenty of space for aerial sparring, there was nothing like being able to simply open your wings and fly without thinking of defensive combat.

She envied Garret his life outside the Palace. *His* existence did not hinge on the Queene's whim. He did not even need to work for his wages, if he chose not to. Being the son of a Queene might not merit a crown, but it did earn a reasonable allowance from the Palace treasury. Ayla had asked Garret once why he continued to work at the Guild. His answer had been, "For you, Ayla. Always for you." The answer had unnerved her, and she had not dared to ask it again.

At the bottom of the stairs was a tunnel, accessible through a hole with a ladder. Ayla folded her wings carefully and slipped into the hole, dropping down to land hard on both feet. A shock rippled up her ankles; she thought belatedly that she should have used the ladder. But it was good to be doing something physical, testing her body just a bit before going on whatever assignment Garret had for her.

Garret's apartment was one of four in this small, square tunnel. There were two on either side, stacked atop each other. One end of the tunnel branched off on a path leading deeper into the Lightworld. The other ended in a wall of water-stained concrete, and climbing ivy grew there, carefully trimmed around a stained stone fountain that leaked a trickle of rusty water. It was one of the nicest dwelling areas Ayla had ever seen, though she hadn't had much reason to explore the homes of the Lightworld.

Garret lived in one of the second-level apartments. There were no stairs. These were exclusively Faery dwellings. Ayla opened her wings and raised herself up, grasping the polished metal bar beside the door. She knocked, and when Garret opened the door to admit her, she used the bar to swing herself inside as she folded her wings.

Garret's apartment was a wonder to her after sleeping in the barracks for so long. The space was L-shaped, the sleeping area hidden from the door by the bend. There was a low, flat table with cushions all around for entertaining—a luxury many Faeries could not afford—and a brick oven set into the wall for heating and cooking. Garret had well-stocked cupboards and a fine collection of wooden dishes, all of which seemed to be on display on the square table in the center of the room.

Ayla hesitated, one hand still on the door. "Am I…have I interrupted your supper?"

Garret smiled and held out his arms, and she allowed him to embrace her, but it turned out as awkward as it ever did. "No, this is for you, Ayla. I have something I wish to speak to you about. Sit down, please."

He guided her to a cushion and took the sword from her, propping it against the wall by the door. He gestured to the table, laid out with fat, round loaves of bread, a bowl of sweet cream and strawberries, a very rare delicacy that grew only in the Upworld. "Please, help yourself."

Sinking to her knees beside the table, she viewed the fare uneasily. "Garret, what is this about?"

"I have had a wonderful day, Ayla." Instead of sitting across the table from her, Garret took a seat beside her, almost too close.

She inched away a bit, tearing off a chunk of bread to focus her attention on instead of Garret's unusual nearness. "A good day? Then you must have heard better news than I gave you this morning."

She chanced a look at his face then, and saw a shadow flicker across it. But he smiled, a bit forced, and held out one of the berries for her. "I must talk to Cedric about that, still. But you and I have much more pleasant business to discuss tonight. My sister, the Queene, has granted my petition."

"Your petition?" She opened her mouth and let him slip the berry inside.

"Yes. I asked her permission to make you my mate."

Her breath hitched. She choked on the berry.

Garret slapped her back until her spasms passed, and gave a dry chuckle. "That was not the reaction I had hoped for."

"I am sorry." Ayla fumbled for a cup on the table and sucked down the honeyed wine within. "You surprised me."

"It should not come as so great a surprise, Ayla. You have known for some time how much I've wanted you." His words ended on a desperate whisper, raw and a little frightening.

Ayla looked away from the intensity on his face, the pleading in his words. There had to be a way to remove herself from the situation with grace. But when she opened her mouth, the words, "But why?" came out, and she felt the current in the air change. She glanced up at him, at the antennae laying against his hair, fluttering in irritation. He could put on all the charm in the world now, and she would know it false. She had angered him.

The beginnings of many tentative smiles twitched his mouth as he tried to find sincerity. "There are many women at Court who would throw themselves on such a change, Ayla. To be mated to the Queene's brother…it could one day mean a throne."

It could, if the Queene were to die. And among their mortal race, death occurred only in battle. *Or assassination.* She pushed the evil thought aside. What she needed was time to think, to weigh the benefits against the risks in this battle. "I do not mean to offend. You've taken me by surprise."

His demeanor softened in earnest then, and he rubbed a comforting—at least, it was meant to be comforting—hand down her arm. "What have I been thinking? Here you are, worried about your position in the Guild with your recent transgression looming over your head, and I make you a silly offer, thinking only of myself."

Ayla swallowed. Had she been unsettled by the consequences of her experience with the Darkling, or by the experience itself?

Garret rambled on. "Only, think of what this means. Ayla, if you were my mate, you wouldn't need to worry about your future in the Guild." He paused to let the point sink in. "Your future would be secure."

So, he was not above playing his wealth and status as an incentive. And why should he be? Ayla had lived at Court long enough to know that wealth purchased many opportunities. Were she to ally herself with Garret, despite her lack of passion for him, she would purchase a life away from the barracks, more leniency within the Guild. Perhaps, even greater favor with the Queene, though Garret already said his sister held her in high esteem. All of these things would make her way easier. Why choose the difficult road, when a clear path lay before her?

Garret pushed her braid from her shoulder,

brushing elegant fingers across her skin. She shuddered, and hoped he would mistake it for more than it was. He did not disgust her, but he made her uneasy. It was not a thing she would overcome quickly. Guild training had taught her to disguise her emotions in battle, and she called on it now as he pressed his lips to her neck.

"Say yes," he murmured against her skin, tracing the line of her Guild tattoo with his tongue. The pattern burned into her memory under his hot, wet mouth. She would never again need a mirror to recall what the mark looked like. "Say yes," he urged, and his palm curved over the top of her thigh, stroking upward as though nothing separated his flesh from hers. Her body, not aware of the emotional distance between them, urged her closer, craving more touch to feed the aftershocks of touches already received.

Her rational mind broke in with a jolt of memory. The rolled parchment clutched in Garret's hand. "I thought you were inviting me here to discuss my next assignment."

He went still at her side and pulled back, his face serene, but his antennae betraying his agitation with a florid display. "Yes, well, had I not spoken with my sister on your account, there might not have been another assignment."

As he rose, Ayla scooted around to watch him

stalk to the chest at the end of his bed. In the Astral, Faeries had slept on mossy banks or in the crooks of trees. At least, that was what the stories spoke of. At the Guild, Ayla slept on dank blankets piled atop a wooden plank bunk. Garret had a real mattress, imported from the surface, with funny metal coils that made the whole contraption shift and bounce. That kind of comfort was hard to come by, and Ayla added it to her list of reasons to accept Garret's proposal. But she did not answer him now, while he still silently fumed with agitation. "Was the Queene very upset with me?"

"More than you know," he replied, but it seemed more for himself than for her. "I must meet with her again tomorrow morning. That will give us the night, if you'll have it, and you'll be able to set out on this in the morning."

She took the parchment from him and unrolled it, though it did her no good. "What does it say?"

"It comes straight from Mabb's hand. She requires the deaths of five Demons. It seems there has been some…encroaching of the Demon population on locations in the Lightworld, at the Southern borders where the Strip does not separate us from the Darkworld. She wants to send a message to the Demon king." He paused. "If you'd rather not take the assignment…"

Not take the assignment! An assignment from

Mabb's own hand was a higher honor than Ayla had ever received.

"I'll have a messenger bring over your things in the morning," Garret continued. "We can sleep a bit late, perhaps visit Sanctuary. It would be appropriate, to begin our life together there."

She forced herself not to cringe at his words. Instead she smiled. "I would not wish to keep Her Majesty waiting."

He nodded. "Her Majesty. It is a post you might one day hold, Ayla. If you would accept me."

"It would be far in the future, if the day even came. You know as well as I do that your sister is immortal. And to speak of her death, even in speculation, is treason." Ayla looked furtively over her shoulder, as if one of the Queene's spies would jump from the trunk at the foot of Garret's bed and drag her to the dungeons.

Or perhaps Garret was one of Mabb's spies, trying to trick her? No, that was ridiculous. Garret had never given her any cause to doubt his loyalty. Living at Court had allowed the seed of suspicion to grow into a sinister garden in her, and she cursed it.

Garret's palm closed over the back of her neck, his tongue snaked over her earlobe. She pulled away. To distract herself from the throbbing in her veins, she congratulated herself on her foresight in bringing a weapon. She could start off for the Darkworld immediately.

"Ayla, I wish you would not go," Garret tried, but he broke off, helplessly indulgent. It was a practiced expression, Ayla was sure, but it did not annoy her. So many at Court perfected their mannerisms in that way, and it was often difficult to drop them when outside of the Palace walls.

She pulled open the door and swung the strap of the scabbard over her chest, the weight of the weapon nearly knocking her over the threshold. "Demons are clumsy and easy to kill. I will not be away for long."

"And when you return, you will give me your definite answer?" Garret's voice took on a teasing edge. He'd already decided what her definite answer was.

Taking a deep breath, she swung out the door and opened her wings. Before descending to the ground below, she turned to him. "When I return, I will say yes."

Nine

❧❧❧

The Strip. An assault on the senses. A feast of sin and vice. A haven for the lowest souls—and the lower soulless—in the Underground. Malachi surveyed it all with pronounced distaste. His companion shouted over the group of mortals clamoring before a covered stand. Keller's voice was heard, his request fulfilled and he handed Malachi a fragile paper cup that looked as though it had been used—and perhaps washed, though Malachi would not have expected so much from the establishment—before.

"Drink up, buddy, drink up," Keller urged, raising his cup before quickly gulping down the foul-smelling liquid inside.

The vapors off the potion stung Malachi's nose. He would not drink it under any circumstance. "I thought you brought me to see the healer, not to become intoxicated."

"She's a healer," Keller said with a shrug. "Might as well let her heal us of liver damage, too. Get our money's worth."

Trade! That other bizarre force that consumed the mortals. How could he have forgotten. "I have no money," Malachi said bluntly, offering the cup back to Keller. "Not to pay for this drink, not to pay for healing."

"Drink's on me," Keller said, eyeing the cup. "Unless you don't want it?"

Malachi gave up the malodorous liquid and watched with disdain as the Human consumed it in one swallow. Keller made a guttural noise, eyes going wide before squeezing shut tight. Then his body shook, like a man dying of exposure, before he let out a satisfied "Ah."

"The healer doesn't work like that," he assured Malachi with a voice that sounded damaged by the strong drink. "Well, she might for me, but she won't ask you for money. She likes the strange ones, and I bet she's never seen one of you."

"Angels fall often," Malachi said simply. What could possibly tempt his brethren to willingly give up their immortality? The flesh of the dirty women, Human and unHuman, who displayed themselves provocatively on their walks up and down the

Strip? Could a creature have inspired such lust in him before his fall?

Yes, his conscience whispered to him. *One could have.* And his rage swelled anew at the thought of sodden red hair flashing above the water, strange eyes flaring to take in the sight of him.

"Mortal blood," he cursed under his breath. Yes, he did lust for her. Desire, so fierce it froze the breath in his newly Human lungs, overcame him at the thought of gripping her pale neck with his big hands and squeezing, squeezing until the fragile bones and fibers within snapped and the life gurgled from her body. Immortal or not, she had mortal blood. He could kill her. Would kill her. He would find a way.

Keller led on through the crowded tunnel, though the way parted easily for them with Malachi in tow. Curious whispers followed them, as well as stares and brazen hands reaching out to touch the curiosity that was Malachi.

"Have they never seen a creature with wings before?" Malachi grumbled, slapping aside a scaly, blue hand that had curled around his biceps.

Unperturbed by the attention, Keller plowed on through a group of pale Humans. "None like yours. I set you up with a sweet patch job. Hey, watch out for these guys, they're Vampires."

The creatures in question opened their mouths,

baring gleaming, pointed teeth. One of them, a female with severely short-cut hair and a tight, leather bodice that pushed her breasts up nearly to her neck, stepped forward and placed a palm on Malachi's chest, her touch icy and dry.

"Want to play with me, pretty birdie?" She laughed, showing dangerous, yellowed teeth. She leaned closer, her open mouth inches from his throat. "Come on now, you know you want to."

"I recognize the death on you, unholy one," he snarled, and the Vampire pulled back with a hiss, as though burned.

"He's a Death Angel, don't touch him!" she shrieked to her companions, and they laughed at her.

One, a male with a bald head marked with a tattooist's blue ink, shoved her away from the group. "He's a mortal, you stupid bitch." This brought another round of laughter from them. "What's he going to do to you? Besides serve as a good meal?"

"I'll be no meal for you," Malachi warned, ignoring Keller's tug at his elbow.

"Let's not get into a fight now, not with opponents who have mouths full of weapons," the Biomech urged, trying to pull him away. "There needs to be something of you left by the time we get to the healer, or else it's a wasted trip."

The bald Vampire chuckled. "Listen to your coward friend. He knows what he's talking about."

A tall, thin male with lanky black hair hissed at Keller, and he jumped, pulling Malachi nearly off his feet in an attempt to get away.

"Were I not mortal," Malachi began, then realized his mistake. Were he not mortal, he would not have had the free will to do these soulless creatures harm.

The Vampire knew it, too. He laughed and grabbed the female by the wrist. Sneering at Malachi he spat, "But you are. And I'll make sure you know it next time we run into each other."

"Yes, thank you," Keller said, practically bowing in his gratitude to the creature. "Thanks for the warning. Mac, let's get out of here."

Keller did not speak again until they were a good distance from the creatures. "Do you intentionally try to get yourself killed or is it just a natural talent?"

"I do not like the undead." And why should he? Their souls were destroyed the moment they chose the Earth over the promise of Heaven. Less a promise now than a far-off dream, but it was no excuse. Things without souls were unclean.

Keller turned and stopped him with a hand on his shoulder. The Human's face, usually a wry mask, took on a look of frightened seriousness. "Like them or not, you're not indestructible anymore, man, and I never was. Do me a favor, the way I'm doing you a favor, and don't get our asses nailed to the wall."

They plunged on through the teeming masses, the jostles and jabs getting sharper, a small cluster of curious onlookers wending their way after them. Malachi did not like having so many eyes on him. "I grow tired of this place. Where is the healer?"

"Just up ahead," Keller called over his shoulder. "That's the healer's sign."

Above the heads of the creatures on the ground, Malachi saw a mass of half-painted metal bars supporting raw, wooden planks stained by drips of water. A second row of stalls and shops were accessible from the scaffold, though foot traffic was less heavy on the upper level than below.

"The shop with the blue hand. That's her," Keller said, grabbing the rail of the ladder leading to the second level. He shouldered his way onto the steep steps and didn't wait for Malachi. There would have been no way to, without being crushed by the other creatures climbing to the top. Though the crowd was thinner above, it was squeezed into a smaller space and moved far too fast for anyone to pause.

Grasping the rail, Malachi rose a step at a time on shaking legs. Climbing was not like flying. It unnerved him, being so high up without the reassuring resistance of the wind beneath him. But that had all been an illusion, hadn't it? He'd never sailed on the wind. His physical body had never been for him but an illusion for the souls he collected. He had moved through the air because he was meant to. He wondered if this mortal body could even fly.

The healer's sign was a configuration of glowing blue, bent into the shape of hand. In the center, more radiant tubes, pink and yellow, formed an open eye that flickered as they approached. The door was a flimsy, black woven screen stretched across a metal frame with a wooden slat across the center. The smell of pungent smoke drifted out. Keller pulled the door open and ushered Malachi inside.

The room was dark, lit only by more glowing tubes, these black, giving off an eerie blue light. The walls were painted in blue, yellow, pink, the colors glowing as if illuminated like the sign outside. A row of chairs lined one wall, stopping at the mouth of a short hallway. There were doors, all closed, painted with the same strange symbols that decorated the entryway. In the center of the main room sat a wooden platform. An elderly woman with short white hair, dressed in a loose white garment, sat in the center of a glowing circle, her eyes closed. She did not acknowledge them as they entered.

"What do we do now?" Malachi asked, his voice

seemingly too large for the room. It rang off the painted stone walls and echoed in the high-ceilinged space.

"Would you just—" Keller shushed him and flapped a hand. In a much quieter tone, he said, "Take a seat. When she's ready for us, then she'll say something."

The chairs were empty. Malachi took the one nearest the door, staring impatiently at the woman. She did not appear to know anyone was in her presence, but maintained her serene pose, legs crossed loosely at the ankles as she sat, face lifted to the sky.

It was a long wait. Malachi shifted on the chair, trying to learn the most comfortable way to arrange his wings, yelping, startled when he bent them. It was easier, he found, to pull his feet up and perch on the edge of the seat, flaring his wings slightly behind him.

"Would you watch those things," Keller whispered fiercely. "Just settle down, okay?"

"Your friend does not possess that grace known as patience," a light, feminine voice observed, and Malachi turned to the woman on the dais. Though her eyes were still closed, she reached one arm to beckon him.

"Go," Keller urged, pushing on his shoulder, and Malachi climbed down from the chair.

Cushions were scattered around the base of the platform. Malachi knelt on one, wondering if it would be a sin to bow his head in deference to her, if it would be idol worship.

"You're making powerful enemies, though you do not know it yet," she said without preamble. "Tread carefully now."

"I have already been warned about the Vampires." Malachi did not care for cryptic speeches.

"I do not speak of the Vampires. Others, more powerful. Winged warriors who seek to destroy you."

The Angels who had torn his wings and cast him out. Truly, she had a gift for telling him what had already passed. "I do not want your false predictions. I came here for healing."

She opened her eyes then. "You wish to be healed."

He nodded. "You are a healer, are you not?"

"I can heal, but not in the way you wish. I cannot restore you to your former self. I cannot make you that creature you wish to be." She closed her eyes again, as if to indicate that their interlude was finished. "You are healed, in as much as I can help you."

Keller did not speak until they stood once more on the crowded, swaying scaffold. They stayed as close to the wall as possible, the river of unwashed bodies flowing around them with loud complaints.

Keller scratched the metal plate behind his ear and asked, "What did she mean? People want to destroy you? What people?"

"Tricks and lies to make herself appear other-worldly." If he hadn't already known the answers to the Human's questions, Malachi might have been less irritated by them. He pushed his way into the pattern of foot traffic, then down the stairs, hoping he traveled in the direction they had arrived from.

"Hey, wait up!" Keller was trapped behind a particularly slow-moving Ogress who turned and hissed at him, the bony spikes down her back lifting in a menacing display. Malachi left the Human, eager to be away from the Strip, longing for the familiar dankness and isolation of the Dark-world.

Malachi found, to his frustration, that he could not read the signs posted at the entrances to the tunnels leading away from the neutral city. He recognized the looks of the creatures, however, and he followed, at a great distance, a group of Human vagabonds into one of the tunnels.

It was good to be alone, to have time to think. The Human, having shown him the ways of mortal creatures, was no longer useful, and this was as practical a way as any other Malachi could think of to be rid of him. Now, with all the knowledge he required to survive, he could concentrate on finding the Faery and killing her.

And after that task is finished, what then? a voice he'd never heard before, a voice that sounded startlingly like his own mortal voice, chided him. *Even after she is dead, you will still be mortal.*

The voice was infuriatingly right. What would be left to him, once he'd killed the Faery who'd damned him? He could not return to the Host. He would never see another of his kind until the day his mortal body withered and released his soul. And then, all that was left was to return to the Aether Globe and wait with the other trapped souls until the Almighty was found.

The Aether Globe illuminated in his mind, brilliant blue and green swirling behind a polished surface like glass. Truly there was no surface, and the souls, milky and seemingly liquid as they slid over and wound around each other, were not contained by anything more than the desire in each mortal being to return to the divine. Every day, the number in the globe grew, every day the slick, cool mortal will that kept them in stretched thinner, until, Malachi imagined, it would burst as a soap bubble might.

As an Angel, he had known all things to be possible, the universe limitless. And now, to his great dismay, he could not imagine the Aether Globe surviving such relentless expansion. His mind was enslaved by the physical laws of the mortal world.

Disgusted, he stared down at his feet, ugly and square, with oddly hairy toes, as he walked. The sounds of the Humans ahead of him grew fainter as they traveled farther ahead, and he listened to the dripping of dirty water as his path wound deeper into the Darkworld.

At a divergence in the tunnel, he found a new sound that intrigued him. Steel against steel, perishable creatures in combat. Though his body had become mortal, his instincts urged him closer at his own peril. He saw the mouth of a dark tunnel, lit with flickering, sickly green, the way the Humans would have gone. And the other path, radiant with a warmer kind of light and the sure, clear sounds of excitement that beckoned him.

He crept closer, cautious, toward the source of the battle sounds.

This way was dry and uphill, and none of those undulating water shadows showed on the walls ahead. Golden circles of harsh, electric light burned around their tiny glass sources, hanging at intervals on strings that swayed them out of Malachi's way as he ducked past. The sting of blood was on the air. *I might attract those Vampiric* creatures the Human had warned him of, but it would not call other Death Angels to the scene. The scent was soulless, inHuman. He sneered at the thought of all the pitiful creatures, little more than animals, really, and their inane fight for the world above.

A haughty expression felt good on his face. He might wear one more often.

As he came closer and the sounds became louder, shadows began to flicker on the walls. A long, lithe shadow, seemingly dancing between clumsy, solid ones. It dipped, spun, ducked, almost playful. What new creature was this, that had grace and skill and beauty in combat in this festering and unlovely Darkworld?

Around another bend, he saw the creature, and rage boiled through his new veins. The light above her head threw a caul of gold over her flame-colored hair that beat behind her as if suspended in water as she whipped through her fighting dance. Her body was impossibly small; standing beside him her head would have come only to his chest, and her arms, though muscular and straining as she wielded a huge blade, seemed thin and fragile compared to his own. Her skin was so white as to be nearly translucent, and two luminous strips stood out against her hair, twitched with a life of their own. Grotesque, leathery wings folded at her back, and his hands itched to grab them, to rip them from her body, the way she had taken his from him.

If the things she fought did not steal his chance first. They were huge, rocklike creatures twice her size, slow, clumsy, but enormously strong and bearing weapons that could smash her, cleave her in two. She darted about her opponents, delivering teasing blows with her sword, always within reach of their monstrous claws that flashed like polished stone blades in the light.

She cried out triumphantly as her sword sank through the neck of one the beasts. Muscles tensed and strained beneath her pale skin as she pulled the blade in an arc, severing the creature's gruesome head. Another of them gripped her arm, and a spray of her blood splattered the wall behind her.

Malachi's mortal heart seemed to cease beating. He was close, so close to his revenge. It couldn't be taken from him now.

The wound laid her arm open to the bone. She stared down at it for a fraction of a second, then turned her eyes to her leering enemies and laughed. It was a chill sound, a mixture of tinkling bells, rushing water and phantom wind howling in the trees. She sprang into motion, faster than before. One creature fell before Malachi could track the flame-red streak of her to him, and he realized grimly that she had not been fighting as well as she was capable. She'd been playing with them.

It was finished in such a short piece of time that Malachi felt dizzy trying to comprehend it. He leaned against the wall, still concealed by the shadows, safely away from the tiny, lethal figure bathed in the dirty glow of the bulb over her head. Frozen, sword still in her hands where it had connected with her final kill—who'd long since fallen, gurgling his death, to the ground—she appeared somehow beautiful bathed in blood.

In the next instant, that beauty vanished as her arms sagged, the injured one still flowing blood, and her head dropped forward. A harsh breath scraped from her throat. She did not look into the shadows, but she spoke. "I know you are there, Darkling."

Her words were like the rustle of dead leaves and cracking ice, and Malachi struggled to understand them. The loss of his ability to understand stung him, opening the wounds in his wings that the Human had patched. What else would he lose? His memories seemed so far away.

"Go, Darkling," she continued, turning her back to the shadows. She hefted her huge weapon onto her back and walked from the cone of light, deeper into the tunnel. "If I see you again, I will kill you."

The warning set his blood afire, forced his feet

to move after her. She would order him, a being crafted from the mind of God, as if he should fear her? He would crush her to pulp under his hands.

When he sprinted through the light, into the shadows, she was gone.

Ten

Ayla waited in her hiding place for as long as she dared. Her wound made her head spin, made everything too bright and sharp. But she could not chance him returning to find her, injured and alone.

He wanted to kill her. He had a right to wish her dead, she reasoned. If someone had stolen the Fae from her blood—what little there was of it—she would hate them until her last breath. But he would not be able to kill her, not in the state he was in. No mortal could kill her, a trained Assassin of the Court of Mabb. Hardly a creature existed that could match an Assassin's blade. This Darkling would try, and he would fail.

Let him. Let him try, slay him, and hold the geis. It seemed a sensible enough solution. She'd already broken her vow twice. Twice, in as many nights. After five years of utter faithfulness, of nary a temptation. For this creature.

And why? Because of pity? The word sent a crawl of disgust up her back. Pity. There was no reason to pity these creatures, these evil, twisted things that lived little better than insects in their filthy holes. When this one died, there would be one less. That was all.

Why, then, did the thought tear a hole in her? Perhaps she was losing her nerve. Perhaps becoming Garret's mate would give her a reason to leave the Guild without answering the questions that were sure to shame her.

No. There is one solution to this, and you have let it escape! She lurched from the niche in the broken tunnel wall and pulled her sword. He couldn't have gone far. His great wings held him back, and his mortal body would tire under the strain of dragging them. It would be nothing but a simple run to catch him, but a moment's work to slay him.

A dagger of pain ripped through her wounded arm. She closed her eyes and used the inward sight to examine it. In her chest the trunk of her life tree glowed vibrant green, but its branches that reached toward her slashed flesh were an autumnal orange, fading to red where sparks of her life force touched the torn edges of the wound and exploded like harmless bubbles. She would not be able to heal this herself.

It would not be breaking the geis to go to the healer before killing the Angel. And it would not endanger her so greatly, either. She strapped the sword to her back and turned, giving only one last look to the way the Darkling had fled.

There was a healer on the Strip who came recommended from the Healer's Guild in the Lightworld. At least, as high a recommendation as could be afforded to a Human, and one would ply their trade to any creature, Lightworlder or Darkling alike.

It was not difficult to escape the Darkworld, if you knew the way, and Ayla knew that way. All of the Assassins did. The Lightworld kept their borders closed and guarded to all but a few. Even the Trolls, those disgusting rock biters in the poorest slums of the Lightworld, respected this convention. Or perhaps they didn't have the brains to protest it. The Strip was full of drugs and liquor and stimulants, the sort of prurient currency that their sloven kind dealt in, so it seemed unlikely they would comply quietly with being kept from it, unless they didn't know better.

The Darkworld, however, seemed wholly unconcerned with the scum roiling over its borders. They allowed Humans, by the hair of Bronwyn! It was a handy thing, for an Assassin who wished to hunt their prey in the lawless confines of the Darkworld, but it made survival there harsh for its denizens.

The Strip, though, held another kind of dangerous lawlessness altogether. Ayla scanned the crowd, keeping her maimed arm close to her body. She pulled her thin vest off and wrapped it tight around her arm. It wouldn't stop the bleeding, but it would perhaps deter the interest of any Vampires she might pass.

It wouldn't deter the interest of the other monsters who leered at her. She used her uninjured arm to shield her nakedness as she made her way through the teeming crowd.

The jostling street traffic seemed endless and impossible. Though the sword was heavy at her back, she pushed off her feet and rose into the air. It, too, was filled with a parade of creatures hurrying up and down the busy Strip, but it wasn't as choked as the traffic on the ground. In the distance, the comforting glow of a Lightworld healer's symbol pulsed neon. It wasn't right that someone not of the Lightworld should use it, but perhaps it was fortunate. Ayla's thoughts were increasingly muddy; she might not have recognized it any other way. Blood slithered from beneath the wet leather wrapping the wound, and the tree of her life force grew dimmer at the trunk as the gentle orange crept closer. Her vision flared and darkened with her heartbeat by the time she landed on the rickety scaffolding outside the healer's door. She did not knock, but pushed her way inside, startling a small group of robotic Humans who sat at the feet of an elderly Human on a raised dais.

"I need a healer," she rasped in the Human tongue, the words like jagged rocks to her mouth.

Then the dark veil fell over her eyes. She was asleep before she felt the bite of the floor.

She'd left a trail. Bloody footprints that grew fainter, then renewed after a puddle interrupted the dry, dusty ground. When those footprints died, Malachi did not change his course. He knew he would find her. The certainty burned in him, driving him deeper into the tunnels. It occurred to him that he was lost and would probably never find his way back to the Human's workshop, or to the Strip. It didn't matter. The desire to kill pushed any potential panic from his mind, pulled a veil of well-being over his eyes as he stalked farther down the twisting tunnel.

Ahead, an echoing, sibilant whisper warned that he approached water. Fear gripped him in the darkness. If he did not see some ledge, if the tunnel floor suddenly dipped and spilled him in… He remembered the bite of dirty water in his lungs and the impossible weight of his soaked wings as they dragged him down.

Still, the rage outweighed the fear, and he moved on, dropping into a crouch to feel the ground before him as he crept closer to his goal. Ahead, the tunnel split, one reaching off to his left, the other a round frame displaying a broken stairway that led to nothing but empty air. She would have had to go down the left tunnel. He was so close.

Something darted across the opening of the tunnel, a darker shadow against lighter ones. There was a splash and a hiss full of the sound of glass breaking. His heart beat faster. She was here.

She wasn't afraid of him. She came closer. His hands tensed at his sides. Visions of those foul creatures falling under her blade surrounded his mind like a cloud of angry smoke, and for an instant he considered running.

Then she was in front of him, her skin so white it lit up the darkness, her braid like a rope of fire where it lashed behind her as she took a last, tentative step, so close he would touch her if he only took a deeper breath.

Her arm moved, slowly, but she did not reach for her weapon. There was no weapon, he saw, his knees going weak with relief. Perhaps she'd left it somewhere to try to make a fast escape.

How she would regret that now. Malachi's heart pounded, blood rising to his skin, fury filling him to overflowing within his chest. Her hand, so small and transparent that he could make out the white bones beneath her flesh, reached for him in what seemed slow motion. The moment she touched him, the heat of her skin sent a scorching arch through him, animated him with her hot energy. He grabbed her, his hands closing completely around the delicate lines of her upper arms. He squeezed, wanting to break her, finding her stronger than he imagined. She moaned, her head falling back as she sagged in his hold, bringing her body full against him.

A magnificent power rushed through him. Not the torture he'd felt the first time he'd touched her, but something darker that stirred his blood. He lifted her off her feet, raised her up to see into her eyes, so she could see the rage in his. So she would recognize him, would know who killed her. His lips pulled back in a smile that was painful.

And then he smashed his mouth against hers, their lips touching before he realized the perverseness of his action. He had sought her out to kill her. Not just to kill her, but to brutalize her, to shame her for what she'd done to him, to make her plead for mercy. But that desire had warped, twisted into something else, something that shamed him, instead. Still, he could not release her, and he could not stop the sudden racing of his blood, the pounding of his pulse in his ears as her hungry mouth fought back against his.

This did not disgust her. She clung to him, her arms breaking free of his hold to twine like clutching vines around his neck as her legs mimicked the action at his waist. That connection, her body pushing against the mortal part of him that strained to feel her, as if under its own power, raised some primitive drive in him that warred with the last, dying shreds of his hatred.

There is still time! the blood-soaked, vengeful monster inside him cried. There was still time to crush her, especially now, when she was off guard. But he was reluctant to break the contact of her hot mouth moving on his. Other Angels had fallen for the touch of a mortal creature. Not in the way he had, but in the way he experienced now. He'd thought them weak-willed and deeply flawed, but now he saw it was not as easy to resist as he'd believed. It was not a matter of will, but a matter of want. He wanted this, to possess her carnally, to hear more of the groans and breathy sounds she made as she ground herself against him. To feel an end to the relentless excitement building in him, though he did not want it to stop.

She pulled her head back, gold eyes flashing.

Her hands gripped the front of the borrowed shirt he wore and tore it to splay her palms on his bare flesh. The ethereal white of her made his skin seem dull and so much more mortal by comparison, but as he watched, the white dimmed and darkened, blackening as her fingers turned to scaly claws.

Panic seized him. He looked up at her face, which had been so delicate and pale, now darkened like her hands. Only her eyes were luminous now, glowing red.

A shock went through him. This creature was not her. The fear that flooded his veins with ice was not fear of this wretched thing that held him, but fear at his own reaction. For when he realized that it was not the Faery that he held, he remembered his original goal, saw how he had failed, and knew that it was better to die here than to ever find her for real.

If he did, he would not kill her. It was not hatred that had driven him to her at all.

The creature opened its mouth to show its dripping teeth, and then Malachi saw no more.

The sky. Ayla had only seen it in brief, stolen glimpses through the metal grate that separated Sanctuary from the Upworld. But she knew what it was, even without those bars framing it.

She was looking at the sky, blue so bright that

its shade was indistinguishable from the light spun into it. Spiderwebs of cloud writhed on a breeze she couldn't feel.

Had she died? Was this the Summerland?

No, the Summerland had disappeared years ago. After the veil tore, as the stories were told, the Summerland had decayed. The leaves had fallen from the trees, the fields of wheat had shriveled and died, the streams had soaked into the dead earth with no way to renew themselves. Then, it had become the wasteland it remained, and no one, not even the Upworlders, went into it.

She remembered finding the healer's shop. Where had she gone from there?

The benign blue sky offered her no answers. She couldn't have made it to the Upworld. If their own guards hadn't killed her, someone would have found her by now. Where was this sky?

"You're on the Strip," a gentle, Human voice said, speaking the Faery tongue surprisingly well.

No matter how passable it was, Ayla couldn't stand to hear it. "Do not speak Fae to me. I understand your Human words."

"Very well." A weathered hand came into her view, pressed against her forehead. "What happened to you that you needed my help so badly?"

Turning her head, Ayla pushed back her hair to reveal the Guild mark tattooed from her jaw to collarbone. The woman beside her was the healer she'd seen before, her mortal skin creased with wrinkles, her white hair cropped close to her head.

The healer's brow furrowed, kind eyes sad and liquid brown in their nest of fine lines. "I don't understand."

"I am an Assassin." The Human tongue was strange on her mouth. She hadn't used it since…

The woman nodded gently and stroked the side of her face. "Don't think about that now. Painful memories do nothing but harm."

It should have frightened her, that this woman could hear her thoughts so clearly. Instead, she turned her face to the sky. "It is so beautiful."

"You know it isn't real." The Human's voice was sad. "You will never see the real sky this way."

"Until we take it back," Ayla growled, turning her head to glower at the woman. But she couldn't quite make herself angry enough; something in her knew the healer spoke the truth. A tear came to her eye as she saw through the illusion of the sky, to the dirty pipes on the ceiling of the concrete room. "Am I healed? Can I leave?"

The woman didn't answer. "Who did this to you?"

"A Demon. He is dead now." The disappointment clutching her chest was so keen, it hurt. "Am I healed?"

"Your body is healed, for now." The woman

pressed her hand to Ayla's forehead again. "This will not be the last time we meet."

Ayla sat up, and, realizing she'd been lying on soft, green grass, her disappointment turned to rage. "Do not insult me with your tricks! I am an Assassin. I could kill you now, before you could ever know what had happened!"

"You won't. We will meet again." The woman drew her hand back, smoothed the skirt of the simple gown she wore. Her face was serene. "You are in danger."

The illusion of the sky was no longer enough to keep Ayla calm. "I am frequently in danger." The grass seemed to melt beneath her feet, the thin trick creating it bowing in the face of the true magic of Fae blood. "I am leaving. I do not wish to further consort with Humans."

The woman remained where she sat. Ayla walked away from her, six, seven steps, toward the dark line of trees that muddled her perception of distance. She did not know her way out. "Where am I?"

"You are safe, for now." The woman did not turn to face her. "That is all you must know."

Ayla reached for her sword, found it missing. The daggers at her sides were gone, as well. "Give me back my things! Let me go!"

"I will show you the way, when you heed my warning."

Her fists curled tight at her sides, she went back to the healer. "I understand, we will meet again. I will be hurt, then? Is that the danger you speak of?"

The woman smiled benignly and patted the ground in front of her. Only when Ayla sat did she speak again. "The danger you are in runs deeper than any wound. You have enemies, Ayla. Powerful enemies."

There would be enemies, Ayla knew, when her union with Garret was announced. Petty jealousy was a way of life at Court, and it would be especially concentrated on anyone of the Guild class who climbed quickly into society. And for a half-Human? Ayla had already considered that.

"A man with wings," the woman said suddenly, gazing toward the false sky as if in a trance. "I see a man with wings. He will destroy you."

The Darkling flashed through Ayla's mind. He'd been angry. So angry. And so powerless. "He will fail."

"He will destroy you, if you do not have the strength to destroy him first." The Human looked sad for a moment, but the expression changed to something hard. "You know what you must do."

What I should have done before. What I have had the chance to do twice now. Twice. She'd broken the geis twice. Had this woman seen that, too, while she'd healed her?

"Let me go," Ayla whispered, and this time the woman did not argue with her. The air around them shimmered, the illusion of the sky and the field evaporating like steam, revealing a room as gray and dank as the rest of the Underground. The woman went to the door, a heavy, steel thing that scraped the concrete as it opened, and motioned for Ayla to exit first. The antechamber was just as she had remembered it, lit weirdly blue with glowing sigils painted on the walls and a number of creatures huddled on mismatched chairs around the perimeter. They looked at her impatiently as she walked toward the door to the Strip.

She turned. She'd almost forgotten about payment. The Guild would frown on her choice of healers—they would grumble that she should have returned to the Lightworld to be healed by a member of the Healing Guild—but they would cover the cost. "I will send someone with money for you," Ayla said, standing straight and proud in front the pathetic creatures assembled there.

The woman nodded serenely. "You know what you must do."

Ayla did know. And she would see it done sooner, rather than later.

Mabb's rages, when they came—which was often—never lasted long. Garret was able to keep calm while she stormed about her bedchamber, dashing her rare and expensive luxuries to a pile of glass and precious scented oils on the ground. She would receive more, in a day or two, from the fawning pilgrims who awaited her long-withheld council.

She would never see them. The workings of the Lightworld would grind to a halt until she finished pitying herself.

"Sister, you are overreacting," Garret soothed, his heart only half in it. The other half enjoyed seeing this loss of control over something he'd caused. "You knew what I planned."

"But I did not expect she would have you!" Mabb sank to her knees, tears gliding theatrically down her white face. "I did not think it would be so soon."

He went to her, wanting to break her neck, embracing her instead. "My sweet sister. Nothing has changed. You will always be first in my heart." *And I will be second to you in yours.*

Childlike and sad, she lifted her face to his. "I have failed the realm."

"You have not." He stroked her hair, barely restraining himself from tangling his fist in it to jerk her head back. It would be so easy. *Patience. Patience.*

"I have. For a hundred years I've ruled here, a

hundred more on our former plane. I do not grow old, but I do not grow young." She sniffled pathetically. "I want a child. I want an heir."

"You don't need an heir. You'll live forever." *And keep the throne to yourself, and make no move to recover the Upworld for us, until we both go mad from living down here like Dwarves in a mine.* Immortality on the Astral plane was an endless feast of delights for the senses. Immortality in this mortal world was akin to living in a tomb. Surrounded by death, their ageless bodies didn't have the sense to shrivel and die.

Mabb pushed him hard, toppling him into the pile of broken glass bottles. Cloying, sweet oil soaked into the sleeves of his robe as he caught himself on his elbows; he'd smell of the stuff for months.

"You're trying to replace me!" she shrieked. "You think that you will be able to win the love of the Court with this…this half-breed! That they will tolerate her as their Queene!"

Be calm. You cannot reason with her when she is this way. "I think that you read too much into this. You know that I cannot be King unless you die…and I would not live without you. You are my only blood kin."

"You cannot be King, because no King can rule! You want this Assassin to be Queene, so that you can use her like a puppet in my stead." She stalked away from him, her hair lashing behind her like a pale wraith caught in a violent breeze. "Why else would you take a mate?"

"For companionship?" He tried to keep his voice even as he stood. Blood rolled down his arm beneath his long sleeves, and he shook his arm to flick it away. "I cannot find it quite as easily as you do." He nodded toward the tapestry concealing the secret entrance to Mabb's chamber.

She moved so quickly he had no chance to defend himself. It was easy to forget that, in days long past, she'd been a warrior first, a Queene second. Her long fingers slashed across his cheek, leaving three stinging trails of torn skin in their wake.

"How dare you!" She struck him again, her venomous claws raking his throat. "I am your Queene, not some common whore!"

"My dear sister." He laughed softly and pressed two fingers to his cheek to check for blood there. "You are anything but common."

"Guards!" she shouted, and his back stiffened. They entered the room immediately, four of them surrounding him. Their spears were held neutral, but their faces were hard.

Mabb stood between the two in front of him and put a hand on his shoulder, pushing him to his knees. "Have your half-breed. But know that she will never claim the throne. They will never accept her! They will never love her enough to denounce me! You will never be anything but my slave. Any ambition you have will be subject to my whim, until the end of time!"

Or your life, Garret seethed. But it was not the time. Later, when his union with Ayla was complete, when his throne was secured. *And then, dear sister, you will see what a powerful force ambition can be.*

The Darkling had to be killed before she could return to the Lightworld. She had no illusions what would happen when she returned. Garret, no matter what he might promise, would not let her go on another assignment. And perhaps that was not the horror that it had first seemed. If she was no longer an Assassin, she could forget the shame of her broken vow and never find herself in the same position.

But before she could do that, she had to find the Darkling and kill him.

It wasn't as easy as it sounded. The Darkworld went on forever, chaotic, unorganized, unmarked, and she did not know where the Death Angels hid themselves. This Darkling was wearing clothes since the last time she'd seen him, so he must have found a place to nest. And the best place to begin searching for him was where she'd last seen him.

The bodies of the demons she'd slain still lay on the floor of the tunnel, though one of them had been partially eaten by something. Ayla turned her face from the oozing corpses and pressed her hand to the tunnel wall, trying to absorb some energy from it, some hint of how to find the Darkling.

Something diseased and foul flashed through her, and she jerked her hand away. It could not have been residue from the Darkling. He was harmless. Mortal. And she'd touched him before. The energy in him had been nothing like this. It had been…

The memory scorched her, pulled blood to her skin, made her ripe to bursting. She pulled the dagger from her belt to give her fist something to clench around. There was no need to worry now about her response to the Darkling's energy. He would be dead. As soon as she could find him.

He'd been intent on killing her, which meant he would not have given up following her. He had not known, of course, that she'd waited for him to pass before doubling back. So, she would go in that direction, the way she'd seen him running. She might find an energy trail that was not tainted by whatever had recently lurked here. And if she did not find him within an hour, well…he could not very well destroy her if she never returned to the Darkworld.

Tell Garret, a panicked voice in her urged. *Tell*

Garret. He is your mate now; it is his duty to find this Darkling and kill him.

Ayla growled at herself, felt her antennae stir in agitation at her forehead. Garret was not her mate. He would be, when she accepted his proposal and went to his bed. But would he take a mate who'd broken the geis? It was difficult to know if Garret's feelings for her ran true, or if he was merely seeking another pretty bauble to add to his collection.

She looked down at herself in dismay. She was no pretty bauble. Garret stood to impress no one by owning her. Still, his declarations of affection were not enough to risk confessing that she had broken her vow to the Faery Court.

It wasn't her fear of losing the security Garret offered. She enjoyed being an Assassin. It would have been more enjoyable, though, if she'd been given any real hope of advancement. Perhaps, mated to Garret, she would be allowed a position as a mentor. But she did not need Garret to rescue her from her life. If he found out that she'd broken the geis, though, he could tell Cedric, the Guild Master, and she could lose her place in the Palace, even, perhaps, be banished from the Lightworld.

She shuddered at the thought. She'd lived on the Strip before. It would never happen again, so long as she had a sound mind.

If you had a sound mind, you would have killed the Darkling in the first place! she scolded herself. That mistake would soon be corrected.

She'd gone farther than she'd intended to when she reached a fork in the tunnel. The filthy energy she'd felt lingering near the bodies of the dead Demons made the air heavy, charged with a foreboding that crackled down her limbs. If the Darkling had come this way, he was most likely dead now.

Something squeezed inside her at that thought, and her heart beat out of rhythm. She used the Other Sight to examine the tree of her life force. All was well, vibrant green limbs arching within her, roots stretching to anchor her to the Earth. Outside of her body, though, was a horror beyond imagining. Oily, blue-black energy swam like water serpents in midair, menacing arcs and coils writhing all around the juncture of the tunnels. Ayla had seen this before, many times. Succubi and Incubi, the shape-shifting Demons that preyed on the lust and sexual energy of their victims, polluted everything they touched, even the air, with their foulness. They were a common nuisance to an Assassin in the Darkworld; the Guild would thank her for killing it.

She scanned the area, unease growing in her chest. There was something else here, something familiar and uncomfortable. The dark energy emanated strongly from a spot on one of the tunnel walls, twined with a faint scarlet.

In her shock, Ayla flew out of the Other Sight. She couldn't make out the creature. She conjured a sphere of light and threw it into the direction of the monster, and gasped at what she saw.

The Death Angel was there, his mortal skin gray, his face a twisted mask of agony. The Succubus clung to him, her greedy mouth inches from his, pulling a thin stream of crimson light from his lips. The creature's naked legs wrapped around the Darkling's hips, her scaly body split upon his flesh.

Ayla had disturbed the creature's feeding. It turned, hissed, a move meant to intimidate the intruder so that it would flee and the monster could continue sating itself. Ayla flipped a dagger from her belt and leaped, screaming at the Succubus as the sphere of light faded above their heads. The thing matched the darkness, moved faster than Ayla expected. A flash of yellow eyes to her right. She turned, lashed out with the dagger. A spray of glowing yellow blood flashed through the dark. It was enough. The wounded creature screamed and fell to all fours, scrambling for escape. Ayla planted a boot on the creature's back, pushing it flat. As the Succubus strained up, Ayla slid the knife under its arched neck and pulled. The thing screeched while it could, hissed as the blade pulled through its throat, and then the head flipped back. With a grunt of satisfaction, Ayla pulled until the clean white bone of the neck slid from the head with a sound of catching gears and sawed the last of the skin and sinew away. She lobbed the head as far as she could make it go, kicked the body from her feet.

The Darkling remained where he'd stood, supported only by the tunnel wall, his eyes squeezed closed, breath harsh as it scraped from his chest. He would not fight.

You could leave him, and he would die on his own. He will not recover from this attack. She shook her head, trying to force the traitorous thought from her mind. She had thought to leave him to die before, but he had survived. To leave him now would be to break the geis a third time.

She wiped her dagger on her leather-clad thighs. It was an insult, somehow, to kill him with the blood of his attacker still on her blades. The Darkling groaned. His head fell forward and his body slumped as if he would fall.

Ayla caught him, careful not to stick him with her dagger and then feeling foolish that she'd taken such care when she would only ultimately kill him.

The moment she touched his skin, she knew her mistake. Even without the Other Sight, she knew the green sparks of her energy rushed to her skin to meet him, and the shock jolted through her. It took great effort to push herself away, and she felt the scorching pull as if something tried to ensnare her.

The Darkling fell to the ground, panting shallow breaths. His eyes opened to slits, then widened at the sight of her. "Enough of your tricks, beast. Kill me!"

The words sent a shiver of cold through her. Beast? Was that how she appeared to him? Then another icy chill gripped her, one of understanding. He thought she was the Succubus. Which meant...

"Hey!" A Human voice echoed off the walls of the tunnel, and Ayla dropped into a crouch, sliding slowly back. The Human wore a strange contraption on his head to illuminate the darkness. When the beam fell on Ayla he stopped. She saw his skinny neck move as he swallowed. He was afraid.

He should be. "You, stand where you are!" she called to him in his tongue, and it took him a moment to respond, as if he couldn't understand her.

"What the hell are you?" He stepped closer, squinting.

Ayla clenched her fists. The Human's curiosity overcame his fear, and that troubled her. "It does not matter what I am. Stand where you are!"

"Hey, I'm just looking for my friend, okay?" He

turned his head and the light followed to fall on the Darkling. "I leave him alone for five minutes and this happens."

"I did not harm him," Ayla said quickly, before she knew why it was important to tell him. "It was a Succubus."

The Human reached down to lift the Darkling by one arm. He was strong, stronger than Ayla would have expected from a Human. "Well, way to get yourself some, Malachi."

Malachi? Ayla covered her mouth and shaped the name against her fingertips. What an ugly sound. *Malachi.*

"Hey, you. Help me get him to a healer." The man paused in his struggle to get the Darkling to his feet. "You, winged thing. Bat girl? Let's get moving."

"I cannot." *Kill them! Kill them both now!* she screamed frantically at herself. But the moment had passed. The chance was gone, and she'd broken the geis again. Still, she could not be seen helping two Darkworlders reach a healer, no matter how many times she ignored her vow.

The Human rolled his eyes and dropped the Darkling to the ground. "I'll pay you. What do you want? Cigarettes? Food?" He looked her up and down, the light on his hat bouncing as he did, and Ayla had to shield her eyes. "A shirt?"

"I do not want any payment from you. I cannot help you." She stood, started to walk away. The man put his dirty hand on her as she passed.

It took only a second for him to fall to the floor, beside the Darkling. The lighted hat knocked to the ground, the yellow beam rocking back and forth over the ceiling of the tunnel as it settled. His eyes were wide with fear above the blade pressed to his throat.

Faced with imminent death, the Human still bargained on behalf of the Darkling. "If you don't help me get him out of here, he's going to die. And when I got here, you didn't look like you wanted him to die." His gaze cast around, to the limp black hand of the headless Succubus only inches from his face. "Did you do that?"

Ayla nodded sharply. "I will kill…Malachi… next."

"No, you won't." The Human swallowed carefully. "If you were going to kill him, you would have done it by now."

Ayla pulled the blade away, narrowing her eyes. "What does it matter to you if one Darkling is killed?"

"He's my friend." The Human extended his hand. "Like we're gonna be friends, at least, until you can help me get him moved. My name is Keller."

"Ayla," she said in her language, her name the combined sound of a drip of water from a leaf after a rainstorm and the gentle rustle of wheat in a field. Or, so Garret had told her. He knew the meaning behind so many things, she never questioned him.

Keller twisted something on his imperfect Human face to make himself appear suddenly incredulous. It was a funny trick, one that explained how Humans could tell what they were feeling without use of antennae. "I don't think I'm going to be able to pronounce that. You're a Faery, aren't you?"

She nodded, perplexed by this strange man.

"Then that, Faery, is what I'm going to call you." He sat up and motioned to the Darkling. "Now, get your skinny ass in gear and help me."

Eleven

~~~~⚭⚭~~~~

They took the Darkling to the Human's workshop. Ayla stood firm that she would not be seen on the Strip helping a denizen of the Darkworld. The Human did not understand. She did not expect that he could.

"Put him on the table," Keller—another ugly name—told her, and she helped lift the Darkling onto the cold steel surface.

"He will not be comfortable there," she observed, finding an overturned crate to use as a seat.

Keller frowned at her for no reason she could understand. "He's dying. I don't think it matters."

"He should be comfortable while he dies." The horrible twisting feeling returned, and she pressed a palm to her chest to ease it.

It will be over soon. Soon, he will be dead and

*you will be free. You will never have to tell anyone
that you broke the geis.*

But he did not die quickly. They waited for hours,
the Human pacing, deliberating whether he could
pay a healer to come into the Darkworld, Ayla
watching the Darkling's chest rise and fall with
jerking motions that grew weaker and weaker, then
renewed again as he fought to save himself. The
Human finally adopted her pose, his eyelids
drooping as he watched the Death Angel's final
struggles.

"You are tired." Ayla managed to pull her gaze
from the Darkling for a moment. "You should
sleep. He will die if you are watching or not."

Keller shook his head, looking sad. How long
could he have possibly known the Darkling, and he
mourned him? Humans were odd creatures. "No,
I don't want him to go alone. It's not fair."

"He will not be alone. I will be here." Only if
she stayed until the end would her conscience be
clear.

The Human waited a few moments, obviously
torn between fatigue and loyalty to his new friend.
"You won't kill him?"

"I will not have the chance." Her relief shamed
her. "I will merely wait to see him die."

The Human went away, muttering something
that Ayla ignored. The Darkling was too large for

the surface he lay on. His wings, strange objects patched with odd bits of metal, crushed against the rolled edges of the table and jutted over the sides. One of his arms hung nearly to the floor, twisted at his shoulder at what looked like an uncomfortable angle.

Ayla contemplated the arm. His skin was darker than it had been when he'd been immortal. He'd been almost as pale as herself then, only more blue-tinged than translucent. Now, tawny-brown stretched over his muscles. Those were hideous, bunched and bulky like a Human's. The Fae races were leaner, muscles stretched taut as lute strings across their bones. There was something about this ugly creature that compelled her, though.

Why hadn't he shrunk from the Succubus? If the creature had been wearing Ayla's face, he had all the more reason to run from it. Hadn't she made it clear before that she would kill him on sight?

The memory of how she'd found him, ensnared in the arms of the Succubus, brought her blood to her face. She did not wish to acknowledge—but could not ignore—the other possibility: that he'd gone to the Succubus willingly, thinking it was Ayla's arms around him.

The Darkling moaned, the first sound he'd made in hours. His face tightened in agony, and his chest jerked, the skin drawing tight over his throat as he pulled in a shallow breath.

Then it was done. His body relaxed with a sigh. He lay utterly still. A disappointing end to a long wait.

Ayla pressed the heel of her hand to her chest, pushing hard to quell the ache that suddenly intensified there. As if her own breath had left her as his had, her throat squeezed closed and dark spots marred the sides of her vision.

Get yourself under control, her mind commanded, but her body would not listen. Sudden wetness sprung to her eyes, which she attributed to fatigue after all this long time waiting. *This is what you wanted!*

Taking a deep breath, she stood, fists pressed to the strangely hollow place beneath her ribs. She approached the Darkling's motionless body, one hand reaching, trembling, toward the arm that fell over the side of the table.

"I am sorry I did not have the courage to give you a good death," she whispered, then felt silly for speaking to a dead thing. As if speaking had broken the spell over her, her fear and sadness fled. She gripped the arm and placed it over Malachi's chest.

The flesh seemed to come alive under her palm. Against her will, the Other Sight sprang into her vision. Bright red sparks of her life raced down her arm to the Darkling's body, feeding him, healing him.

She could not let go. At first, because her skin seemed fused to his. Then, because his hand gripped her wrist. She tore herself from the Other Sight, but she could not free herself from his grasp.

The Darkling sat up, his expression murderous. Still, he held her. "What have you done to me?"

She couldn't find her voice. Assassin's instinct screamed at her to reach for her dagger, but another instinct warned her not to move. Not because she was afraid of him. She was oddly unafraid. And that was, perhaps, something that should have frightened her.

"I have not done anything to you," she said, forming the ugly, Human words carefully. "You were hurt. Your friend, the Human, helped you."

"You hurt me!" he shoved her, and she let herself fall. It was a concession that put her far from his reach and seemed to appease him some.

"I did not. It was another creature who fed off of you. It wore my face, but it was not me." She stood slowly, hands in front of herself to ward off any further attack.

For a moment, it seemed he would not believe her. His hands flexed to fists as he stared at her, unable or unwilling to comprehend the truth. "It was you."

"If it was me, I would have killed you, not…" She couldn't think of the word in Human, and the Fae word was too vulgar, made it too real. This Darkling thought he had shared intimacies with her that she'd never experienced with anyone, even of her own kind. The thought brought flames to her face. "It was a creature of your world that did this."

He stood, then slumped down, crouching so the tips of his wings barely touched the floor. Everything about him seemed heavy, as if invisible roots held him to the floor. "This is not my world."

Though the Human language was limited, simple, the pain in his words filled the air. Ayla knelt down, trying to see his face behind the hair that had fallen in front of it. He did not look sad. Grim and angry, but not sad.

"I am sorry for you." The urge to comfort him with her touch was almost unbearable. But if she touched him, she would not have the courage to kill him later.

No. She would never have the courage. She hadn't killed him before. She wouldn't do it now.

Her failure shocked her to the core. She stood, backing toward the door on numb legs. This was the Human half of her, certainly, that could not overcome the weakness of emotion to finish what she had begun. The pity and fear that Garret, in his capacity as her mentor, had banished from her life, beaten from her when it had been necessary, ravaged her tired brain. If she did not leave now, she might kill this Darkling who had somehow broken down every one of her defenses. If she did not leave now, she might not kill him.

Her hand was on the door when he spoke again, his voice soft and pained in the quiet. "Stay."

Her fingers tightened on the door handle, desperation to be away from here clawing in her chest like a wounded animal. "I cannot."

That was what she'd meant to say. The word that came out was "Why?"

"I do not know," he told her, honest and raw. "I wanted to kill you."

"If you will kill me, I will not stay." She couldn't stop the smile that twitched the corners of her mouth. Strange. She hadn't smiled in so long.

The Darkling made a frustrated sound, low in his throat. The hair stood up on Ayla's neck. "I will not kill you."

For a moment, all Ayla could remember was her first glimpse of his eyes, solid, glassy-black in the darkness, taking her by surprise. But the image fled before his new, mortal face, lined with pain, his eyes Human and tortured.

Slowly she went to him. Trembling, she reached toward him. This time, when she laid her hand on his skin, his body was not hungry for her life. The only shock was the unpleasant heat of him, nearly burning her palm, and the strange urge to touch more of him. It was enough to make her pull away.

"You spared me. In that tunnel," he spoke slowly, his voice rough. "Why?"

"If I could answer your question…" She paused, collected herself so that her voice did not sound so childlike and unsure. "If I knew the reason, I would have killed you."

He stood slowly, his body shaking. He had still not recovered fully from the attack.

Ayla stepped back. At his full height, the Darkling towered over her. Without thinking, she opened her wings and bent her spine, a primitive instinct to make herself larger, threatening.

He laughed.

Her first instinct, to be angry with him, fled at the sound. Genuine laughter was rarely heard in the Lightworld. Laughter was to mock, belittle, prove superiority. He laughed at her, and she did not feel she needed to defend herself against it. It was silly to fear him when she could so easily kill him.

"Why did you heal me, if you wish me dead?" the Darkling asked, his face suddenly serious again. "Did you want me whole, so that it would be fair?"

It was Ayla's turn to laugh, though she did not. "I am an Assassin. We do not concern ourselves with fighting fairly."

"That does not sound honorable," he sniffed.

"Honor does not imply fairness, just as fairness does not imply honor." She moved to the other side of the room. The Human kept such strange objects in this workshop, and she could not resist touching a few. "How do you know that my touch healed you? Because I touched you, and you awoke? You look at things through a mortal's eyes."

Before she could sense the attack coming, he had her pinned, bent backward across the sharp edge of the workbench with her hands trapped behind her. "I am not a mortal!"

"Then why did you nearly die?" She shoved herself forward, hard, and he flew across the room, throwing his wings open in a futile attempt to cushion the blow as he hit the chain fence that covered the concrete walls. The wings were still injured, though. He fell to the ground, groaning in pain, blood dripping from the tips of his black feathers.

Ayla did not offer him her hand. Instead she watched patiently as he pulled himself to his feet. His features twisted in rage. If he'd had less intelligence and more strength, he would have tried to attack again.

"I did not heal you by my own choosing. I think I healed you. I felt great sadness at the thought of your death, and some magic worked in my blood.

It was not intentional." The words pained her as they scraped from her throat. "There is something between us…something that is not natural. When I touch you, everything in me, my life force, my essence responds to you. It is not something I should ever like to feel again."

It was the truth, though she had not thought of it until the words came out. The raw, scorching tension that wound through her when she was near him made her unsteady and tense. The old healer's words came to her as if through a fog: *a man with wings.*

Of course this Darkling would destroy her. More frighteningly, when she was near him, she did not care.

"You do not understand." She shook her head, cursing herself as she went to the door.

"I do!" His voice sent daggers of agony through her. "I understand what you feel. Since the moment you stole my immortality, I have felt it."

"Then I will not make you suffer my presence any longer." She opened the door, though her instincts became confused, ordering her to stay at his side.

"I do not suffer," he whispered.

She turned slowly. He looked at her shamelessly, the pain and pleading in his eyes bare and startling.

Those disturbing feelings he claimed to feel climbed up in Ayla's chest, into her throat, choking her. The memory of how she found him, the monster with its legs wrapped around his waist, threw the burning in her into sharper relief.

"Then I leave for me. Goodbye, Darkling."

She let the door slam closed behind her and chased the echo of its hollow knell down the tunnel, toward the Lightworld.

Malachi stood staring at the door, knowing she might still stand just on the other side. If he opened it, he might see her shadow flicker off of the walls, or see a ripple in the sewage where she'd disturbed the water.

"Women." Keller came out of his chained-off alcove. He had witnessed it all. That made the rejection burn more.

"She is not a woman," Malachi growled, knowing the anger in his voice sounded ridiculous. If she was not a woman, why did he want her the way mortal men wanted mortal women? Why did he no longer wish to kill her, but overpower her in another way?

Something flashed through his mind. Mortal memory was a frustrating thing. Details were lost to the haze of a Human brain, but there, in his mind, he had her over the workbench, twisting in rage beneath him. His blood pounded toward the source of the excitement rising in him. He could almost smell her hair.

"She's not a woman, but she's a female. They're just about the same thing." Keller gave a low whistle and went to touch the blood on the wall. "Thanks for keeping the place nice while I was away."

"You were here. In that room." Malachi pointed in the direction of the alcove, wondering at the short memory span of Humans. Would his own be so easily lost? What if she never came again, and the memory of her was lost?

Keller looked him over, as if trying to discern something important with his uncomfortable gaze. "We need to work on your sense of humor. Or, at least, get you to stop thinking so literally."

Malachi scowled and dropped to the floor. He wanted this man to go away, so that he could think more on his Faery. When he was stronger, when he was safe, he would go into the Lightworld and find her.

"You're never going to be that strong, friend," Keller said quietly, shocking him to attention.

Malachi flared his wings open, tried for the terrifying voice he'd always had as a Death Angel. "You know my thoughts! Witchcraft!"

If he had still been a Death Angel, the Human

would have feared him. But what he had been mattered not. Keller laughed, not a single, rumbling laugh that he seemed prone to. Great, whooping laughter that echoed around the room. Tears came to his eyes, and he wiped them away with the backs of his hands. "Are you going to burn me at the stake or something? 'Witchcraft,' he says!"

"Do not laugh at me, soothsayer!"

This brought more unexplainable laughter, until the Human was doubled over, hugging his midsection. After a long time, he managed to get control of himself and became upright, scrubbing at the tear tracks on his cheeks with the ends of his too-long sleeves. "It's not…witchcraft. It's just something I can do. And it's one of the reasons I'm down here."

"You were rejected by the world above?" Malachi had seen many Humans in the Underworld, but he'd never given thought to why they were there. Could Humans be so cruel as to cast their own kind to their enemies?

Keller shook his head. "I didn't give them the chance. See, up there, they have these…Enforcers. Magic is illegal, even if it's unintentional. You step out of line, you get taken away. And the people who get taken away don't come back. Some people say they come down here. I've never met a Human who got thrown down here by the Enforcers, though, and I've met a lot of Humans."

"Your abilities are unintentional?" Another thought that never occurred to Malachi. Could someone really be so cursed?

"Ever since I was a babe in swaddling clothes. Not a fun gift to have, by the way." Keller went to one of his metal supply lockers and pulled out a half-empty bottle of something. He pulled a cork free and the acrid scent of alcohol filled the room. "I kept it mostly hidden. No one can really prove you can read minds, right? So, I just made extra sure to look surprised when I opened my birthday presents, even though I knew what I was getting, and to never mention to my grandma what my mom really thought of her."

Malachi did not know how to respond. Keller handed him the bottle and Malachi took it, reluctantly drinking some down. Whatever the potion was, it scalded his throat and brought water to his eyes. A pleasant warming began under his ribs, though, and he found his second swallow much more enjoyable.

"Well, then I turned eighteen, and when you're eighteen, you have to register with the Enforcers and take this test." Keller took back the bottle and swallowed a huge gulp. "I'm thinking everything is going to be okay, but as I'm sitting in the waiting room, I hear the guys thinking in the next room. They're thinking, 'What if we just take the kid out and dump his body somewhere? No one's going to miss him, and we won't even have to prove he's a mind reader.' I start getting real nervous. These guys knew what I was, and they were having god-awful sadistic thoughts about how they were going to kill me. I kept looking at my watch, and then the receptionist—that's a lady behind a desk who answers phones and stuff—the receptionist keeps looking at me funny every time I look at my watch.

"Finally it's time for my appointment. I'm sitting in their uncomfortable waiting room chair, on the edge of my seat, bouncing my knees, sweating, I'm a wreck. And then the guy thinks, 'might as well go get the poor bastard, see if we can wrap this up before lunchtime.'"

"What did you do?" Malachi found he had leaned closer to the Human, that his knees bounced the way Keller's had in the story. He took another drink from the bottle, warmth creeping into his face.

Keller shrugged, as if the tale were boring. "I ran. And of course, that was the test all along. They wanted me to run, so they would know. I wasn't out of the building a full five seconds and a group of fully armed Enforcers were busting down my path. I ran into an alley and found a sewer grate that was loose. I dropped down here to hide, and I never got around to going back up."

"Why not?" Why would any Human wish to stay down here, when the clean fresh air and water waited for them above?

Keller gestured to his missing arm. "A woman. Bad choice, I know. But I stayed. And I like it here. I can be myself, don't have to worry about hiding my 'talent.'" He made a motion with his fingers, both the Human and mechanical ones, as he said the word. "I can live a 'normal life.'"

"You join parts of things to other living things," Malachi pointed out, a laugh of his own coming to the surface.

"There, I knew this would work on your sense of humor," Keller said, lifting the bottle up to the light. "I've got to figure out a way to keep my bar stocked better."

An idea sparked in Malachi's brain. An idea that brought a smile to his mouth so wide that it hurt. "You can read minds?"

"Human minds, yeah," Keller said, taking another drink from the bottle.

The idea crumbled, leaving disappointment in its wake. Malachi no longer cared for the warmth in his stomach.

"She's part Human, you know," Keller said, as if he weren't interested in what he was saying at all. "I can read her."

"Tell me where she is!" Malachi found himself

on his feet, his hand around the Human's throat before he could stop himself.

Keller's feet, barely touching the ground, kicked at the air as he strangled. Malachi set him down, feeling at once remorseful and foolish for what he'd done.

"Jeez, are you trying to kill me?" The Human rubbed his throat, eyes bulging. "That's not the way to ask for a favor, you know!"

"I am..." Malachi struggled for the word. "Sorry."

"You are," Keller agreed. "Look, I'll help you. But you need to know more than where she lives. Look at you! How are you going to get into the Lightworld to find her?"

Malachi was already outside the door, ready to drop into the filth to wade toward the Lightworld, but Keller had him by the arm, pulling him back into the workshop. "Not yet! Come back in here and listen to me!

"You can't just rush off to the Lightworld. Their guards will pick you off the second they see you." Keller's heavy sigh echoed through the tunnel. "Come back inside. We need to work up a disguise for you, and a plan. And, let's be honest, you need some serious help in the hygiene department, if you're going to win her over."

"Hygiene?" How much more equipment would

be required? "I will go to the Lightworld and bring her back here. I do not need hygiene!"

For a moment, it appeared as though the Human was laughing. Then, he looked frustrated and sad. "Come inside. There are things I need to explain to you before you go after this chick. What's her name again?"

Malachi realized he did not know.

Twelve

━━━❧❧❧❦❦━━━

When Ayla returned to her bunk in the Assassins' dormitories, her things were gone. Pixies would leave a calling card, to make the theft sting more. This was not the work of Pixies.

"Something missing?" Garret's voice, as warm and friendly as it had ever been, grated on her now.

It was simply her missing things, and her anger at the theft. That was all. "I've come back to find everything pinched. I'm not in a good mood about it."

Garret's arm slid around her waist, a touch he would have never allowed himself before. "Perhaps they haven't been stolen. Perhaps they've been…moved." His mouth was so close to her ear that his breath stirred the hair at her temple.

Moved. Of course. How could she have forgotten all that had transpired before her disastrous trip to the Darkworld?

"Moved?" She tried to sound pleased. "Already?"

Garret pulled her to face him. Puzzlement clouded his eyes, but he kept his expression carefully composed. "I thought we'd made an agreement. You...accepted my proposal."

She hadn't. Not yet. She'd promised to, when she returned, but she hadn't. And he'd taken her from the only real home she'd known, without asking her permission.

"I need to report to Cedric. Can I meet you later? At home?" The word burned her tongue.

His smile was polite. It did not reach his eyes. "I had planned something for us, and I do not wish to wait."

If there was anyone in the Lightworld she could not say no to, it was Garret. And he knew it, and used it to his advantage.

"I need to get this filth off of me," she tried, knowing the effort was futile.

His eyes lit up as if he'd anticipated this answer. "Then it is a good thing I've planned to take you to Sanctuary."

She sensed a cold, blue frost racing across her veins. Surely, in the Other Sight, she would have seen the branches of her life tree withered and winter-black. "So soon?"

It was a tradition, when their kind wished to mate, that they declare their intention to the Old Gods. But the Old Gods were gone, so—foolishly, in Ayla's opinion—couples declared their intention and cor ˈˈ ˈˈted their union in Sanctuary, where the spirits of the Old Gods were said to reside.

Garret sensed her distress. He could not disguise his irritation with her, though he tried. His antennae twitched the way they always did when he felt she was fighting him. "I am eager to make our union something more than that of a mentor and his student, as I thought you were. Unless something has changed?"

The way he asked made it clear what he meant. If she turned him down, she was a fool. She could not disagree with him. As his mate, she would gain entrance to a life she could never dream of earning on her own. And if her life before the Assassins' Guild had taught her anything, it was how to survive. There were much more unpleasant ways to do that.

"No. I am surprised." She tried for a smile like she'd seen on the ladies at Court, knowing and promising all at once. It felt stiff and unnatural on her mouth. "I did not think that when I visited Sanctuary for this purpose that I would be covered in filth."

He laughed and put his arm around her shoulders. "Come. We will find a messenger to deliver the news of your conquest. Then, we will go to our home and perhaps you will find some more appropriate attire there before we go to Sanctuary. Ayla, this is truly the happiest day I can remember."

Something stirred in her chest at that. She'd made him happy. It was not often that she had the chance to do that for anyone. If she could hold on to that feeling, perhaps it would be enough.

And if it were not, at least she would still have a home.

Garret's apartment was warm and clean, more so than usual. Ayla was aware that this was for her benefit, to impress her, as were the various colored robes and exquisite toiletries, probably collected from his sister's ladies-in-waiting. She thought she should question how he had obtained them, but she forced herself to think about anything else, so that she would not be upset by the answer. Strangely it did not sting her pride to think he might have exchanged intimate favors with Mabb's servants. She could not summon an ounce of jealousy.

Rather, it hurt her more that she lacked any feeling of possessiveness. The very fact that she was not upset, upset her.

"I did not know what you preferred," Garret said, moving quickly to the bed, where her new clothing was laid out. "Each one is fine, but none match your beauty, Ayla."

She almost laughed at that carefully practiced remark. "They are very fine." She reached out to touch one, but he quickly shooed her hand away.

"Perhaps you should wash a bit, first," he said, squinting in distaste at her muddy, bloodstained hands. "There is water in the pitcher on the hearth."

Outwardly obedient while chafing inside, she went to the hearth and poured the slightly warmed water into the clay bowl beside it. "You said you brought my things here. Where are they?"

She did not have to wait for her answer. The few possessions she owned were stacked carelessly beside the door, as if in the hopes they would show themselves out in shame at the face of the splendor around them.

After washing and tossing aside her filthy leather, she slipped one of the new robes over her head. The delicateness, both the light blue color and the fine weave of the fabric, seemed only to highlight the coarseness of everything about her. The calluses on her fingers, the scars on her bare arms.

If Garret noticed, he did not seem to care. "Let me help you," he said, stepping behind her to fasten the fabric at her shoulders. His hands lingered there. "This was the life you were meant to lead, Ayla. If your mother had only chosen another Faery to mate with, you could have achieved it without my help."

"It was not my choice to be born this way," she snapped, before she could help it.

Garret was quick to soothe her. "Of course it was not. But it is something to think of. Something to…guide your actions. In the future." He turned her to face him. "You have mortal blood in your veins. You will always be prey to mortal temptations. Do you understand what I am saying to you?"

She did not, not completely, but enough, at least, to be vaguely insulted. She nodded, anyway. No good would come of such an argument.

They started out for Sanctuary in casual conversation. Garret made no further mention of her shameful parentage, no thinly veiled criticism of her past actions. They talked as they had when they had first come to know each other, after the initial awkwardness of new acquaintance had faded and been replaced by tentative and exciting friendship. Ayla found herself more relaxed in Garret's presence than she had felt in a long time. Since before his attitude toward her had changed from that of a teacher to a suitor, she realized.

Though Sanctuary was thought to be a gift to all of the Lightworld, it remained cut off from anyone not in good standing with the Fae, as it had appeared in the Faery Quarter. It had started, Ayla had been told, when a seed from an Upworld tree fell into the Lightworld. Sunlight and rain followed it through the grates separating the Humans above from their enemies below. As the tree grew and seeded new growth in the cavern it occupied, the Fae took it as a sign that they had not been abandoned by the Old Gods. Sanctuary went from a curious and pleasing accident of nature to a sacred place, a promise that the Fae had not been forgotten.

The first time Ayla had been to Sanctuary had been before she had begun her training in the Assassins' Guild. Cedric, the Guild Master, had brought her so that she could renounce the life she had lived outside of the Lightworld, and pledge her allegiance to the Queene of the Fae. She could not have dreamed that on that day, when her feet had touched grass for the first time, the first time that sunlight had warmed her face, she would one day be mated to the brother of the Queene.

"It is beautiful, isn't it?" Garret whispered reverently as they approached the oval of brick that framed the entrance to Sanctuary. Elsewhere in the Lightworld, it was still night. The daylight borrowed from the Upworld filtered down to them long after it gilded the Humans' blocky towers. But the wide expanse of metal grid that stretched over the opening above Sanctuary let in the daylight in its own time. A thin, white haze wreathed the trees, and from somewhere inside the small wood came the sound of a brook.

Wide, broken steps led precariously down to the grass, and Garret helped Ayla make her way over them. They stopped on a level bit of concrete to slip off their shoes to feel the crisp prickle of grass and the soothing cool of the soil beneath. She turned her face to the pale sunlight filtering through the grates, smelled the air. It wasn't fresh, but fresher than the staleness of the tunnels. It would be a shock to return to that, Ayla knew from past experience. When you've never breathed fresh air or seen sunlight, it is too bright and wholesome in reality. When you return to what you knew before, it is too dark and never quite the same as it was.

When she left Sanctuary this time, things would be changed again. On her first visit, she'd come as a refugee, left as citizen of the Lightworld. Now, she came lonely and would leave mated to her constant companion for the last five years.

"Not long from today, we will come to this place to ask for a blessing on our heir," Garret said quietly, resting a proprietary hand on Ayla's stomach, as though a babe already grew there.

It wasn't something Ayla had given any thought to. Fae only bred when they wished to, not out of necessity. That would not happen today, though, and she locked the worry away to the back of her mind. Far off possibilities would not hang over her today, when she could concentrate on more pleasant things.

"Have you ever been up there?" Garret ask, pointing to the grates that separated Sanctuary from the Upworld. "It is beautiful."

She turned to him, unsure why he asked the question, hoping it was an invitation.

He nodded indulgently. "Go. I will wait for you here."

Though it would have been more polite to stay behind, Ayla's curiosity was too powerful. Tentatively unfolding her wings, she let them buzz against her back before opening them completely and taking to the air.

The feeling of pushing herself higher and higher, not limited by the low ceiling of a tunnel, was indescribable. The tapestries lining the halls of the Palace depicted this kind of flight, but Ayla had never allowed herself to imagine it. It was an unspoken rule of the Lightworld, not to long for the old days, in order to make their imprisonment more bearable. It had been easier for Ayla, who had been born in the Underground, to ignore the instinct to fly; she had never, in all of her visits to this place, thought to fly here. After this, would she find the short trips—up to a door, over a span of water, to avoid a crowd—satisfying anymore?

But it was a false freedom. Though the limit had been raised—she was far above the trees now—it still existed. Ayla reached the grates and poked her fingers through the metal grid. Separated from the world of the Humans by metal bars and half of her blood. What would it have been like, to be born wholly Human? She'd imagined being born completely Fae, but she'd never thought of the other side of the coin.

Garret called to her, and she looked down. A Human in her position would fall and die, their fragile mortal body smashed on the ground below. She folded her wings and let go of the grates, falling like a star from the sky—as such an event had been described to her—her stomach leaping, limbs seizing in terror. It seemed much farther with her eyes closed, and she wondered what would happen if she didn't save herself. Would she die before the healers arrived? Certainly there would be no consummation of her relationship with Garret today, no formal announcement to follow. It would be at least a week of rest and healing, if she survived.

"Ayla, stop."

She twisted, opened her eyes, saw the tops of the trees rushing at her and opened her wings. The pull of air against the stretched skin stung a bit, but it slowed her fall, giving her a moment to collect herself. It wasn't Garret's voice that had called to her, but she saw no one else.

Garret looked up as Ayla's feet touched the ground beside him. He didn't appear worried in the least that she had just fallen from the sky. It could not have been him that warned her.

He took her hand to lead her into the trees. Here was the heart of Sanctuary, where it was said the Old Gods hid, waiting for the day they could return safely and crush the world of man.

"I hear the water," Ayla said absently, her feet tingling where they touched the charged ground. Something in the trees shifted; she thought she saw a face in the leaves before it disappeared in the breeze. Soon, they came to the source of the water sound, a tall, jagged stone with a narrow crack in the face. A thin, arcing stream fell from the lowest point of the fissure to disturb the face of the pool below. Ayla wondered where the water came from, but the thought fled, her mind overwhelmed by the power that crackled in the air.

At the edge of the pool, Garret pulled off his robes and slid into the water. He grimaced as the slight current caused by his disturbance of the surface pulled at his wings.

Ayla knelt on the bank, watching in envy. Garret's wings were fragile, like dragonfly wings, with the rainbow sheen of chemicals on water coloring them. She reached back to touch her own, tough wings, skeletal monstrosities covered with tawny skin, as if they belonged on a mortal.

"Are you going to come in?" Garret asked, a hint of impatience in his voice.

The faster she got in, she reasoned, the faster she could hide her hideous wings from his scrutiny. He'd seen them before, but if she managed to cover them before he commented on their appearance she would save herself much embarrassment.

The water was pleasantly cool and clean. She slid off the bank, for the first time not thinking of how the wet would seep into her clothing and cause hours of misery as it dried. She left her robes on the bank and sank down, until her head was completely covered. Beneath the surface, she opened her eyes and watched her hair float around her like rust-colored seaweed.

When she broke the surface, Garret was beside her, laughing. "I forget that you probably do not visit here as often as I."

She swam to a low rock shelf beside the waterfall. "I do not have much time."

"You will, now," Garret said, breaking off to duck his head under the water. When he emerged, he swam beside her and pulled himself to sit on the rock. "We'll come as often as you like. As often as will make you happy."

Her heart sank at his words. She couldn't say she'd ever been happy, even as a child. Her happiest day had been when her people—her true people—had grudgingly accepted her into their world. Even then, any good feelings she'd had on that day had been tainted by the knowledge that she was still, in many ways, an outsider.

Garret smoothed her hair behind her ears, then cupped her jaw between his slender hands. "I know at times it seems I can see nothing but myself. But I have been your mentor for five years now, and you would not be alive if I were as self-absorbed as you believe me to be. I see your pain, every day, and it has grown over these years. I do not want to see you in such a state, not anymore." He leaned forward, his lips hovering just over hers. "Let me take it from you, Ayla. Let me make you happy."

It was the last chance she was likely to get. And looking into Garret's eyes, so kind and, for once, earnest, she wanted to be truly happy with him.

She seized the chance.

In a moment, she was beside him on the rock, their wet skin sliding together as he pulled her into his lap. There could have been some spark of feeling, but the novelty of another person's hands on her, and the disturbing knowledge that it was Garret, her mentor, someone she'd never thought of in such a way, squashed anything but a slight giddiness that fluttered in her stomach at the thought that she was about to experience something that until now was a secret to her.

Garret had touched her before, in training, to show her a move or correct her grip on a weapon. The way he touched her now was possessive and hungry. He did not linger overlong on just one part of her. His mouth slid from her neck to her breasts, his hands smoothed a restless path to her hips. All the while, he whispered against her skin, promising to be a good mate, trying to reassure her, to ask her not to be frightened. She wasn't frightened, but she didn't wish to correct him, for fear of disappointing him.

It all happened so suddenly that she almost missed it. A strange buzzing set up in her head, angry and red, and she realized she'd never experienced a sound that had a color before. Then, her body felt it was no longer under her control, and she feared she might faint. She gripped Garret tighter, and he strained against her, but she could not tell him that it was not from his ministrations that she felt dizzy.

He moved her to straddle his lap, parted her thighs with his hands. The male part of him jabbed clumsily between her legs, and she panicked. "Please, wait a moment…"

How could she tell him that it was too fast, too frightening suddenly? How could she tell him that the edges of her vision were beginning to curl and blacken like burning paper? She opened her mouth to ask for just a minute to catch her breath, a moment to get her bearings, but the tip of him found entrance and before she could take her next breath he gripped her hips and pulled her down, splitting her open just as everything turned red around her.

The water arcing over their heads turned to blood, the black sides of her mind closed in around and behind it, bending it until it was her hair, floating in the dark void that surrounded her as it had beneath the water of the pool. Below her, instead of endless black, a sea of bloodred feathers stretched as far as she could see, and she plummeted toward them, crashing through the surface without touching a single one. The feathers turned black—where had she seen black feathers?—and rained over her as she knelt above Garret in the pool. The searing heat where their bodies joined flared, burning up the tree of her life force inside of her, and when she raised her head, sobbing, from his shoulder, it was not Garret she clung to.

It was the Darkling.

In a flash, he was gone, replaced by Garret, who shuddered and groaned inside of her. Gone, too, was the burning in her soul. With the vision gone, all that remained was the stinging pain in her abused flesh where Garret slipped from her body. The ebony feathers that had covered the ground like black snow had been nothing but a dream, as well. She shook her head and pressed her fists to her eyes, willing her mind to balance.

"Ayla, are you all right?" Garret pressed his palms to her temples. She felt his energy trying to force its way into her, to heal her, but it was spiked and cold and blue, and she did not want any part of it.

"I am fine. I am…overwhelmed."

This pleased him. He laughed a little when he said, "It is understandable, with such a new experience."

She heard little else of what he said as he pulled her from the pool and gently helped her dress.

What had the vision meant? Surely not that she wished to mate with the Darkling! The creature was physically disgusting, and his very nature was contrary to the principles of the Lightworld. One God? A wish to return the Earth to the Humans? No, she could never bring herself to even imagine such a desire.

The man with wings. The old woman's words echoed in her mind. Surely, then, this was a warning. This Darkling would destroy her, and the happiness she would surely have with Garret. But how? Would Garret learn what had taken place in the Darkworld and reject her? No, he did care for her, and he would not wish to lose something he cared about. Would the Darkling kill her? It seemed less likely after what had taken place. But the old woman had known, and she had possessed a powerful magic. This Darkling would destroy her, and her vision was no coincidence.

Garret dressed quickly and returned to her side, his antennae twitching in concern. "You look so serious, Ayla. Perhaps more is bothering you than you care to tell me?"

"No," she began, shaking her head, "I am only—"

She was not able to finish. Garret lifted his hand to her hair, lips compressed as though trying to stifle laughter. "How did you manage to get this tangled in your hair?"

When he pulled his hand back, he held a night-black feather.

Thirteen

Human rituals of hygiene were nothing short of torture. Keller guided Malachi from one insane and uncomfortable task to another. Washing with a rag and a basin of water, so that his skin prickled from the cold. Raking a comb through his matted hair until he was sure the skin would come away from his skull. Dressing in new clothes Keller grudgingly gave over.

"It is too tight," Malachi grumbled as Keller pulled the shirt over his head. He sounded like an unhappy child. He did not wish to bother with all of these inane vanities. The longer he waited, the farther she would go, disappearing into her strange world forever.

"No, no." Keller fussed with the fabric, pulling it down. "Maybe. But look, you're not trying to win a beauty pageant here. You just want to be clothed."

Malachi picked at the sleeve of the garment. It was a shirt like Keller's, with no buttons on the front, so it had to be dragged over the head, a disconcerting process that made Malachi feel as though he'd ducked his head under water for a moment. The back bunched around his shoulder blades, where his wings attached, but Keller made two quick cuts and pulled it down. The fabric hung as a flap between his wings, but at least it was not tight anymore.

"I have these," Keller announced, producing a pair of pants that appeared to be missing half their length, "or these."

Malachi chose the second option. They were far too large, but better than too short and ragged at the ends. He put them on, and Keller produced a length of frayed cord to thread through the loops at the top to prevent them from slipping down. Malachi pushed his hands through his hair, and Keller swatted them away. "We just got that untangled. Hang on." He pulled a thin, stretchy band from the handle of a tool lying on the workbench and used it to gather Malachi's hair into a single tail at the back of his neck. "You look good, Mac."

Vanity! Another new experience. He allowed himself to smile at the compliment. "Thank you. Now, you will take me to the Faery."

"No, we're not done yet." Keller went to a cabinet and rifled through it, cursing. When he emerged, he held a long length of burgundy cloth in his hands. Unrolled, it proved to be a cape with a hood and a faded gold emblem of a star painted on the back. "From the Dragon Court. Their Human messengers wear them. Nobody's going to bother you with one of these on."

Malachi took it from him and swung it over his shoulders, flattening his wings.

"No, don't put it on now!" Keller snatched it and rolled it into a hasty bundle, looking around as if some invisible person might have caught them. "If you're seen with this on in the Darkworld, you'll get killed. Put it under your shirt and keep it there until you reach the Strip. Oh, and don't let any real messengers see you with it on, either. Their employers don't like people messing with their stuff."

"Then how did you get this?" Malachi took the folded cloak and tucked it under his shirt.

"I won it off a messenger in a card game." A moment later, guilty and angry, Keller snapped, "I stole it off him, after he passed out."

"Brave of you." Malachi headed toward the door. "Now, you will take me to her."

"Now, just wait a minute." Keller had not moved, stubborn Human. "I'm not going with you. I can tell you where she is, but there's no way that

I'm going to be able to sneak in. It's going to look suspicious already, you looking as Human as you do, and I'd rather both of us remain in one piece. I can't tell you exactly where to find her, but I can tell you enough that you'll be able to find her on your own."

"On my own?" The idea held some excitement. If he went by himself, he could act as he pleased, with no bossy Human to impose restrictions on his behavior. He could find the Faery and steal her, and, as nothing would matter once that had been achieved, he could do what was necessary and efficient to make his way back with her.

"You can't kill anyone," Keller said gravely, and Malachi cursed the Human's ability to look into his thoughts.

"Tell me what I need so that I can find her." Malachi's hands clenched to fists at his sides. The waiting was interminable. He needed her. The feeling of her hands on him, the way she had felt against him as he'd pushed her against the workbench…those moments tumbled over and over in his mind, driving him mad. He needed her.

Keller canted his head to the side, more thoughtful than he'd appeared a moment before. "You love her."

"Love?" A small laugh escaped with the word, a huff of denial he had not meant to express. "I do not know about mortal love. I need her. And you must tell me where to find her."

With a loud sigh, Keller relented. "I see a door, up high, no stairs. There are four doors where she's at, but this one is up high. There's a pipe leaking water, and it's in an area where a lot of Faeries live."

Something plummeted in Malachi. "Is that all?"

Keller nodded, spreading his hands helplessly. "All I can give you. I saw trees a little while ago, but it couldn't have been real, because she was—" He broke off suddenly. "Better be going now, if you want to get into the Lightworld tonight."

He wanted to ask Keller what he'd been about to say. If she were hurt or needed help, he would want to know. But the prospect of the journey was too enticing as he slipped out the door.

"Dragons speak Latin. I assume you know it?" Keller called after him.

Though his gift of language had fled, Malachi still remembered that tongue, preferred of the Human church on Earth a century ago. "Yes."

"Use that when you enter the Lightworld. The guards won't question you. And take the entrance to the Faery Quarter, that's your best shot. Ask someone on the Strip, they'll tell you the way."

Malachi nodded once and turned, slogging through the deep water.

"Hey, Mac!" Keller yelled, and Malachi turned back. The Human smiled. "Good luck."

Malachi took the sentiment to heart as he made his way toward the Strip. On his first journey to the Strip, he'd been desolate and bewildered. He had not cared that something might spring from the shadows to devour him. After seeing the Faery, touching her, his heart beat with new desire to live, to be with her again. Was that the "love" he'd seen Humans display for each other while he'd done his duties for God?

Perhaps, but perhaps not. So much of the love he'd seen examples of seemed destructive. Women lying dead at their own hands, in despair over love. Men killing their wives, their children, driven mad by the ending of a relationship. That was not love.

What he felt for this Faery was just as consuming and terrifying, though. Did that constitute love, or mere infatuation? Love seemed the sort of concept that would need time and nourishment to grow. He could not love her.

Lost in his thoughts and plans for how he would find her once more, he did not realize how close he'd come to the Strip. The easiest part of his journey was over, he realized with some dread. He slipped into the stream of people and pulled the cloak from his shirt, but he did not put it on, not yet. First, he had to find the passage into her land,

and it seemed unlikely that the messenger of a Dragon, a denizen of the Lightworld, would not know how to find their own home.

A young, female Human with shining golden hair stood beside a stall containing ribbons and jewels, all the many material goods that female creatures enjoyed possessing in order to appear more attractive or wealthy than others. This girl would not question him, too intent on selling her wares.

"Excuse me." He smiled at her. Smiles seemed to get Humans further with each other.

The girl's face brightened, and for a moment something about her seemed so familiar that prickles rose on the back of his neck. In the next second he felt nothing. She was merely a girl, dazzled by the sight of someone who looked good, if Keller could be believed in such matters.

"Yes, sir. What can I show you today?" Something about her words implied more than polite helpfulness.

If she was interested in him on a base, mortal level, she might be more inclined to speak to him honestly. He leaned forward, pretending to be interested in something on the cart. "I fear I have lost my way. Might you be able to show me into the Lightworld?"

Her eyes glittered. "What do you need in the Lightworld that you cannot find here?"

"True love." He thought it ridiculous as he said it, but her face shone with true emotion.

She reached one work-roughened hand into the stall and pulled out a metal pendant on a ribbon. "Any alley off the south side of the Strip will lead you to the boundaries of the Lightworld. And take this."

Her quick movement toward him surprised him, but he bent down so she could slip the ribbon over his head. "This will help you find your true love," she whispered close to his ear. When she stepped back, she looked into his eyes as if trying to convey some deeper meaning to him, but a moment later she turned and darted around the other side of the stall. He started after her, but the pull to the Lightworld was too strong, now that he knew how to get there.

He unrolled his borrowed cloak and fastened the ties around his neck, glancing for a moment at the pendant the girl had given him. A curled vine, covered in thorns. If it were a sign, it was a disappointing one.

He pushed across the traffic of creatures in the main thoroughfare of the Strip until he reached the wide alleys that would lead him into the Lightworld. Posted at the mouths of these paths were signs in many languages. He found one he recognized and read:

Behold the proclamation of Queene Mabb: No enemy of the Lightworld shall pass these gates. No creature born of Dark shall be suffered within these walls. Heed these words or perish.

It might have served a frightening warning to some, but mere words would not stop Malachi in his pursuit. He pulled the hood of his cloak lower, flattened his wings around his shoulders, grateful that the cape brushed the ground and concealed their tips.

Despite its name, the Lightworld was as dim as the Darkworld. Cleaner, though, and drier. And though Malachi had never seen sentries or any sign of an organized militia in the Darkworld, within five hundred feet of the mouth of the tunnel, two soldiers awaited him.

He began to practice his words in his mind, what he would say. Would they ask him his name? What Dragon he worked for? For the first time, real doubt crept into his mind. But the sentries eyed his cloak and stood down without comment, even looking a bit afraid of him as he passed. It might have been his size—the sentries were slender as children, even with the added bulk of their armor—or that he worked for so fearsome a creature as a Dragon.

He knew of Dragons and knew they were not to be angered.

His first task managed, he set to the next. Where, in the whole of this Lightworld, would he find his Faery? At the juncture of two tunnels, four directions to choose, he stood paralyzed. It would be easy to become lost here, and dangerous, as well. He looked about the tunnel, hoping for some identifying sign, wishing he had brought something to mark his path.

Unbelievably the sign was there, as it was around his neck, as well. Painted arrows and corresponding symbols—a rose here, going farther south; a tree, pointing east; a large red X toward the Strip—decorated the concrete at the tops of the tunnels. And there, pointing him west, a curled, thorny vine, identical to the pendant the girl had given him.

Gripping the pendant in his fist, he started down the tunnel.

All Ayla wished to do once they arrived back at Garret's apartment—no, *her* apartment, *their* apartment—was to crawl into bed and sleep for a day. The experience at Sanctuary had sapped her of her energy, but Garret wished at once to present her to Mabb.

"Come, please. She will be so happy to embrace you as her sister." Though he said it with as much sincerity as he could muster, Ayla knew it was not the truth.

But she wished to please Garret, so she combed her hair and left it loose, as the ladies at Court did, and put on a fine silver necklace that Garret presented for her. Forcing her weary, swollen feet into the silk slippers he offered, she wondered if it would always be this way: presents for obedience, swallowing her discomfort to please him.

"While we are there I can report to the Guild Master," she mused aloud as they flew down from the door.

Garret sniffed. "I wouldn't think it necessary. You outrank him now."

"Yes, but I have completed an assignment." She swallowed the lump in her throat. "My final assignment. It is my duty to report."

"My sister—"

"And I would not wish anyone to speak ill of you as a mentor." Striking at his vanity was a low tactic, but he had always taught her that there was no shame in doing something she knew would work.

He smiled. "Ayla, you know where my weakness lies. For my pride's sake, you will go and see Cedric."

At the Palace, the stares of the Court members

were open and disbelieving as Ayla walked the halls beside Garret. The whispered gossip was not so much whispered as hissed so it could be heard as they walked past:

"I never thought Mabb would allow it!"

"To think, he could have had anyone, and he picked *that*."

"Half-Human? What a tragedy."

She kept her head high. In the past few hours she had let her guard down some, and now the barbs wounded her far more than they would have on an ordinary day. She blamed her fatigue for the tears that collected in her eyes and stiffened her spine.

"You are beautiful," Garret murmured close to her ear as they slowed before the doors to the Assassins' Hall. He pulled her close and pressed his lips to a tear that slipped down her cheek. "You are my beautiful Ayla, and I would have you no other way."

It was a lie, but it helped her gain her composure as they entered the Hall.

The reporting for the day had already begun, and the Hall was crowded with interested courtiers and Assassins ending assignments or awaiting new ones. Ayla moved through the crowd to sit and wait on a bench in the queue, but Garret pulled her forward, marching her down the aisle in the center of the room, toward the table where the Guild Master was seated.

Cedric was a Faery so old that it was said he'd been on the shore the day Amergin won Ireland with his feats of Human wizardry. He'd walked with Lugh and had once been a lover of Bronwyn, Goddess of the Northern Sea. He kept his position at Court to be near Mabb, his true love, or so it was said. Ayla supposed that now she might know the truth behind those rumors, if she found the courage to question Garret on them.

"Garret!" Cedric's kind face broke into a wide grin. Though ancient, the Guild Master's looks were eternally youthful. His hair, sun-kissed-gold despite the lack of sun, was long and just unruly enough to avoid looking severe. His face was not as beautiful as some Faeries'; the jaw was too wide and sharp, his nose not quite straight. But he was handsome enough to attract the Queene's eye, if the rumors were true. His kind blue eyes moved to Ayla, and his smile faded the smallest bit with surprise. "And Ayla. It is an unexpected surprise."

"Surely you've seen my student in my company before," Garret said with a chuckle. He put his arm around Ayla's waist before she could protest the display, and the hall erupted behind them with speculative murmurs.

"I had heard rumors. Congratulations, friend." He nodded to Ayla. "You were a promising member of the Guild. You will be missed."

"That is why she is here." Garret disentangled his arm and stepped forward with her, leading her as though she were a child. "She has come to make her final report."

"Yes, of course." Cedric nodded to the paymaster seated at his left, then motioned to the records keeper at his right. "We have received word of your victory, are ready for the recounting, Assassin."

An almost painful sense of sadness gripped her, freezing her lungs in her chest. She would never stand here again. In a month, her fellow Assassins would have forgotten her. She cleared her throat and attempted to speak without her voice quavering. "I was instructed to kill five Demons in revenge for encroachment upon the territory of the Lightworld."

"And did you complete this duty?" Cedric barely waited for her "Yes" to continue. It was a formality. "And at what time did you complete this duty?"

She hesitated. The time that had passed between her assignment and her return would be questioned. Could she lie convincingly enough? Garret had believed her, but he was blinded by his certainty that she would never do anything he did not wish her to do. Suddenly aware of the expectant look on the Guild Master's face, she said, "One day and one night ago."

His gaze flicked to Garret, and then back to her. "And why did you not report yesterday?"

Everyone in the hall would believe her if she said the consummation of her mating with Garret had taken precedence over her position as an Assassin. Already some of the courtiers seemed to be leaning in to hear, so that they could titter at the implications and congratulate Garret with knowing winks as he left the hall.

Still, Garret would ask her later why she lied, perhaps even demand that she tell the truth so that his perfect record as a mentor would be unsullied.

While she mulled over her answer in the space of a few heartbeats that felt like ages, Garret stepped forward and spoke for her. "She was wounded in the Darkworld, and had to hide herself in order to heal. It is lucky indeed that she was returned to me safely." He reached for her hand and lifted it to his lips as if to kiss it when a voice from the back of the room shocked him into dropping it.

"Ah, that would explain the energy expenditure that was reported by my spies last night." Queene Mabb herself, surrounded by guards and several of her ladies-in-waiting glided down the aisle toward them. The assembly knelt in a wave, and Garret quickly pulled Ayla down to bow beside him as his sister approached. Unlike the rest of the Faeries in the room, however, Garret stood, one hand still on Ayla's shoulder to keep her in her supplicatory position.

From where she knelt, Ayla could see only the Queene's skirt and cape, and one white hand. The skirt was of a silk so fine that it appeared liquid violet, the cape a deep shade of blue and heavy, with silver thread twining around amethysts and quartz sewn to the fabric. Gold and silver shimmered on her fingers, long silver chains dripping with more amethysts wrapped about her wrist.

"Your Majesty. What a pleasure to see you again. May I present my mate—"

Mabb spoke as though she had not heard her brother. "There was a large amount of Fae energy detected in the Darkworld last night, Guild Master. Perhaps you should instruct your Assassins better in our policies."

She swept past, and Ayla dared a glance in her direction. Her white hair was long, nearly touching the ground if not for the knot that bound it into a sharp point near her ankles. A circlet of silver with a mass of looped chains rested on her head, and her wings were concealed.

Ayla looked at Garret. His antennae were red and flat against his hair. He was angry with his sister, and no amount of graceful posturing would cover it.

As if sensing his anger, Mabb stopped and turned. Ayla averted her gaze quickly.

"Garret, I need you. Send your mate home."

Ayla could judge the moment the Queene had left from the buzz of excited conversation that exploded into the air.

Angry and humiliated, Garret pulled Ayla to her feet. It was not the gentle, loving touch he'd given her before. His grip on her hand caused her bones to creak. "Go home. I will finish things here."

Stunned at the Queene's sudden appearance and her quick dismissal, Ayla only nodded. She'd taken a few steps away from him when Garret stopped her. His tone was calmer, his touch softer. "I will return to you tonight, never fear." He kissed her, then whispered against her lips, "I hope to find you awake and…eager for my attention."

She left the Palace alone, afloat on a sea of new whispers at her back.

Fourteen

The signs were not as easy to follow as Malachi had first thought. After too many dead ends he'd nearly given up, until the sound of water turned his head and feet around.

There, at the end of a dim tunnel, he saw the four doors, two on each side, one above, one below, and the pipe leaking water.

Which door was hers? It was above, so Keller had said, but which of the two? One mistake might bring the guards, and he'd seen many in his traversing of the Lightworld. To come this far, to be so close after hours of searching, and to have his progress snatched away would be more than he could bear.

In the hours since he'd entered the Lightworld, he'd imagined the moment when he would see her again. Would she come to him, tortured by the same emotions he'd suffered since they'd first touched? Or would she kill him, as she had sworn to?

It mattered very little. If he could not have her, he would no longer need to live.

He wondered if he had not been lying to the shopgirl when he'd said he sought his true love.

Throwing off his cape—the way was clear enough—he stretched his wings carefully. If they did not work, then what? He would find a way, even if he could not reach the door through his own power. Though they were heavier with Keller's patching he managed to give his wings an experimental flap that brought him off the ground. Another try, and he was level with the first door, heart nearly bursting with relief.

There were no windows in these dwellings. It would have made it easier to check for her. The residents of the other homes were either away or asleep. The night must have fallen while he walked. Near each door, a single metal bar was set into the concrete. Malachi gripped it, let it take some of his weight as he considered his next move.

A single strand of flame-colored hair was wrapped around the bar, just above his thumb.

The shock of the sight nearly sent him tumbling back to the ground. This was the door. He pushed it open without further thought and used the bar to steady himself as he stepped in and closed his wings.

Only when he saw the cheerful domesticity of the scene did he halt. Two pairs of boots, both belonging to a male, rested on the bricks near a dying fire that lit the room. Stepping farther into the dwelling, Malachi caught sight of the end of a bed. A proper bed, like the Humans above used, not a pallet of dirty blankets like Keller had in the back room of his workshop. Dangling over the edge was one slender white foot.

If she lay there beside a male of her own kind, he would kill him. He no longer cared about Keller's orders. Keller had no understanding of the feelings that roiled in him. He would kill the Faery at her side, then Keller for not warning him.

Malachi turned the corner to face the alcove where she lay, alone. Instantly, the murderous rage in him evaporated. She lay on her stomach, her wings folded against her back. A blanket twisted across her lower body, and her hair spread on the dark sheets as though fire had spilled like water there.

He approached carefully, not wishing to wake her. Not yet. He wanted to imagine the scene, to see her waking in his mind, her face rumpled at first in confusion, the expression giving way to joy when she realized he'd come for her. He wished to hold the image in his head for a moment, for he could not be sure he would see it with his eyes.

Slowly he reached out a hand and touched the foot that hung over the bed, cupping it in both his hands. Her flesh was warm and soft, and he knelt to press his cheek to it.

In her sleep she turned, murmuring something in her dreams. Malachi stood and placed one foot on the mattress, testing to make sure that his weight would not disturb her. He crouched at the foot of the bed, his wings slightly opened to keep his balance, and reached for a tendril of her hair. He lifted it to his face, taking in her scent, then looked to her face.

Her eyes were open, wide and afraid. She sat up slowly, never breaking her gaze from his, as if she faced an opponent in battle. A mere day ago, she might have, but Malachi could not believe that, not wholly. Even at the height of his rage after she'd left him for dead, even then he could not have killed her. There was no explanation for it, no reason such feelings could have consumed him at his first sight of her. But none of that mattered now.

She rose to her knees, clutching the thin covering in front of her like armor, and inched toward him with a hand outstretched. It seemed an eternity as those small, white fingers inched toward him. An eternity of watching the pulse beat wildly at her throat, an eternity of feeling his own heart leap as if trying to escape his chest to reach her.

Then he felt her fingertips on his chest, warm through the fabric of his shirt, and he covered her hand with his own. That brief contact broke some dam inside him, and without thinking of what his actions might cause, he grabbed her, wrapped his arms around her back and pushed his mouth over hers.

She did not fight him as she might have done, as he should have expected her to do. Her hands lay on his chest, but she did not push him away. Her mouth was as greedy and desperate as his. He twisted his hands in the mass of her hair, wanting to ensnare her further, to have so firm a hold on her that no physical power could wrench her from him.

It was as though all of his blood rushed to meet her, wherever she touched him. As if his heart would cease beating if he stopped touching her.

"Ayla!" An angry voice that spoke in the sound of rushing water broke through the ragged quiet of their breathing. She stiffened in his arms, tore her mouth away.

A male Faery stood in the doorway, his expression twisting through a spectrum of disbelief, horror and rage. Malachi's gaze fell on the huge sword propped against the wall beside him, and the Faery's eyes flicked to it immediately after.

Ayla—even in his sudden terror, the rapture of finally knowing her name swelled in his chest— pushed him, shouted a word he did not understand. Then, she spoke in a strangely accented version of his own tongue to order, "Go!"

A world of promise hung in that word. She did not banish him, but protected him. She feared for him.

She shouted no warning to the Faery at the door, who had no time to lift his blade before Malachi knocked him aside. Faeries were immortal, but fragile, built to blow on capricious winds rather than stand against them. The creature's head smacked the bricks of the hearth and he crumpled.

Somewhere, an alarm went up. Malachi dropped from the doorway, landing on his feet with a painful shock that shuddered up his bones. He could not stand. Opening his wings, he took to the air awkwardly.

Ayla stood in the doorway, robed in her shining hair. Her white skin lit the air around her.

"Come with me," Malachi said, the words scraping past a barrier of fear in his throat. "Please."

She looked inside, where her injured man lay. "I cannot. Go." When he did not move, she screamed it at him, the cry seemingly wrenched from her heart. "Go!"

As he flew away, he looked back. She watched him, tears sliding in long trails down her face, putting out the light that surrounded her.

"How did he find us?"

Ayla sat motionless on the floor. She'd donned her fine, blue robes and now they fanned into a jagged circle around her knees, a sea separating the island of herself from the onslaught of Garret's cold anger.

"How did he find us?" he repeated. Not "How did he find you," but "us," to emphasize the magnitude of her betrayal.

When she did not speak, he struck her. If any other creature had raised his hand to her, she would have fought back, but how could she fight her mentor, the one person who'd believed in her, taught her and loved her since the day she had come to the Lightworld? She deserved the stinging slap that burned her cheek like a brand. It would leave a mark and display to the world the depth of her betrayal.

"On the same evening that I dedicated my whole heart to you, the same evening I bound my life to yours, I come into our home and find you with a…a monster! An enemy of our world!" He stopped and took a deep breath. "You owe me an answer. How did he find us?"

She spoke quietly and slowly, so that she could listen to the words as she said them. She would not let herself be misunderstood or make a mistake. "I do not know how he found us."

Another slap.

"It is not a lie. I am not withholding the answer to hurt you. When I returned from the Darkworld, I had no clue that I would be living here, with you. I could not have told him." She waited for another blow, but it did not come.

With a heavy sigh, Garret agreed. "Yes. That is true, I moved your things here without first notifying you." After a moment, the cold calm returned. "Do you know him? Do you know why he would seek you out?"

"I know him," she whispered. She had not braced herself for the next slap, and the shock of it brought a ragged gasp from her throat. She swallowed thickly and began again. "I broke the geis by sparing his life once, and again when I healed him last night."

He hit her again and again, and she let him. She had betrayed him, there was no denying it. Besides, the pain in her heart was far greater than any pain he could inflict upon her with his hands.

Strange, though, that her sadness was not from

the pain she'd caused Garret. Her heart ached for the Darkling, who was certainly dead by now. Mabb's guards would have found him, if not in the Faery Quarter then when he tried to cross the border into the Strip. They would have taken him to one of Mabb's dungeons and tortured him, not for information, but for entertainment. Perhaps the Queene herself would have been present to see the deed done. Only when there was no value left in causing him pain would they let him die. Even now the process of his death had likely begun. She could still taste him on her lips.

"We will never mention this to anyone."

For the first time, Ayla looked up to meet Garret's eyes. His face was gray and drawn. Blood crusted on his skin beside fresh rivulets. The wound on his head had opened while he beat her.

"I will go to Mabb myself, and lie for you," he repeated. "You have no idea what she would do to you if I did not."

"She would have me executed." After their meeting in the Assassins' Hall it seemed she would have found an excuse to soon enough.

Garret was not listening, lost in his own thoughts, which he spoke aloud as though he were mad. "I will go to the Guild Master and speak with him on your behalf. To be sure that you are protected." He turned to her then, as if noticing her presence for the first time. "Is there anything else I should know?"

His rage was spent now, so she could ask without physical retaliation. "After you speak with the Queene…then what?"

He turned away. The wound at the back of his head was ugly, the flesh split. He needed a healer. "Then we will continue as I had hoped we would. You will never be left alone again, though, Ayla. I will never trust you enough to let you out of my sight."

But you will leave me alone. You will leave me alone when you go to the Palace. A horrible thought came over her. She could leave the Light-world tonight and never return. She could leave everything behind.

"You will stay here," Garret told her quietly, as if he could read her thoughts. "Even you are not foolish enough to walk away from a throne."

"But I am not—" She stopped herself. Garret seemed so intent on her ascension to his sister's throne. Ayla did not wish to know why he was so sure of it. "Shall I send a healer for you?"

"I have my own healer. I will consult him on my way to the Palace, once I have composed myself." He reached into the trunk beside the bed and pulled out a stocking cap, which he pulled down to cover his wound. "Time apart will help me cool my anger."

She waited, numb with despair, as he pulled on his boots and went to the door.

"I will find this Darkling, if the patrols have not," Garret said. She did not look up at him. She knew she would see triumph and anger on his face, desire to cause her pain. "I told you once that you are prone to temptation because of your Human blood. I see now that I must remove these temptations as they arise. Let his death be a lesson to you, should you seek to betray me again."

Ayla did not answer him. She listened to the sound of the door closing, counted to ten, then twenty, waiting until it was safe to move.

Thoughts of the Darkling tormented her. Would he curse her for not helping him? Her heart beat hard against her chest, her pulse echoing in the fresh bruises on her face. She could not help him, but if she would, this would be her only chance. She could walk to the Palace, prostrate herself before Mabb and hear herself pronounced a traitor and sentenced to death. If she were to be charged with a crime, let it be a crime she felt just in committing. Let her save the Darkling, if she could.

Practicality overrode sentiment as she pulled on her slippers and raked her fingers through her mussed hair. She could not help the Darkling, and why should she? It had not been her choice to place him in danger. Garret had not washed his hands of her entirely, despite her betrayal, but storming into a royal dungeon and defending the life of the creature would be a push too far. Perhaps when the old healer had warned her of the man with wings who would be her ultimate destruction, this was what she had meant. Not that the Darkling would destroy her himself, but that he would be the impetus of her downfall.

At the Palace, it seemed to Ayla that word of her shame had arrived ahead of her. The stares she received were gleeful and hostile, but she knew they tittered at her bruised face. Garret would never admit publicly that his mate had strayed from him with a Darkworlder, and the Court likely assumed she had been beaten for displeasing the Queene in today's audience.

Truth, cold and plain, sent panicked shivers down her limbs. It seemed a winter had settled over the tree within her, its branches cracked in the bitter wind of her fear. She might confess all to Mabb, and her position as Garret's mate might pardon her. But later, if Garret chose to cast her off and find another mate, one that was not tainted by scandal and gossip, one who was fully Fae, what then? Would she still be spared a traitor's death? How far could his protection reach?

She ducked into a darkened doorway and

pressed her palms to her temples. Her heart pounded as though it would burst from her chest, her head throbbed with fatigue and confusion. The Darkling was most certainly dead. She must stay. If she stayed, she might die. She should go. Every second brought a different bend in the path she knew she would take, throwing her off of her course.

"What do you mean, you haven't found him? What about the border guards?"

At the sound of Garret's voice, Ayla flattened herself against the arch of the doorway. He passed without noticing her, and why would he? He did not expect her to be there, and so it would not be so, in his mind. His arrogance affected his eyesight.

Cedric, the Guild Master, walked beside him, head down, serious. "The border guards are not under my command, but I agree, this is a matter for the militia, not for the Guild."

Garret had said no such thing, and his voice rose. "It is the duty of all capable fighters in the Lightworld to find this creature and bring him to justice! He attacked Ayla! Defiled her! Do you really wish for him to escape?"

The Guild Master paused, head still bent as though the floor might yield a diplomatic answer to him. "I am sorry for the pain this has caused you. But as far as we can tell, the Darkling has left the

Lightworld. I cannot risk the lives of my Guild without an order from the Queene."

"You have influence enough there." The sneer was plain in Garret's voice. "Why not use it, and leave her bed with orders for a full scale invasion!"

Garret stalked away then, down the corridor, leaving Cedric behind. The Guild Master stormed in the opposite direction, and Ayla wondered which she should look after.

The Darkling had escaped. That much was clear from the exchange. Also, that Garret had concocted a story and put it about before his sister had a chance to speak out. Queene or not, Mabb had a reputation for slander. No one would believe her now, when Garret had already begun to spread his version of the story around the Court.

With relief at both ends of the scale, the decision was harder to make. But only for a moment. As long as he lived, the Darkling would return for her. She felt this truth the way she still felt his hands on her. He would try again to reach her, and be killed in his attempt.

She would go to him. To ask that he never contact her again? To stay with him and never return to the Lightworld? Days ago, the prospect would have horrified her. Why leave the world she'd fought so hard to become a part of?

That was a decision she could make later. For now, she had to make her confession to the Queene.

It would have been easier to lie to Mabb, as Garret would lie to the rest of the Court, but this was not a matter of simple politics. The geis was a sacred oath, made not only to the Queene, but to the Old Gods, wherever they might be. To break it was to renounce your allegiance to the Lightworld, and that could only be forgiven by the Queene, in person. Woe be to anyone who broke the geis and did not confess. If their transgression was discovered, the punishment was worse than death. Ayla did not know what could be worse than death, and no one had told her, but she did not wish to find out.

The Queene's formal audience was closed for the evening, but with her new status at Court Ayla could gain entrance to the Queene's private quarters. The parties Mabb hosted for the elite were lavish and legendary. Too late Ayla remembered her disheveled hair and bruised face. If nothing else, it would make Garret's falsehood seem more plausible.

Mabb's chambers were located at the heart of the Palace. Ayla had never been there, but the guards appeared to know her—likely briefed by Garret on his last visit—and escorted her inside

The antechamber was huge, the floor and arched ceiling covered with tiny octagonal tiles placed there when it had been part of the Human world. Courtiers mixed in small clusters around the perimeter, to have a better view of who entered and left, no doubt. Their robes and gowns were garish, their jewelry catching the candlelight like golden starbursts. Ayla ducked her head to hide her face, pulled some of her hair to cover the bruises on her cheeks. In attempting to make herself unnoticed, she attracted the interest of the predatory gossip-mongers, and she heard their whispers as she passed.

"That is the Royal Heir's mate? What was Garret thinking?"

"She looks like a common Strip whore."

"Look, you can see the Guild mark, there, on her neck!"

"Has my brother not taught you to bow in the presence of royalty?"

A sudden hush fell over the room. Her stare intent on her feet, Ayla had not realized they had led her directly to Mabb, who now looked at her as though she were some insect.

Ayla bowed quickly, and when she rose she did not meet Mabb's gaze. "My apologies, Your Majesty."

"You may look at me. We are sisters now, after

all." Mabb said this loud enough to be heard by everyone in the hall, but she needn't have raised her voice. The courtiers had ceased their conversations, ready to hang on their Queene's every word. Leaning close to Ayla's ear, Mabb hissed, "Let us go. This is no place for private conversation, and I would have one with you now."

Mabb turned, her deep violet skirts flaring behind her. Her white hair was coiled in two braids like deadly serpents at the back of her head, and instead of her crown, two daggers with green jewels in their hilts kept them wound into place. As Ayla followed, another guard fell into step beside her. Flanked by the two, Ayla felt a distinct unease. It was as if she were being arrested, and she hadn't yet confessed her crime.

Mabb led the way through another room, this one an official-looking hall with a raised dais and long trestle tables. "My informal assembly," she explained, waving a dismissive hand through the air as they passed. "To meet with my council and advisors. Not that you should concern yourself with this. You will not be advising me. You are *family*."

The word dripped venom, and the poison hung in the air as they entered the next chamber, a small, crescent room with doors lining the arc. A grouping of chairs and a decorated table sat awkwardly in the middle, and Mabb passed these by, as well. "When you come to call on me, this is where you will wait to be seen by one of my ladies. They will discern if I am in a mood to see you that day, or if you will leave notice with one of my servants. The latter will almost always be true, in your case. I will not have time for you."

In the peak of the arch stood a huge double door, and the guards at Ayla's side hurried forward to open them at Mabb's signal. As Ayla and Mabb passed through, they stayed behind.

The doors opened onto a short hall with an arched roof. All along the bricks that lined it from floor to ceiling were gaps in the plaster. Mabb pointed to one and, without facing Ayla, remarked casually, "At my signal, poisoned arrows would come springing out at you. It is my last line of defense against those who seek to harm me."

Ayla stayed silent. Mabb produced a silver key from her sleeve and unlocked the plain metal door at the end of the hall, and they entered a new room.

Mabb's personal apartment, Ayla realized, unexplainably excited to be allowed into such a hidden and private place. The excitement faded, however, as she remembered why she was there, and that she was not welcome to begin with.

Finally Mabb turned, looking Ayla over with a critical eye. "You do not talk much."

Ayla phrased her response carefully. "I was content to let Her Majesty speak, as there was nothing of greater value I could contribute to the discourse."

Mabb held up a hand. "I did not ask you a question, Assassin, I made a statement. I trust you are able to tell the difference?"

Ayla nodded.

"No wonder my brother has already beaten you. You are very annoying," the Queene said with a beleaguered sigh. Mabb's skirts made a soft brushing sound on the grass-covered floor as she walked away. Everything in the room seemed to have come from the world above: the decadent fabric panels covering the walls, the gold accents and ornate, Human furniture. The chairs were not the simple stools favored by winged creatures, but tall-backed objects that would be impossible to perch upon comfortably. It was as if a piece of the Upworld had fallen by mistake into Mabb's Palace.

The Queene stood before a heavy, wooden cabinet with an ornate lock. The key jutted from its hole; Mabb had no fear, obviously, that someone would breach this inner sanctum.

"Has my brother informed you of what your duties will be, now that you are to be Queene?"

Though she was not versed in Court treachery, Ayla saw the hundred traps that lay in the question, and knew well enough to avoid them. "I do not understand. Your Majesty is the Queene." Ayla did not speak what else she knew, that Mabb was immortal and therefore her reign could potentially last forever. To speak of such a thing might lead Mabb to think of assassination, and Ayla wished to avoid the subject entirely.

When Mabb laughed it was angry, mocking. "He has at least taught you how to lie. I am still Queene because there was no one to replace me! Now that the Royal Heir has a consort at his side, she can be made Queene, and I will be tossed aside! Do not lie to me and say that you have not planned this!" In her fury, Mabb ripped one of the daggers from her hair and hurled it at Ayla.

It was easy enough to dodge it, but the Queene's rage had shown itself to be an unpredictable storm. Ayla proceeded cautiously. "I have no desire to become Queene. I am a simple Assassin—"

"I did not ask you to speak!" Mabb screamed, stalking a few steps toward her. Then, as if remembering something, she stopped and smoothed her loose, frayed braid behind her ear. She turned and opened the cabinet and drew out a stone tablet, which she clutched to her chest like a babe. "I know well what you are. A lowly Assassin, born on the Strip to a Faery mother long since banished from my kingdom and a Human father who died in the gutter, racked with disease from Human vices. If my brother had chosen a mate from the noble class, even one of my ladies-in-waiting, he could have disguised his intentions." She held out the stone tablet, motioning for Ayla to take it. "Read this! Read this and tell me that my brother is not playing me false!"

The stone was heavy, and Ayla fumbled with it a moment before she could right it in her hands. She glanced over the inscription for only a moment before handing it helplessly back to Mabb. "I cannot read," she said, feeling more ashamed of the fact than she ever had before.

Mabb's smile twisted cruelly. "Of course you cannot. But regardless, you would not be able to decipher these markings. It is in an old language, one that few in this stinking world remember." She took a breath, closing her eyes as if to calm herself. When she opened them again she was regal, royal despite her ragged hair and flushed skin. "It tells a prophecy of a time when the Fae would be forced to live underground. For centuries it was assumed that the prophecy foretold the invasion of Humans in our beloved Éire, that forced us to spread over the Earth and shelter in cairns and lakes and sea caves. But as even you, with your limited intelligence, can guess, it alludes to this time, that we are trapped below the Human cities, scavenging for sustenance and comfort, barred from nature and sunlight, entombed like the dead!"

Mabb's hands trembled as she placed the tablet back in the cabinet. "The prophecy speaks of one who will save our race, free us! A mighty warrior Queene who will lead a campaign, scouring the Earth and making all right once more."

Mabb, in all of her fine silks and delicate jewels, her body frail and small boned, was the furthest thing from a warrior that Ayla could imagine, but she had more sense than to speak such a thing to the Queene's face.

"This great heroine," Mabb continued, her eyes growing bright in her fervor, "will be born of both worlds, above and below. And her name will be remembered in the hearts of Fae and Human alike, for all eternity. And I intend to be that Queene!"

Though Mabb had not asked her a question, Ayla could not keep silent. "But it could not be you. I desire as much as anyone to see the hopes of the Lightworld restored by some great figure, but you are Fae."

"Do you dare to claim that this fate might be yours, instead?" Mabb came forward, drawing the other dagger from her hair as if she would stab Ayla. "Do you dare to insinuate that I cannot free my people?"

Queene or not, Ayla would show no fear to an

opponent. "I am merely stating the facts that you yourself spoke. While I am not proud enough to see myself in your words, the prophecy says it will be a half-Human Faery that fulfills this roll. Your Majesty is many things, but certainly not Human."

Mabb laughed, mocking again. "You know so little. My brother is full-blooded Fae, that is true. My mother, whore that she was, conceived him off one of her guards. But her lusts ran to the bestial, and she coupled regularly with a Human male she kept here, in the Palace. I was the product of their perverse union."

It was almost so sensational as to insist Ayla call the Queene false, but Mabb worked the ties of her gown, opening it as if she did not stand in the presence of a near-total stranger. "Have you never wondered why I do not display my wings? Why I keep myself covered at all times?" The ribbons of her bodice slipped through their grommets as she violently jerked them free, one pair, then another pair, the fabric gaping apart and exposing the white skin beneath. "No one, not even my ladies-in-waiting, see me completely exposed. It is too shameful, despite my great destiny, and I would not have anyone know the low, common origins of my birth."

She shook the gown free and turned slowly. What Ayla saw made her gasp out loud. There was the proof to Mabb's sensational story, jutting from her back, twisted and half-formed. Two small, pathetic flaps of white skin hung from protruding bones, their blunt, round ends betraying them as Human. They did not move of their own accord, but Mabb reached to smash them flat against her back as she drew her gown up, the skin swaying sickeningly as they folded over each other.

Ayla said nothing, only stared as the Queene pulled her gown closed and retrieved her daggers to right her hair. Only after she'd consulted her looking glass and found everything in order did she address Ayla once more.

"You will speak to no one of what you have seen. In time, I shall think of a crime great enough to banish you from the Lightworld, and then you will be nothing." Satisfied at this pronouncement, she went to the wall, where she slid a false panel aside. "You may go. Through here. I will not have you in my private audience."

Frozen, Ayla's feet would not move. If she told Mabb now of her failure to uphold the geis, the Queene would have the excuse she wanted to exile Ayla. Or, she might choose instead to have her executed.

Before, the prospect seemed less horrifying. For breaking her vow, the punishment was deserved. But to be sacrificed to Mabb's vanity? That was something that Ayla's small, hard-won pride would not allow. She squared her shoulders and left the room via the secret passage, which spit her out near the Assassins' Hall. Then, she left the Palace altogether.

The streets of the Lightworld were quiet. Most of its inhabitants slumbered now. Ayla ached to do the same. She thought of Garret's bed, how soft and warm it had been, how she'd slept so hard she hadn't dreamed. It would be so easy to return, to submit to whatever punishment he chose to inflict, as long as she could sleep for now.

But he'd warned her that she would never leave his sight again, and she did not doubt it. As long as she was close to him, she was close to Mabb's treachery. The Lightworld, once her home, now seemed alien and dangerous.

She passed the tunnel that would lead her to Garret's, and walked to the boundary of the Lightworld. There were more guards at the openings to the Strip than normal, all waiting to catch the Darkling. Ayla flashed her Guild mark as she walked past, and they stepped aside for her.

Just a short walk, and she would be out of the Lightworld altogether. The border seemed so innocuous. There was nothing stopping her walking back, past the guards, back into her life. No physical impediment that could keep her out, not yet,

But so much had changed that her old life was as separate from her as the Underground from the Upworld. At each step she knew she could not turn back, every movement an indelible mark.

She reached the Strip. She took a breath. All she had known was already behind her, all that remained was a future so insubstantial that it could not even hold fear. She did not look back. Another two heart beats, another breath, and it was decided, final. Ayla stepped from the tunnel, into the Strip.

Fifteen

❧

Garret stormed through the halls of the Palace. The whispers of Ayla's appearance had been bad enough. When he'd returned home to find those rumors confirmed by her absence, the entire situation had become so much worse.

She would have confessed, of course. Ayla's idealism had always been her greatest fault. By now, Mabb would know that she had broken the geis. By now, Ayla had ruined him.

He assumed that Mabb would be secluded somewhere in her private apartments, privately rejoicing in his downfall. Instead he found her among her fawning courtiers, laughing and talking, animated by some manic inner drive.

"Garret!" She moved to him as quickly as her heavy gown would allow, eyes sparkling with crazed light. "I was hoping to see you this eve-ning!"

He studied the faces of the courtiers carefully, but their vapid masks gave away nothing. Likely they did not notice the change in their Queene's behavior. They saw only her glittering exterior, and the things she would give them. Parties, banquets, little favors when they wished to slight their neighbors or gloat over their relationship to the Queene.

When he was on the throne—when Ayla was on the throne—things would be different. Mabb's fa-vorites would find themselves in far less comfort-able situations, and the new crop would worship their monarchs, as subjects should.

For now, though, his sister was Queene, and he bowed to her respectfully. "Sister, have you seen my mate this evening?"

The change that came over Mabb was immedi-ate. She whirled away from him, her skirts snap-ping like vipers behind her. "Guards! My audience is over for the night!"

Garret followed her without being told to. The servants they passed on their way to Mabb's private chamber scurried out of their way. They, like Garret, had spent enough time with her to guess her ever-changing moods.

Only when they were safely locked in her room

did she address him. "Why was she here? She spoke directly to me, in front of all of the Court. It was a mockery!"

"She confessed to you in front of the Court?" Though she was foolishly brave, Ayla was not a fool.

The frown on Mabb's face told him all he needed to know. Ayla had not confessed. Ayla had come here and, what, tried to gain his sister's favor?

He cursed silently. If his sister did not know what his mate had done, plans could still proceed.

"Confess?" Mabb laughed. "What could she have confessed to, besides her bedraggled state and ugly clothes? You didn't buy those for her, did you?"

Her pride must have been wounded deeply for her to stoop to such a barb. "Where is she now?" he asked.

"I sent her away." Mabb flounced to her dressing table, reaching for a vial of perfumed oil. "I do not care where she went to."

He paced to the secret door; the panel was ajar. "Did she leave with an escort?"

"I would not waste my guards protecting your…pet." Mabb scoffed and opened the bottle, sniffing delicately. "What do you think of this one?"

"I think you have made a very foolish mistake." He came to stand with his hands on her white shoulders.

Her gaze met his in the looking glass, anger giving way to confusion, then concern. "Garret, you're trembling."

It happened so much faster than he'd have ever dreamed. In all his years of planning and imagining, all his carefully constructed fantasies could have never prepared him for how beautiful, how incredibly freeing it was when the moment came. His hand closed over one of the daggers in her hair. She turned, face frozen in shock, a horrified plea ready to burst from her lips. It died, as she did, strangled by a tide of angry black that spilled from her throat. Her life force gushed liquid, falling to dead leaves on her gown.

She clutched at him as her limbs shriveled and twisted like vines left to die in the snow. That unnerved him; he'd always planned on poison, so that he wouldn't have to watch it happen. Still, he remained stoic as her brittle fingers caught his garments, trying to drag him into the beyond with her.

But there is no beyond to go to, sister, he thought, and for a moment felt real pity toward her. What must it be like, to pass from one world to another. From this world, where she was never meant to be, never meant to be mortal, to a place that did not exist. To be forced from one plane with no other to turn to. To leave, with no destination. Because it did not exist.

With a last, rasping breath like wind through frozen branches, she fell back, curled onto herself and darkened, an empty husk inside her fine gown.

It was finished, in the space it would have taken her to scream for her guards. It was finished, and there was no undoing it.

More troubling now was Ayla's disappearance. Perhaps she'd run to her Darkworld lover to escape her fate. His fists clenched at his sides at the thought, and he stalked out of Mabb's bedchamber. He would rather see Ayla dead than see her with that creature.

He calmed himself before he exited to the public rooms, and nodded to a passing servant. "Her Majesty would like to be alone for the rest of the evening."

The servant bobbed her pretty dark head and continued on her way. She did not know that she spoke to the Royal Consort, soon to be ruler of the Faery Court, once the last obstacle was removed from his path. Now that she had run off, perhaps fled the Lightworld altogether, that would be far easier.

He had planned to rule through Ayla, use her as

a puppet. She did not have the knowledge or the ability to run the Faery Court. But now, his path to the throne was so much clearer. He would not have to rule through a Queene. He could break with tradition and rule in her stead.

The Dragons might give him problems. The creatures were too clever for their own good. He would put it about immediately that the Darkling who'd infiltrated the border had been disguised as a Dragon messenger. He even had the creature's cloak to prove it. That would cast enough suspicion toward them to suppress any allegations they would make, at least until after the coronation.

He found that when he reached the Palace gates, he was reluctant to leave. What a strange, possessive feeling was inspired by becoming King. Foreboding nagged him as he stepped across the threshold, into the streets of the Lightworld. He crushed it down.

The throne awaited him. All that was left was to claim it.

Left. Another left. A right. Through a sharp bend. *A man with wings. I see a man with wings.*

Ayla shook her head, swiped at the dirty air before her. She stumbled over the hem of her gown for what seemed like the thousandth time, crashed to her knees in the mire.

He will destroy you.

She pushed the Human's warning behind her, climbed to her feet with a cry of pain that came as much from her aching legs as from the gnawing hole in her chest, as real as if someone had cut her heart out with a knife.

A knife. She had no knife. No weapon. No defense. She could easily die here, in the Darkworld, without anyone to know or care.

And whose fault was that? Throughout her life she'd done all she could to keep distance between herself and the world outside of her. Those who had wished to protect her—Garret and her father—she had rejected. Those who could have been friends, she'd bristled to. There had never been a lover, a confidant, never anyone to wonder where she'd gone.

A lifetime spent trying desperately to be a part of and apart from a world that would have happily been done with her years ago.

The water rose over her feet, weighing down her gown. The life of fine things and comfort that had lasted all of a day became more of a weight on her now than it had been before.

A part and apart. Left in the middle, as always.

Ahead, she saw the water shadows she'd memorized before. Water kept its own secrets, and they could be learned by careful observation. Now, these gentle ripples reflected in eerie black-blue on the dim wall of the tunnel pointed her to the Darkling.

If he'd survived. No, he had survived. If he had not, Garret would have found her by now, gloated to her, beat her. But if the Darkling did not want her, then what? She'd given up her world forever, and she could not survive in the Darkworld with a Guild mark on her body.

That was not true; she could survive, but it would be another hollow existence. Her heart had grown less fond of those, now that she found she had a heart.

Left, into deeper water, up to her waist. Something bumped her below the surface, and she hastened her step as much as she could, wading through the muck.

The Human healer had been just that; Human, foolish, as likely wrong as she was right. There was more than one male Ayla could name who had wings. It might not be the Darkling that would be her doom.

At the mouth of the tunnel that would bring her at last to Malachi, her stomach went weak. She pressed the heels of her hands hard against her cramping middle, willed the nervousness away. Had he felt this way, when he'd come to her?

She gritted her teeth and moved on protesting

legs through the resistance of the water. She'd set out to make this journey, and she would not let a moment of doubt stop her. She hadn't so far.

The door to the dingy room he lived in blended so well with the concrete of the tunnel wall that she almost missed it before the water shadows lapped upon themselves and commanded her back. She stood for a long moment, the damp creeping up the thirsty fabric of her gown, hands flexing in the air on nothing. Then, timidly, she stretched a hand out. Her fingers had scarcely brushed the rusted metal when the door swung open with a deafening screech and Malachi grabbed her, pulling her into his arms without a word, crushing his mouth over hers.

Her dirty, wet gown slapped against his bare legs; it did not matter. Her hair tangled in front of her face and he had to push it aside; still, he did not stop, did not set her on her feet again. The door closed, though she did not feel the strength of his arms leave her for even a moment.

Of course he would not reject her. He had followed her into the Lightworld, had risked his mortal existence to find her. How could she have expected anything else?

They were bound, by some strange, indescribable force, had been since the moment her touch had made him mortal. Now, that bond caused an ache in her that made no sense; now that she was close to him, their separation seemed more painful. Now that he touched her, it seemed they would never be close enough.

He carried her to where the Human slept, although he was not there now. The little alcove was empty, aside from a pile of torn blankets on the bare concrete. Malachi set her down there, ripped the filthy gown from her body.

With Garret, it had all happened so fast as to cause her to panic. The suddenness of this did not frighten her as much as it excited her. If she closed her eyes, she felt she was falling. If she opened them, she felt she would break apart.

His hands were on her everywhere, and hers on him. His body, so strange and ugly in comparison to the smooth, lean lines of a Faery male, was surprisingly exciting to the touch. The hard rounds of muscle beneath tightly stretched skin teased her fingertips as she dragged her hands down his arms, his chest, his stomach. She gripped that part of him that made him male, and a harsh sound wrenched from his throat. She opened her wings and let him push her back onto the blankets, where he fell between her legs.

He was huge, longer and thicker than Garret had been. She rose to meet him, the breath forced from her chest as he filled her.

Her world compressed to the maddening push-pull of him moving in her, the hot, coiled serpent of pleasure that pulsed and tightened in her. She screamed and panted and clutched at him, and he, just as ferocious, clutched back, his fingers digging tight into her hips, holding her impaled on him as he surged even deeper into her. Her body spasmed around him, and she jerked, gasping for breath, twisting in his grasp, lost under waves of feeling too intense to be pleasurable, too pleasurable to be painful.

His movements quickened, battering inside of her, as if he sought to break her apart. Then, with a shout, almost disbelieving, he bucked, lifting her hips off the blankets, and she saw the tree of her life force flare bright white, ignite into flame. She held him as he collapsed on her, crushing her to the blankets. He shuddered inside her still; she could feel the beat of his heart.

He came to his senses and rolled to his side, dragging her to lay atop him. He wrapped his arms around her, then his wings around them both, closing them into the dark.

The alarm went up just before morning broke. Garret had waited all night to hear it. Now, it seemed like the death knell that it was, but meant for him. He removed that thought immediately.

His plan would not fail, not now when he was so close.

At the knock on his door he rose from his place beside the fire, cast a look at the carefully rumpled—but not too rumpled—bed, mussed his hair and unfastened his robes. Cedric and six of Mabb's private guards hovered at the opening, their faces grim.

This was what Garret had been practicing for, as he sat at the hearth. The stricken expression came to him as easily as if someone had painted it on. "Gods, what has happened?"

"Your sister, the Queene, is dead." Cedric's eyes were rimmed in red, awash in tears. The weakling couldn't hide his sniveling devotion to Mabb even when carrying out his official duties.

Garret clutched his chest, stumbled back. "No. No, it cannot be."

"I am sorry, Garret."

He smoothed his hair back, forced tears to his eyes. "But Ayla…she is all right?"

Cedric looked past him, into the apartment. "I do not know. I expected to find her here. We must secure her, before the Assassin finds her."

"Assassin?" Garret let his eyes grow wide, forced some tears. "Are you saying that Mabb, that my sister, was assassinated?"

Cedric nodded, once, sharply. "That is why we

must find Ayla and secure her. She is your mate, is she not?"

"Yes, of course she is, but…" The taste of the declaration on his tongue was sweeter than the air in the Upworld. "But she was at the Palace. I sent her there for her own safekeeping, after the Darkling…"

"Ayla was not at the Palace. It is possible she fled." Cedric had never been the smartest of Faeries, and he clearly struggled to follow. "You say that Ayla was at the Palace last night?"

"In Mabb's private chambers, when I left them." Garret took a shuddering breath, which surprised him with its intensity. He was better at his role than he had expected. "You cannot possibly believe that Ayla—"

Cedric held up a hand to stop him. "It is imperative that we find her. Do you know where she would have gone?"

Garret had to hide his smile behind his hands in a display of weeping. It was all working out so much better than he'd planned.

Sixteen

❧❧❧

In her sleep, the harsh lines of anger that so often contorted her face disappeared. Malachi wasn't sure if it made her more familiar or more alien. He touched the soft skin where her wings met her back, and they twitched where they lay folded against her body, as if they would spring alive of their own accord.

Such strange things, bodies. When she'd come through the door, he'd wanted nothing more than to hold on to her, to prevent her from leaving. But his body…now that had wanted to drive into her, to pound, to punish her for letting him go, to make a mark on her that would label her as his for all time. When it was over, though, he realized he hadn't wanted to hurt her. He never wanted to hurt her. And then he'd been ashamed and fearful that he had done just that.

She stirred a little on his chest, such a slight weight against him, but comprised of so many sharp, jutting parts. He shifted her to his side to lie in the curve of his wing and rest her weight there, and her eyes came slowly open.

The two small, thin lines of light that sprouted from her forehead twitched and glowed white. He reached out to touch one, but her hand got to them first and smoothed them back against her hair. "My antennae," she said, but he could barely understand her.

"What does it mean, if it glows this way?" He pointed to them again, and she ducked her head, said something he could not make out.

He touched her hair, smoothed it down, over her wings. Occasionally they looked at each other, and she would smile, almost shy, which seemed absurd after what they had just done.

It was enough. Strangely it was enough to lie in the quiet with her, to have the assurance of touching each other. He tried to remember his talent for languages, but it was gone. He could only say her name, and it didn't sound right from his lips. But it made her smile.

He thought she'd fallen asleep again when she spoke. "I cannot…go back." Her faltering speech was clearer, as if she concentrated harder to get these words across in the mortal language. "No home."

He tilted her face up to his and kissed her. And what a strange impulse that was, to press your mouth to another's, to want to do such a thing. "You will stay with me. Your home is with me," he whispered to her, and pulled her hand to rest over his heart so she would understand.

Where that home would be, physically, remained to be seen. Keller would return soon. The niceties of mortal interaction would prevent Malachi from demanding that the Human keep them both there, as much as he wished to. He would have to find a place for both of them to be safe, and he feared it could not be in the Darkworld.

They could live on the Strip. He had seen other mortals doing it, sleeping out of the way of the foot traffic, begging for food and scraps. It did not look difficult.

Keller would not turn them out before Malachi made his decision. The Human was too honorable for that. He also had connections that might find alternatives for Malachi and Ayla. There were benefits to knowing someone like Keller.

"There is so much you do not know." She touched the side of his face, hers filled with pity.

He dropped his wings, letting the faint light

from the workshop enter their seclusion. A dark stain on her cheek, that he hadn't noticed before, crumpled a tight fist in him. "What is this?"

She combed her hair quickly over the blotch, her fingers tangling in the snarled mass. He gripped her wrist and forced her hand down. "What is this?"

She made a noise like the sound of fire ravaging a grass field, which she translated for him as "Garret." A rough, protective instinct balled up inside of him, ready to bring him to his feet, to charge out, to find the creature who had struck her and to rend the flesh from his bones.

As a Death Angel, he had seen many types of violence. He wanted to subject this Garret to all of them.

Then he remembered her face in the dim light of the small Faery dwelling. It had been smooth and white and unblemished. The Faery he had thrown against the bricks, that had been Garret. And he'd done this because of Malachi.

He stood and helped her to her feet. She limped beside him to the workshop, and he lifted her onto the table. She hissed when her bare skin met the cold metal, and he laughed. He couldn't help it, though she scowled at him.

Besides her bruised face, her hands and knees were scuffed and scabbed over, and her feet were torn and bloody. Malachi looked through Keller's boxes and cupboards until he found the Human's store of items for patching the body. There were various metal instruments, much like the ones strewn about the shop, but also long strips of torn fabric that he could use as bandages.

"I can…" she began, but quieted when he lifted one of her small feet in his hands and turned it in his palm. Dirty blood collected in the wells of her toenails. He wet one of the cloth strips with clean water from Keller's dwindling supply and carefully wiped the filth away from her wounds. He did the same for her knees and her palms, taking his time to carefully clean the abrasions there before wrapping them with bandages.

When he finished, he found her gown. It was a sodden, torn lump on the floor, unsuitable for wear. In Keller's boxes he found a large shirt that fell easily to Ayla's knees when she put it on, though she could not open her wings.

"Your friend. He will not be angry?" She shrugged her shoulders and picked at the fabric.

Malachi didn't think Keller would be, but he mentally prepared to make some sort of apology. The Human seemed to forgive much with just a few kind words.

The door scraped open and the Human in question entered. "Looks better on her than it ever did on me."

"Because she is more beautiful," Malachi said.

Keller reached into the leg of his strange wading pants and pulled out a wet bag. He opened the seal at the top and produced the dry contents, two smaller packets. "Ramen noodles, straight from the top! It was lucky I got these, too. Some Upworlders were protesting and pouring sacks of food down a manhole onto the Strip. Almost got knocked out by a can of Chef Boyardee. I didn't know they still made that stuff."

Malachi noted that the condescending stare Ayla had fixed on the Human matched his own.

Keller seemed oblivious. He removed his hat with the light attached and tossed it carelessly onto one of the workbenches. As he stepped out of and hung up his waterproof pants, he kept talking. "So, interesting rumor humming all up and down the Strip. They say that the Faery Queene bit the big one."

"The big what?" Ayla's look of bored disinterest had turned into something more urgent at Keller's mention of the Queene.

"Died. Dead." Keller made a face. "Shit, that's right, you don't sprechen ze Human very well, do you? Somebody—" He reached for a jagged knife that lay on the workbench, mimed stabbing it into his chest. "Killed her."

Ayla stepped back, shaking her head.

"She is upset." Malachi rounded on Keller. "You have upset her."

"Hey, I'm not the one who upset her, chief. The guy who killed the Queene did because…" He squinted his eyes at her. She shrank back, gave him an angry look. "Oh my God."

"Do not!" She rushed at him, her antennae raging bright red, and then knocked him onto his back on the hard concrete. She straddled him, her fist raised above his face as he shielded himself with his hands.

"Get her off me!" Keller shouted, but Malachi had already moved to help. He seized Ayla's upthrust wrist with one hand and dragged her to her feet.

"Do not look in my mind!" she snarled, twisting in Malachi's grasp, still trying to get at Keller.

The Human wheezed as he climbed to his feet. "I won't read your mind. But you need to be forthcoming with the details here."

She turned her face away and said nothing.

"Look, you're standing in my shop, wearing my clothes, my bandages. The least you could do is tell both of us the truth." Keller flicked his gaze from Ayla to Malachi and back again, and wet his lips. "Your Majesty."

Beneath the confining shirt, Ayla's wings shifted.

Malachi did not like this talk of dishonesty. It was unpleasant, and made his stomach ache to think that Ayla might have lied to him about something.

"She does not have anything to tell you," Malachi said gruffly, putting an arm around Ayla's small shoulders. "Leave her alone."

To his surprise and displeasure, Ayla ducked his arm and faced them both. "My…mate. Garret. He is brother to the Queene."

Mate? The word burned in his mind. That Faery, the one who had struck her, the one who had not valued her and protected her as he should have. The one he would someday rend limb from limb.

"And?" The hint of the smile Keller gave her was dark, unsettling. "Now the Queene is dead. So, he's the King?"

"No. I am Queene." She looked as though she were admitting to a crime, rather than divulging a royal heritage. "It passes to the female."

Did she not see what a wonderful turn this was? Malachi lifted her in his arms, ignoring how stiff she remained. "You can go back now! You are not without a home."

"She can't go home." Keller raised his hands to protect himself as she lunged at him again for reading her mind. "I saw it before, I swear, I saw it before!"

Malachi's hands closed over Keller's shoulders before he thought to grab him. He pushed him against the door, held his face inches from his. "You will tell me what you saw!"

"Queene." Ayla's voice was like a wraith sliding through the Darkworld. Malachi set Keller back on his feet and turned to face her. Her eyes were sad and downcast. "I am Queene."

"What does that mean?" Malachi asked aloud, though he wasn't sure who he asked.

"It means that she can't stay here." Keller lit up one of his "smokes" and puffed away at it, the acrid smell filling the air. "There were already troops on the move on the Strip. They're looking for you. And I don't really want them to find you here."

"They will not find her." Malachi's mind worked feverishly. When he'd had no will, no control over his fate, things had been less complicated, and much less frightening. The thought of losing Ayla, now, when he finally had her… "I will take her deep in to the Darkworld. We will return when they stop searching for her."

"No, you won't return here, man." Keller shook his head. "Listen, I've done a lot for you. A lot. And I really do like you, despite your many, many faults. But this, this isn't something that will just blow over. They're going to keep looking for her. The Queene of the Lightworld, that's, like, a big deal."

"I am supposed to return her to the one who did this to her?" Malachi gripped Ayla's chin and turned her head to display the bruise there.

She swatted his hand away. "I will go."

The bottom of Malachi's stomach dropped. "You cannot go. You cannot return to that."

"I will go," she said again, folding her arms across her chest. "The Human is right. They will keep looking for me. There will be a war if they think I am being held prisoner. There is no danger for you, if I go."

No danger? If she left, he would follow her. To his death, if he had to.

"Listen," Keller said, sensing the mounting tension in that strange way he had, "this isn't the time to argue, okay? You're both tired, probably hungry. Let's get some food, get some rest, and we can work this out in the morning. There's no way they're going to make it this deep into the Dark-world tonight, not at the rate they're going. It's like they're afraid to get their shiny boots dirty."

They did not speak further on Ayla's plans to return that night. Keller brewed the food he'd found into soup, and they ate their portions in relative silence. Keller kept up a forced chatter for a bit, but gave up when it did not lift the mood. It was just as well, to Malachi.

They went to sleep on a few borrowed blankets

on the floor of the workshop. Having Ayla nestled at his side, in the crook of his wing, seemed so sure and real to Malachi. It was impossible to believe that she might leave him alone again.

But when he woke, not hours later, she was gone.

At this hour, the Strip should have been crowded, alive. Ayla knew this because it was where she had spent the first part of her life. Sleeping in doorways, tagging after a Human father who had no idea how to care for his child. Who preferred to spend his nights gambling and his days hiding from debt collectors. Who encouraged his child to steal, subjecting her to the lowest, most degrading life on the Strip so they could simply eat and sleep in safety.

She would never live that way again. Malachi had only been mortal a matter of days. He did not understand the pain of an empty stomach night after night, the humiliation of a life spent trying to survive.

Tonight, the Strip was dark. News of the troubles in the Lightworld had no doubt frightened the residents into their homes. Those who didn't have homes had found places to go where they would not be seen.

Mabb was dead. Who would have wanted to

kill her? Certainly not her babbling admirers at
Court. They had nothing to gain. In fact, no one had
anything to gain from her death. Mabb had led the
Faeries, and the Lightworld, in the final battle
against the Humans, and though it had been unsuc-
cessful, she had kept their race from total extermi-
nation. She'd been their leader then, though
something had broken in her since. Surely those
who had been there could not have forgotten that.

It must have been some creature from another
of the quarters who'd done the evil deed. No Faery
would have.

One might have. And you know which. She
pushed the evil suspicion aside. It didn't matter
who'd wielded the weapon. Someone had killed
Mabb, and now Ayla was Queene.

And Garret her Royal Consort. What a sham
that life would be. She would return to the Lightworld, throw herself on his mercy—what little that
he had—and become a prisoner of her rank and
commitment to him. But she would find a way to
bring Malachi to her, or, failing that, to sneak away
to him when she wished to. She would be Queene
and none, not even Garret, would be able to oppose
her.

He would be angry. He would survive it.

Ahead, a Faery regiment patrolled the Strip.
They were dressed too fine for their surroundings,

too imposing and militaristic. She squared her shoulders and approached.

"There she is!" one in the front shouted, and the whole group of them ran after her. Her instinct was to run, as well, but she walked calmly toward them. They would not harm her, not once they knew who she was.

But when they reached her, they did not ask her any questions. They forced her arms behind her back and secured them roughly with a length of rope. Her bound hands and her wings, impeded by the shirt she wore, disrupted her balance and she fell. None of them moved to catch her. She crashed into the cement face-first. Blood dribbled from her nose and mouth as she drew a choked breath.

"You have mistaken me…" She squeezed her eyes shut as a wave of nausea came over her. "You have made a mistake. I am Ayla, mate to Garret, sister of the Queene."

One of them kicked her in the chest as she struggled to get on her feet.

Never before had Ayla truly feared for her life. Perhaps there was no reason to fear the loss of something that had held so little value. But as another boot connected with her hip, knocking her again to her face on the ground, she thought of Malachi, of never seeing him and, more importantly, of never being able to tell him why she'd left, and she feared death more than she'd ever feared any enemy in battle.

One of the soldiers hauled her to her feet by her hair. She cried out, then was ashamed to have displayed her pain for them. She would memorize their faces, she resolved, glaring at each of them through eyes swelling shut, and they would be punished. But they pulled a stifling hood over her head and tied it tight around her neck, choking her, and all plans for revenge gave way to the need to concentrate on every breath.

She did not need to see to know where they took her. They marched her across the threshold of the Lightworld, and Ayla entered that place that she had resolved never to return to as a prisoner.

Seventeen

～ઉ૭ુુઉ૭ુ～

She had been there. And now she was gone.

Malachi stared at the door as though he could conjure some sort of image of her there. Had she looked back on his sleeping form in pity? Regret? Or had she plunged into the darkness without a thought for him, her only desire to return to her Faery world, a realm he could never enter?

Having tired of him, she had abandoned him. Having sated her curiosity, she had gone back to the life she would rather have had.

No, he could not force himself to believe that. She had come to him for the same reason he had gone to her. Because they could not be separate, could not survive as two. They would be together or perish.

Keller stepped out of his alcove and lit one of

his cigarettes. For a long time, he said nothing, and Malachi was content to have it that way. What could the Human possibly say that would soothe the sting of his wounded pride?

"Are you going after her?" he asked after his cigarette was half-burned.

Malachi did not answer him.

That proved no barrier for the Human, who, Malachi was convinced, would talk to an inanimate object if he found a subject fascinating enough to expound upon. "Did I ever tell you how I lost my arm?"

Turning his head only slightly, Malachi gave the man a sideways glare.

Keller ignored him. "See, I'd been down here for probably a year before I really got the swing of things. In that time, I'd been living off scraps on the Strip, hiding from all these really scary and unusual creatures that I had only ever heard stories about. I mean, I knew they were down here, but when was I going to come down here, right? And here I was, living with them.

"It was really about a year before I noticed there were other Humans. Everyone looks so different, so dirty and they dress weird compared to where I'm from, so I didn't get that some of them were just like me. That's when I met this girl. Winter Rose. Oh, she was gorgeous. She was one of the

Gypsies. She was tiny, came up to my shoulder. And she had this long hair—it was bloodred, almost black unless you saw it in the right light, just a riot of curls down her back. I saw her at one of the stalls on the Strip, stealing food. She was so quick, I didn't realize what she was doing at first.

"I was starving, so I followed her. If for no other reason than to learn how she'd done it, right? She went into the Darkworld, but I didn't care. I just tagged after her, thinking I was being a real sneak. She knew I was there the entire time. She led me all the way back to their camp, and I stayed with them until… God, I think it was six months, something like that.

"Then one morning, I wake up, and they're gone. The entire camp is deserted. They packed up in the night and left. And she took my arm as a souvenir. She drugged me. I didn't even know she'd cut it off."

Malachi scoffed. "What would she want with your arm?"

"She was a flesh collector. The whole pack of them were. I never realized it because they never let me in on it. The Gypsies down here, they're not like the ones topside. The ones up there will take your money, down here they'll take your parts, if not all of you. I was lucky, she really had affection for me, kept them from harvesting more." He shrugged. "I guess they made trades with necromancers who needed to feed their risen dead."

Keller sighed and stubbed out his cigarette. It was good, Malachi hated the smoke. "Yup," the Human said with another heavy sigh. "Stolen arm or no, I should have followed her. I loved her."

"You are trying to make me follow Ayla. But she has not stolen my arm. She has not asked for me to find her. She left, though she knew I would want her to stay." Malachi turned back to the door. "If she did not wish to stay with me, why should I chase her?"

Keller went to his workbench and began opening drawers, moving tools, making a show of being busy without doing anything. It seemed a talent of Humans. "I think she left because she was worried about what would happen to you if they found you here."

Malachi made a noise of disagreement.

"Suit yourself. All I'm saying is that in sixty years, when you're still regretting this, it's going to be too late. Not for her, of course, but you, you won't be much to look at. Don't hold your grudges until you can't find her again, that's all I'm saying."

Keller reached for his wading pants and stepped into them, saying no more.

Good. The foolish Human oversimplified things. Did he not understand that twice now,

Malachi had let down his guard and had his fragile mortal emotions crushed in pursuit of Ayla? That he could spend his entire existence in hope, knowing that any change in the winds might destroy that hope forever?

"That's life, Mac," Keller said quietly, reaching for his hat. "At least for us lowly mortals. And you can either keep getting that hope dashed, keep getting shit kicked in your face, or you can just cut yourself off from life."

"That is what you did," Malachi said, annoyed that the Human had once again breached his mind. "You survive."

"I survive," Keller agreed, placing his hat upon his head and clicking on the light. "But I wouldn't call it living."

The Human pushed open the door with his metal hand and motioned to Malachi with his whole one. "I'm heading out. I can go with you as far as the Strip."

"They have found her, Your Highness."

Garret turned his head, just a few degrees. His neck was stiff from bowing. "Thank you. Bring her to the throne room."

Careful to say "the throne room," not "my throne room." He would play this out as cautiously as he possibly could, until the coronation. Only after he'd reluctantly accepted the job of King of the Lightworld would he let his guard slip.

He rose from his knees, muscles protesting after being immobile for so long. All afternoon, after the healers had discovered their songs would do nothing to bring the Queene back, after her maids had tearfully robed the withered black husk of her one last time, Garret had knelt beside his sister's bier, forehead resting on his clasped hands, back shaking with dry sobs every now and again to display his grief to the courtiers and commoners who streamed through the great hall to pay their respects.

Their respects. If they had known Mabb, they would not have respected her. Her moods that could change like the wind, her refusal to believe logic and rational truths when presented to her, her vain insistence that she would someday bring the Fae to the surface when all of her efforts were directed only to fancy gowns and lavish parties, these were not things that commanded respect.

Once, she might have been worthy of their adulation. But that time was long ago.

The throne room was another of the cavernous spaces hollowed out by the Humans above in a time when the Earth belonged to them, but Mabb had taken special care to bring some dignity to it. One of the few things in her reign that could be called "dignified," in Garret's opinion. In the early days, when it had seemed they might mend their ties with the world above and their tradesmen were still allowed to travel freely between the worlds, Mabb had chosen to outfit this room with walls of polished amethyst tiles and a slick, polished quartz floor. She'd loved those two stones most of all, for their gentle energy and the image of status they projected. She'd believed that to surround herself with amethyst was to proclaim an affinity with the mineral's psychic energy. "No one will lie to me if they believe I shall see directly through it," she'd crowed to him once, and he'd wanted to divulge right then exactly how many lies he'd gotten past her. But maybe that had been the trick of it.

The throne was also quartz, a huge, raw chunk of it, chipped and fashioned and polished enough to be comfortable, but with clusters jabbing from the sides and arms like warning spines to any that would approach closely. It had crossed from the Astral with them, and Mabb had not cast it off when she'd created her underground Palace. There was a crack in the back, where it had been damaged by the Human leader who'd called himself Madaku Jah during the Human uprising. That a Human had infiltrated their Upworld Palace and nearly taken the Queene's life had been the decisive blow in that fight.

Garret posed himself on the throne, his posture strong, but his expression that of a weary and broken man. "How sad the Royal Consort looks," they were bound to say. "Yet how determined and powerful."

He quashed a smile that came to his lips a second before the doors opened.

Two guards led Ayla, each holding the end of a rope that looped around her body. Garret would not have known it was her unless he'd been told, as she wore a strange Human garment that obscured her wings and a hood over her head. Behind them followed a jeering throng made up of courtiers and commoners. One of the guards tugged his end of the rope, and Ayla stumbled to her knees. The crowd hurrahed, and Garret felt an unexpected stab of sympathy for her.

"Guard! Stand down!" He stood and pointed at the other soldier. "Untie her. Remove that ridiculous hood!"

A murmur went through the assembly. They would either revile him or pity him. He believed it would be the latter.

The soldier untied Ayla, leaving the hood for last. When he removed it, she was still almost unrecognizable. Her nose was smashed and bloody, her eyes swollen to purple mounds. Dried blood stained her mouth, and her head lolled from side to side on her neck as she tried to keep her footing.

The gasp that came from the crowd confirmed Garret's guess. They pitied him, that his mate would have fallen so low, and that he was subjected to the horror.

Mabb's—his—council stood in expectation at the side of the room, distancing themselves from this spectacle. One of them, a short, round little Pixie whose name Garret always forgot, cleared his throat and stepped forward. "As acting monarch, it is your job to sentence her as you see fit. If what you have said is true, if she allowed a Darkworlder to infiltrate our borders and coupled with him willingly, if she killed your sister the Queene, you must accuse her of these things and punish her."

"Kill the—" Ayla gasped and coughed, clutching at her bruised neck before righting herself and stating, in a much quieter tone, one that every ear in the throne room strained to hear, "I did not kill the Queene."

"Lies!" a shrill voice rang out over the collection of similar denouncements. But Ayla stood in her place, resolved. She could play the game, perhaps as well as he could.

"Ayla." He let his voice break a little on her name, struggled to keep himself together for the crowd. What a play this had turned out to be! "Ayla, you have been charged with assassinating the Queene of the Faery Quarter. You have also been charged with helping a creature of the Darkworld enter our borders, and with…" He walked slowly off the dais, toward her, his expression fixed and sad. "And with lying with a creature from the Darkworld willingly."

Another outraged burst from the crowd. Garret could not force himself to listen to it, too intent was he on Ayla and the hatred in her eyes. Hatred! After what he'd offered her, what she'd thrown stubbornly aside!

He held up a hand to silence the hall. "These accusations are grave. And they are, indeed, too much for me to contemplate now in the wake of my—of all of our—loss. And I cannot pass a judgment upon you without serious consideration. Therefore, it is my decision that you should be held prisoner until such a time as this matter can be fully investigated and your sentence can be delivered in as unbiased a manner as I may be able to accomplish, under the circumstances."

Another roar of disapproval, and he shouted to be heard above them all. "Please, I ask that you place yourself in my position!" This muted them, almost instantly. "My beloved sister has been… brutally destroyed. My mate has been found, fugitive from the Lightworld. Please, let me grieve my sister before I am to condemn the one soul—" he leveled his gaze on her then, made sure she could feel the import of his words "—whom I have loved above myself."

She spat at him.

That sealed her fate, he reflected with pleasure as the guards trussed her once more and shoved her from the hall, through the snatching, tearing throng. If she had wept, that would have ended her, as well. But the defiance, oh, how they would loathe her for that.

When all of them had gone and the large, stone doors closed behind them, Garret sat down once more upon his throne and smiled to himself.

The cells of the Faery Quarter dungeon were badly lit by torches and smoky because of them. The beds were rags tossed on the floor, the food nothing but stale bread and cups of water. In short, it was but a small step down from what Ayla had lived in her entire life. It was not so horrible as others might have thought it, and so she was afforded plenty of time to think, rather than wallow in misery at lost comforts.

They thought she had killed the Queene. In hindsight, perhaps that was what Mabb had wished all along. She'd had her leave, unescorted, unseen, by that secret passage, had she not? She'd threatened to ruin her. She'd suspected Ayla of wanting her dead.

But no, what benefit would it be to Mabb to frame Ayla for her own murder, when at the end of it all she would still just be dead?

That left Ayla only one other option, and as much as she hated him—and now she really, truly hated him—she could not resolve to believe it.

She'd thought no one could stand to profit from Mabb's death. How naive. Of course, there had been two who could profit, and handsomely. The first being herself, for she would be Queene and supreme ruler of the Faery Quarter and, in all reasonable things, of the Lightworld. The second being Garret, for when Ayla was Queene, he would be her consort, second highest.

She knew she did not kill Mabb, so it had to be Garret.

How to prove it, though? Who would believe that Garret, who was making such a show of his grief that he should have grown up in a troop of players, not in the Palace, would have killed his beloved sister? But a lowly half-Human who'd wormed her way into the Lightworld, scratched out a pitiful existence before being offered a world of luxury and privilege beyond her dreams? How easy it would be to believe she had become suddenly, clumsily greedy for more. Easier still to imagine her seducing her mentor, beguiling him until he brought her inches from the throne. It was then that she had sank her poisoned dagger into her Queene's heart, then that she had dared reach for the crown.

It was sensational and impossible, and that was the thing that lent it the most credence. That was why Garret had chosen her from the start, mentored her, then mated himself to her, when he could have had any other, more desirable Faery in the Court. No other Faery would have become so easy a target for suspicion. He must have planned it for months.

Footsteps echoed through the rough-hewn stone corridor outside her door, and she cocked her head to listen. Her bread and water had already been brought to her, and her jailer's epithets and taunts had run out hours before. Had Garret changed his mind? Would she be put to death now?

The lock on the door twisted. When it opened, the dim light hurt Ayla's eyes, and she shielded them.

"Get on your feet! It's your Guild Master who's come!" A boot connected with her side, already sore and bruised from previous beatings, and she could do no more than lay where she was and cry out.

"That is unnecessary." Cedric's voice was even, calm. Perhaps he had come to kill her. She'd heard of an Assassin being executed before by the Guild Master.

"I did not kill the Queene!" she cried, climbing to her knees despite her pain. She opened her eyes as much as they would and groped in the darkness for something to get her balance on. Her hands found Cedric's tunic, and she half climbed him, ashamed at her own feebleness.

The Guild Master's large, warm hands closed over her own, gentle even now that she was a prisoner. "Leave us," he commanded the guard, and when the door had shut again, he lifted her to her feet. "Ayla, Gods, what have you let them do to you?"

She could not have fought back. He must have known that. And so, she did not explain. Nor did he expect her to, she surmised, when he continued, "Please, I must know…what they are saying is false, is it not?"

She nodded, wetted her lips. She had to speak slowly, as her throat was hoarse and sore from the rope they'd choked her with. "I did not kill the Queene. She took me to her chamber, it was true. But I did not kill her."

"No one saw you leave. No one saw anyone but Garret go to her, and when he left, you still had not." He was not condemning her, but gently probing for the answer that would prove to him, beyond all certainty, that she told the truth.

There had long been rumors of the Guild

Master's relationship to the Queene. If there was truth to them, Ayla was about to discover it now. "You know, as well as I, that the Queene has her ways of disguising that which she does not wish to be seen."

He nodded once, his expression strained in the dim blue light of his antennae. "If you wish to save yourself, then you need to tell me, now, plainly, what your meaning is."

"The secret passage." She blurted it too quickly. It felt as though it were something to hang on to, to save her. But she'd said it, and she said it again. "Mabb made me leave by the secret passage. She did not want me to…disturb her guests."

Cedric turned away, his back rigid, then he pounded both of his fists against the cell wall. "Mabb, you silly, vain fool!"

"You know I could not have killed her," Ayla was quick to continue. "You know that I have always endeavored to serve my Queene. And you know that I would never betray the Lightworld—" She stopped herself there. It was not in her nature to lie.

He faced her again, a calm mask in place. "What of this talk of a Darkling? They say you snuck him into the Lightworld and lay with him in Garret's bed. Is that true?"

"I did not help him cross our borders. He did

that of his own volition. And I did no more in Garret's bed than what Garret himself saw. That is, the creature touched me, he kissed me and then he left, frightened off by Garret's return." Her face burned at the memory. "I confess I did wrong by not killing the creature when I first happened upon him in the Darkworld, but that, and only that, is the extent of the vows I have broken."

"It is a serious vow." A sad smile touched the corners of his mouth, and his antennae twitched. "But less serious than what you are already accused of."

He helped her to sit down on the filthy pile that served as her bed, then walked toward the door. "Rest. I will see that justice is done in this situation. It falls to you now to heal and to wait."

When he closed the door behind him, Ayla rose to check the lock. But he had not come on a mission to free her.

Heal and wait. But there was something else, too: she was to trust him, as he was the only Faery who seemed to be on her side in this.

When Malachi woke, he found he could not sit up. When he opened his eyes, it took a moment to realize that he *was* up. His arms stretched above his head, bound together in an iron clasp, fettered to a chain pulled through a giant loop. His legs were similarly shackled, but attached to the stone wall that scraped his wings with any movement.

When had things gone so wrong? At the Strip, when Keller had tried to talk to the Faery soldiers who detained them.

Foolish Keller. Malachi shut his eyes, almost cried out at the thought of his friend. The screams, the blood. If only he'd done as Malachi had told him, if only he'd run back to the safety of the Darkworld.

Malachi had been paralyzed with horror and grief for the Human. It had been easy for the Faeries to capture him.

A metal brazier of glittering coals stood in the room, not far from him. A set of iron bars lay across it, glowing menacing red. They would torture him, he had no doubt. For what purpose he could not say, but a Death Angel knew the look of torture.

A Faery came in. This one was not a soldier. He wore silk robes, no helmet. He had a haughty expression on his face, and this was what Malachi recognized.

The Faery closed the door of the cell behind him and came close to Malachi, so close that he wished his hands were free. With a smug grin, the Faery pronounced the mortal words carefully. "Do you have any idea who I am?"

"Garret," Malachi answered, just as slowly, delighting in the change that came over the Faery.

Shaking with rage, the little creature struck him. The blow stung, but only for a moment. It would not leave a mark. Knowing that he sealed his own fate, Malachi laughed.

"You will not think it funny when I kill her," Garret spat, turning away from him. "You will not think it humorous when she watches you die!"

Malachi strained at his bindings, but the chains held fast. "No! You will not kill her!"

"And you will stop me?" Garret forced his hands into a pair of stiff gloves and lifted one of the brands from the coals. He looked it over a moment, as if he could examine the heat. Then, without further preamble, he forced the spike into Malachi's side.

The pain was unlike anything Malachi had ever thought to imagine. His flesh split under the point of the brand, then fused to it. When Garret ripped the instrument free, he pulled flesh with it, and hot, wet jets of stinging blood splashed from Malachi's wound.

Garret dropped the brand back onto the brazier. The scent of cooked flesh rose into the air. "When I have finished with you, she will not recognize you. And you will be far from capable of saving her."

Eighteen

The door to her cell opened, but the hall beyond was not the dingy hall of the prison. It was a corridor of clean, gray stones leading straight from her door. She rose on trembling legs and walked, not daring to believe her own freedom, out. At the other end of the corridor, light streamed in. Beautiful sunlight such as Ayla had only seen through the grates above Sanctuary, and sand so blinding white that she had to cover her eyes.

Beyond that sand, water. Open sea, just a bit more blue than the sky, but ever more violent and mysterious, tossing into and over itself as it argued its way toward shore.

At the edge of the water was a woman. Tall and fair, her golden hair nearly the same shade as the sand, her skin the white of the foam crests on the waves. She wore a white garment that blew with her hair in the wind. She turned her face and her full, pregnant body into the breezes the ocean gave her, arms open. When Ayla stepped from the cave, she turned and beckoned her closer.

"Where am I?" Ayla asked, coming to stand beside the woman much closer and quicker than she'd anticipated.

The woman opened her arms to the winds again, her face pink from the sand and spray. "It is the sea."

Ayla had heard of the sea before, seen it in tapestries. That this woman assumed she did not know made her feel foolish and angry. "I know it is the sea! Why am I here?"

"Because this is where all things must begin. And end." The woman closed her eyes and laughed. Somewhere, a gull cried. Or a...

"Malachi is in pain." Distress nagged at her. "I must go to him."

"He has his own end and beginning." The woman nodded to her with a knowing smile. "But you knew that."

"You speak in riddles, as always." But wasn't that a riddle, that Ayla had just spoken? "Leave me, Mother. I do not wish to hear that I am about to end."

"How do you know that you will end?" The

wind stopped now, the sea calmed. The woman turned to her. She took one of Ayla's hands in her own and lifted it, guided it to Ayla's stomach. "How do you know that you are not here for a beginning?"

The waves began again, showed her shapes now. Two featureless bodies, moving as one, sliding over and over each other, bursting apart. Ayla's body tingled at the sight. She remembered the tree of her life force exploding inside of her as her physical body seemed to explode with Malachi.

And then, through the Other Sight, she saw it. A tiny, burning red fruit at the base of her tree of life. A small light, furtive, needing protection. But it was there.

"What does this mean?" Her eyes filled with tears. She knew, without the woman telling her.

The woman knew, as well. She turned back toward the sea, gazed out at the serene calm there. "One day, you will return. And so will your daughter."

And then Ayla woke, still curled in the dark of her cell. And she wept, for in the Other Sight, her daughter was still there.

Torturing the Darkling was not as enjoyable as Garret had hoped. The thing was not evil. It was not wholly good, either. It simply was. Mortal and afraid of pain, it reacted as expected to every gouge and burn.

He had given up hours ago, and now he stood in his new lodgings—the apartment of the Royal Consort, which Mabb had never had use for—stripped to the waist while a lovely young servant sponged the blood and grime of the dungeon off his body.

"I must say," he told her, reaching to touch a tendril of hair that had escaped her plain little cap, "that this is the most enjoyable bath I have had in a while."

She said nothing, but her antennae flamed red against her forehead.

"It almost makes me forget the pain of my horrendous loss." He captured her hand where it held the rag against his abdomen, urged it lower, to slip beneath his trousers. "Almost. Will you help me forget entirely?"

The door scraped open, and the servant jumped back, embarrassment and guilt branding her face. A guard entered. "Guild Master Cedric to see you."

Cedric. How inconvenient an article he was turning out to be. Garret pulled his robe up and slid his arms into the sleeves. "Yes, quickly. I have other matters to attend to."

The Guild Master entered, and said, "I have come here to talk to you about the Queene."

Immediately, Garret wished he had sent him away. "Which one? Mabb, or my mate who killed her?"

Cedric stepped slowly forward. "In truth, I do not believe that Ayla killed your sister."

"Is that so?" Feigning disinterest, Garret went to the small table beside his bed and lifted the half-empty goblet of wine there. He wondered if he should have more sent, perhaps with a bit of wormwood added to ease his way with the serving maid. "That is odd, considering the number of witnesses who saw my mate enter my sister's chambers and never leave. Who can swear that she was the last alone with the Queene before her death."

"Ah, but was she present when the Queene was found?" Cedric did not seem inclined to drop the bone so quickly. "If what they are saying is true, that she was not noticed leaving the Palace all evening, then she must have been present when Mabb was found."

"How do you arrive at that conclusion?" He was stalling. Cedric would see it, too, and he cursed himself for it.

"Logic. She was not seen leaving, therefore she never left. So she must have been there when the Queene was found. If she was not, then the possibility exists that she left before the Queene was murdered." Cedric turned to the door. "Think wisely on this matter, Garret. I have seen Ayla since she has returned. Anyone who has used the Other Sight near her knows that she is with child. It would be a shame to murder your heir."

The door slammed shut, as if in agreement with the denouncement the Guild Master had not been in a place to make.

"If that will be all," the servant said in a rush, moving quickly past him.

But not quick enough. His hand closed over her arm, too hard, he knew, hard enough to make a bruise. He smiled down into her terrified face, exhilarated by the power her fear gave him. "No. That will most certainly not be all."

It was the creaking of the cell door that woke Ayla once more. She could not tell if it was morning or night. Only a little over a day in total darkness and she'd lost track of time.

"Get up." A boot to her side. She'd decided, in the darkness, that she was no longer the wretched thing that had been imprisoned here, but a creature of vengeance incubating, taking stock of every wrong done to her, waiting for the right time to strike back. She stood, looked the guard in the eye.

He did not stagger under the weight of her hatred, and that disappointed her. "The King wants you."

The King. Mabb was barely dead and already Garret's ambition showed. How had she not seen it herself?

She had not seen it, she realized as the guard bound her hands and dragged her from the cell, because she had no similar drive to treachery in herself. To have assumed from the beginning that Garret would revel in his sister's death, that he would be so greedy as to snatch the throne from her not-yet-cold hands was to have imagined doing so herself. If she had truly imagined the Queene's death, she would have been horrified. If her reaction had been to rejoice at what she would gain from it, she would have been able to see Garret with a clarity so sharp as to put the Other Sight to shame.

When she had been arrested and brought to the dungeon, her captors had fitted a hood over her head, presumably so that she could not find her way out. This one did not bother.

Perhaps she was not meant to come back.

"I will not die a traitor's death," she said, lifting her chin. She did not look at the guard. The Queene would not look at her guard.

The corridors were long and winding, the walls not concrete, but raw, brown earth that Mabb had ordered cleared for her royal dungeons.

Perhaps if she did not have so many enemies,

she would not need so large a prison, some cold, unkind voice prodded from the back of Ayla's mind. In the past, she would have carefully examined her thoughts and found sympathy for the Queene, the good Queene who had done so much for all of the Fae races. Now, having seen past the lies and idol worship the Guild had forced down her throat, she let the thought stand. It was a lesson, she reasoned. If she did not make any enemies, she would not have to worry about meeting the same end as selfish, paranoid Mabb had.

It was then that she realized for the first time that she intended to be Queene. Not just for these few moments before what was sure to be her execution awaiting her, but for as long as she lived.

And she did not envision ruling beside Garret.

When they reached a large set of doors at the end of the hall, Ayla was surprised to find they did not open onto the Palace courtyard, where executions took place for jeering spectators. Instead she recognized the gleaming floors and tapestried walls of the Palace. She opened her mouth to question the guard and then, remembering her earlier resolution to not acknowledge him, followed him into the Palace proper.

No one was about. Ayla wondered if it were the hour, or the collective mourning for Mabb that kept the courtiers at bay. She imagined them falling over the dead Queene's bier, each vying to seem the most devoted, the most grief-stricken.

She would not tolerate such foolishness.

They passed the Guild halls, the great halls and the throne room. Just when Ayla began to wonder if the guard would lead her to the courtyard after all, he stopped before a single door set inconspicuously at the side of a dead-end corridor. He rapped on it, looked nervously down the hall, and when it opened, shoved her unceremoniously inside.

It was a bright room, lit with the light of the Humans above, the buzzing tubes overhead fed from the large, rusting metal boxes on the wall. A long table—probably left over from the Humans, as well—dominated the floor, and at the table sat six Faeries she'd never seen before, all dressed in matching robes, and two she had seen before: Cedric and Garret.

"Sit down, Ayla," Cedric invited her, smiling kindly. "Guard, untie her, she is no threat to us."

"As she was no threat to my sister?" Garret muttered, and one of the robed Faeries nodded in agreement.

The Guild Master's face creased with momentary annoyance. "We agreed to a civil meeting, Your Majesty."

The guard slipped the ropes from Ayla's hands grudgingly, jerking the rough cord against her bruised wrists. She winced and gingerly rubbed her skin, but then her mind turned to her appearance. The fine robes Garret wore called attention to her shabby dress, the heavy rings on his fingers cast her bloodied, filthy hands in an unfavorable light. She pushed ineffectively at her matted hair and shrank down in her chair, then, remembering her position, sat up tall and fixed each of the Faeries with a haughty glare.

"Your Majesty," Cedric began, addressing Ayla now, "the Faeries before you are members of the late Queene's private council. It is at their request that you have been released from imprisonment and returned to the Palace until such a time as Mabb's death can be more fully investigated."

Blinking, Ayla turned to Garret. Before she could speak, he waved a hand lazily and looked away. "Do not presume to thank me. It was my wish that you should stay in the dungeon like a common murderer."

Though she was sure her voice would creak like the hinge on a weathered door, she spat at him, "Has your love for me disappeared so completely then? When only days ago you pursued me relentlessly?"

Garret stood, pounding the arms of his chair, eyes blazing with fury.

"Ah, this is the Garret I know!" Ayla stood as

well, a hysterical laugh welling in her chest. It exploded from her, filled with hate. "See the proof of his affection on my cheek!"

"Sit down, the both of you!" Cedric roared, and then, remembering his place, bowed. "I am sorry, Your Majesties, forgive me. But this is a delicate situation, and we must keep our tempers from becoming involved."

"Delicate situation? What is delicate about being wrongfully charged with regicide?" Ayla gasped. Her earlier bravado abandoned her, and her limbs trembled.

One of the council members spoke up, a stiff-faced female who appeared disgusted by the display she'd just witnessed. "The Faery Court cannot be without a Queene. Mabb was our banner, and as word of her death spreads, so, too, does the threat we face from the other races in the Lightworld who wish to command the whole. We have no other female heir to the throne."

"Grania is right, we have no recourse but to release the Queene and let her take the throne," another put in, a round, red-faced male who wiped at his brow with the hem of his sleeve.

"No other recourse?" Garret once again pounded the arm of his chair. "Why should I not be King? Mabb's blood flows through my veins, not hers!"

"She is your mate," Cedric pointed out quietly. "If you did not envision that she might someday become Queene, that was a lack of foresight on your part."

A council member spoke up. Her crystal-blue eyes flashed from her white skin, her antennae twitched and quivered with intelligence. She seemed no more than a child, but she spoke with a confidence that surprised Ayla. "The Faery Court must have a Queene. The prophecy of succession is quite clear that the one who rules must also be capable of producing an heir from her body."

"Mabb was incapable of producing an heir from her body, but you kept her on the throne for centuries," Garret raged. "Besides, this…creature has lain with a Darkling! The validity of any heir she produces must always be under suspicion!"

"Better a dubious heir than no heir at all," the first Faery put in, fixing her shrewd gaze on her King. "You must agree with that, in your position."

"Is it agreed, then, that Ayla should rule for the time being? That she is the true and rightful Queene, and all charges of treason are to be dropped until an unbiased investigation can be conducted?" Cedric looked to each of the council members as he spoke, as if he could bend them to his will with his eyes.

"We are not in unanimous agreement," a voice

rose over the murmured approval. It was the Faery seated beside Garret, a thin thing like the blade of a sword, with a large, pointed nose and hair so black and greasy it appeared to be made of wet ink. He cast Ayla a snide glance and addressed the council. "If these…rumors of the new Queene's infidelity are true, then I move she should be kept under house arrest in the Palace. We cannot risk her further tarnishing the reputation of the Lightworld."

"I agree with Llewellyn." The voice belonged to the small, wise Faery who had argued with Garret before. "Not for identical reasons, but as long as we face attack from the other races of the Lightworld, our new Queene should not leave the Palace."

The room erupted into argument, starting off with a few isolated grumblings and rising in volume and intensity until Ayla wanted to put her hands over her ears and scream for them to stop.

Instead it was Cedric who called for them to quiet, his deep voice echoing off the cement walls. "It is agreed, then. The Queene shall stay here, in the Palace, under house arrest for her own safety, and resume her proper place beside her Royal Consort."

"If she'd known her proper place she wouldn't have spread her legs for a Darkling," Garret muttered.

The look Cedric gave him was murderous, but he could say nothing that would not be grossly disrespectful. "We are adjourned, then."

Ayla sat in stunned silence as the council filed out. The childlike Faery gave her a curious look-over, her wise eyes seemingly absorbing every detail about the new Queene. Then, they were gone, and Ayla forced herself to her feet as Garret strode to the door.

He stopped, barely an inch from her face, and hissed, "We both know that bastard you carry does not belong to me."

It had all changed so quickly. Days ago, Garret had been the one person in all of the Underground who'd cared for her. The only one who had ever professed to love her.

Now, that face that had once held only pride and deep affection for her twisted in rage, and though she knew all the treacherous things he'd done, it stung just the same.

"Just as we both know that I did not wield the knife that killed your sister."

She managed to stay on her feet long enough for him to raise his fist, and then, glaring at Cedric, storm out. Once the door closed behind him, Ayla collapsed.

Cedric was at her side in an instant. "Let me take you to your chambers, Your Majesty."

They did not go through the entrance to the Queene's apartments. "I do not wish for you to make your first appearance as Queene bedraggled from prison," Cedric explained as he led her to the secret passage and pushed it aside, then deftly replaced it once they were inside.

It became more clear to Ayla then what the passage had been for. "How many others know of this way?"

Cedric did not meet her eyes. "Only those who need know it. We could have it sealed, if you wish."

"I will decide later." When she'd had time to decide if it would be of use. When she'd had time to understand her new position and all it entailed.

"Cedric?" She put a hand on his shoulder to stop him before they reached the end of the passage. "Could I… If I wished…can I pardon an enemy of the Lightworld?"

He hesitated, his face frozen in a mixture of horror and indecision. Wetting his lips, he replied nervously, "While it is certainly in Her Majesty's power, it would be…unwise to make any pronouncements without the full support of the council—and the King—behind you. Especially in your current position."

"My position," she echoed with a wry smile. "And I have you to thank for that. If I should thank you at all."

Cedric shook his head. "Do not thank me. I do not wish for your mate to rule any more than you do."

Her mate. She supposed Garret was still that, no matter how they felt about each other now. Perhaps they had set some record for their kind, falling out of love so quickly.

If she'd ever loved him at all. Now, when she thought of Malachi, she wondered if she'd felt love for Garret.

"I apologize, Your Majesty." Cedric bowed quickly, his expression full of concern.

Somehow, this disheartened Ayla more. "Yesterday you were my superior. Today you feel speaking plainly to me is improper. I had judged you to be a smarter man."

A smile touched the corners of Cedric's mouth. "You are tired, Ayla. Perhaps now is not a time for judgment, but quiet reflection."

This was the Cedric Ayla knew. He helped her through the doorway into the Queene's chambers. The feeling of walking through a ghost burned over Ayla's skin. Not the ghost of Mabb, so recently murdered there, but the ghost of what Ayla had been when she'd last stood in that room, confused, perhaps frightened, clashing against what she was now.

"I have something I must do." She turned to Cedric, aware of how she must look with her tattered shirt and matted hair, dirt streaking her skin. But she feared what Garret would do in retaliation, feared that Malachi would not be safe for long. "I must go into the Darkworld. There is someone there who is in danger. I do not trust Garret to let him live peacefully there."

Cedric looked as though she had struck him. "So, it is true then?"

For a moment, she panicked. He would take her to Garret and the council now, tell them that she had confessed. In Garret's fervor to have her destroyed, he would convince them to believe that her guilt in lying with a Darkling implicated her guilt in Mabb's assassination. Her neck would fall under the sword before Garret held his evening audience.

But Cedric had been loyal to Mabb, despite her sins, and somehow Ayla knew that he would show this same loyalty to her, as well. His head dropped in defeat. "I did not want to believe it."

She put her hand on his shoulder, afraid he would recoil from her. He did not. "It is difficult to explain all that has happened to lead me here, but you must know that I have not wished to betray the Lightworld. I broke my geis when I failed to kill the Darkling, that is true. I do not make excuses for that. But I cannot kill him. Not now. What I feel for him does not change the fact that I am now, as I have ever been, loyal to our race."

"How can you say that?" Cedric fixed her with a despondent stare. "How can you wish to consort with the creatures of the Darkworld and still claim to care for your race?"

"Because I have seen that all in the Darkworld is not against us. Some living there are simply trying to survive." She closed her eyes, willed him to feel the desperation she felt to make him understand. "Please, I need to know that Garret cannot harm him."

After a long moment, Cedric nodded, but he would not meet her eyes. "You should not go to the Darkworld now. Garret will be watching you. But I will be watching him. If he makes any move toward the Darkworld, if he sends anyone for him, it will not go unnoticed."

"Thank you." Her tired limbs moved of their own volition toward the bed. As if someone had anticipated her arrival, the bedclothes had been changed and pulled down. As her body settled into the enveloping softness of the featherbed, fear pricked her. She was safe with Cedric, and safe from Garret's machinations through the actions of the council, but servants could be bought. The servants who prepared her chamber, the servants who would be her ladies-in-waiting. Any one of them could enter as she slept and do Garret's bidding.

As if he had read her thoughts, Cedric seated himself before the door and resolutely crossed his arms. "Do not worry, Your Majesty. I will not abide another assassination while I am in service to the Faery Court."

It was all the assurance she needed to fall into a deep sleep.

But her dreams were troubled with thoughts of Malachi, and the unease that grew and wound through her mind.

Nineteen

The days and nights blended into a stream of pain, rolling fluidly from one agony to the next. Sleep did not offer succor; the pain, a red phantom, lurked behind his eyelids, draining his blood and strength.

His torturer did not return. The coals in the basket whitened and died, but their heat still taunted him in his flesh. His arms ached from the chains, his hands throbbed with emptiness, wanting blood that his body could not force into them, his feet throbbed with fullness, the skin stretched tight and pale over his swollen flesh.

Movement was pain without relief, staying still was another pain altogether.

He thought of her. Did she look for him? Of course she would, but would she find him? If she did not, would he die before he could be subjected to further agonies?

Death had been his life for centuries. Now, a mortal, it held terror and fascination. He wanted it, with every pulse of his wounds, he wanted it. But he wanted more to be free from pain and yet living. He wanted to be in Ayla's arms, whole and unblemished by the ordeal he'd been subjected to.

But it seemed that the things he truly wanted were out of reach forever, and so he would settle for death. A release from the mortal body that had endured far too much to remain alive, yet clung to hope that did it nothing but disservice.

There was no sound, no light. Even if he'd had the strength to open his eyes, there would be no light.

He kept that close, for he knew that when there was light, it would mean he was free.

When Ayla woke, her body ached as though she'd completed a hundred training exercises. She'd not moved in her sleep, and now her joints were stiff, her body feeling far more fragile and Human than a Faery, even a half Fae, ever should.

Cedric was at her side in an instant, offering her a goblet of water. "Your Majesty, if you have had sufficient time to rest, perhaps now is the appropriate time to present you to the Court?"

Pushing her hair from her eyes, she took the goblet and gulped down the contents. "I cannot face them like this. They will already be waiting to tear me apart."

Cedric nodded. "Of course, you will have a bath first, and clean clothes. There are a select group of servants in the Palace that I know to be trustworthy. Only they will be allowed access to your private rooms. I assure you, you will be perfectly safe."

"You are leaving?" She did not mean to sound as accusatory as she did, nor as needy. But Cedric had proved her lone ally in the turmoil of the past days, and the thought of being abandoned by him shot panic through her. "They hate me. How can I appear before them without you?"

"The courtiers are easily swayed by the riches of the Court. Show them that you are strong, confident, and appear before them in the finest gowns and jewelry. They will fight each other to declare allegiance to you." He straightened and walked to the vanity table where Mabb had sat so recently. "There is one favor I would like to ask of you, Your Majesty."

"Your help has been indispensable so far. Without you I'd still be in the dungeon." Ayla shuddered at the thought. "What do you want?"

He opened one of the ornate boxes on the vanity

and removed a pendant on a chain. He held it up for only a moment, just long enough for Ayla to see the knotted pattern of the twisted bronze and the shining stone in the center. "I gave this to the Queene." Cedric closed the pendant in his fist. "I would like it back."

"Of course." It was as if his fist had closed around her, squeezing the breath from her. She could watch any amount of physical pain inflicted on a creature. This type of pain that forced Cedric's mouth into a tight line, pinched the corners of his eyes, this was unbearable to see. "And thank you, for all you have done."

"I want to see Mabb's murderer exposed for what he is, just as you do." The malice in his voice made it clear that the time for avoiding the issue had passed. "I vow that I will not tire in my efforts to promote and support you as Queene."

After he had gone, leaving Ayla alone with the trustworthy servants he'd once again vouched for her safety with, there was time for his statement to sink in. Cedric believed that Garret had murdered Mabb. If he believed this, then others surely would, as well. Others must suspect him.

The servants arranged a bath for her. The exhaustion of the past days melted into the water, rubbed away with the grime and evaporated with the scent of the rich oils slathered on her skin. By the time she'd been dressed—in a gown of gold cloth that must have been Mabb's, for the back laced tightly and covered her wings—and the tangles combed from her hair, she began to feel a bit of her former confidence coming back to her. Confidence that had been strangely lacking since she'd accepted Garret's proposal.

Confidence that fled at the door to the throne room.

"Courage, Your Majesty," one of the young Faeries behind her whispered, and Ayla was glad that Cedric had chosen her. She held her head high as the doors opened.

The Queene's door was situated behind the dais on which the throne was perched. A young guard, hardly old enough to serve, ran from his post beside the entrance to the herald who stood beside the dais.

"Her Majesty, Queene Ayla," the herald's voice boomed, like the blow of the executioner's sword.

Rustles and murmurs ran through the assembly like the rushing of water, growing louder and louder, became cries of outrage and cruel laughter. Ayla's step faltered, only for a moment, until she saw Garret.

Seated in an ornate chair at the edge of the dais, his mouth twisted in wry approval of the Court's reaction, he looked every bit the smug villain that

Ayla knew him to be. And it was his satisfaction that spurred her to continue, passing him with barely a glance, to ascend to the throne.

Someone in the gathering could not contain themselves and cried out, "Murderer!" but a guard removed them, creating a scuffle that attracted the crowd's attention long enough for Ayla to regain her composure. When the hall fell silent, when every pair of eyes—Garret's included, though she would not look at him—were fixed on her, she stood, and spoke.

If her voice trembled, she did not hear it. And though she'd given no thought at all to what she would say, and though she rarely spoke to anyone, somehow she found the words without faltering.

"Fellow...Fae." She settled on that simple word, and saw a glint of approval in the eyes of some of the courtiers. "I do not remember a time when our race was not confined underground. I have never fought in historic battles. I have lived my life in service to the Lightworld as an Assassin, and the battles I have fought were not honorable, but they did promote the safety of each of you. As Queene, I swear I will protect our race with ten times the fervor I have ever displayed when dispatching an enemy.

"Too long our race has been underground, long-ing to reclaim our proper home and place, but living more like the Humans who dared to confine us. Too long we have stagnated, growing more and more adapted to our squalid existence. I vow to you today that I will work, for centuries, if I must, to bring all of the Lightworld into the Upworld, and to take back the lives that the Humans have stolen.

"In return, I do not ask for your adulation, your trust or even your respect. I only ask that you reserve your judgment of me until I have been given the chance to prove to you that my devotion, and my love for our race is true."

With the conclusion of her speech, it was as if all of her strength had left her with her words. She sat back down, the weight of the silence in the hall pressing down like an oppressive hand.

Then, it was broken, like a crack beginning in a block of ice, the smattering of unsure applause spreading and splitting the silence, growing until the air in the hall was torn asunder by the roar of approval emanating from each of the courtiers.

Now Ayla looked at Garret, to make sure the satisfaction was gone from his expression. He glared at her, at the assembly, then stood and stormed from the hall, through the door to his chambers.

Ayla motioned to the servant who stood beside her throne. The Faery came forward and bowed her head.

"Is there an entrance from the King's chambers

to the Queene's?" she whispered, and the girl nodded. "Ask that it be guarded, until it can be sealed up."

"Yes, Your Majesty."

When it seemed the adulation of the crowd would never end, Ayla left the hall. Cedric's estimation of the Court had been correct, but Ayla wished to believe that they had seen the truth behind her words, and that perhaps she could be a Queene after all.

"I must give her credit," Garret said with a laugh, not addressing anyone in particular, though there were servants all around him. "She spoke well. Cedric had a hand in it, I'm sure, but her performance was good. They believe she can be Queene."

No one answered him. It didn't matter. The servants in his chamber were busy setting things back to right, after he'd upset everything he could reach. He'd been enraged, but now, that rage gave way to careful consideration. All was not lost. She was still under suspicion of regicide, whether she'd stirred the hearts of the Court or not.

And he had her Darkling. If she felt for him enough to risk her life returning to the Darkworld for him, she may be willing to bargain for his life.

"Guard." He motioned to the one at the door.

There were two on the inside, two on the outside. If he were in Ayla's position and she in his, he would kill her outright. He was leaving her no chance. "There is a prisoner in the dungeon, a Darkling. Bring him to me. Let no one see what you are doing."

Perhaps Ayla would no longer challenge him, once she realized all that was at stake.

It was near midnight when Cedric knocked on the doors of Ayla's chamber. She was in bed, but not sleeping, though the day had exhausted her.

"The Royal Consort wishes to meet with you," he said gravely. "Right away."

Drawing the blankets around her, she sat up. "I will meet with him in the morning. I am his mate now only in name. He cannot call for me in the middle of the night as though I—"

"He has your Darkling."

The words brought a mixture of elation and dread through her. Malachi was here, in the Palace, but Garret's prisoner. Then, another possibility occurred to her, and she felt as though she'd received a blow to the stomach. "Is he alive?"

Cedric nodded. "But barely. I must warn Your Majesty that he is in pitiable condition. He may not live."

She snatched her robe from the end of the bed

and pulled it on. "What do you mean, he may not live? Has Garret harmed him?"

"Yes." He paused when she stopped, one foot out of the bed. "You must come."

The walk through her chamber to Garret's was the longest Ayla could remember. She wanted to take Cedric's hand and squeeze it in hers, but he did not walk beside her. He walked behind her, in front of the two guards that accompanied her, murmuring directions when she appeared to not know the way.

When they reached the door to Garret's chamber, Cedric approached her more closely and whispered, "I must warn you, Garret has tortured this Darkling. You have seen terrible things as an Assassin. Think on them as you prepare yourself."

She had seen terrible things. She'd done terrible things. She would know in an instant what terrible things Garret had done to Malachi.

The guards in Garret's chambers scowled at her, some whispered as she passed. Cedric had been right in carefully choosing her servants for her.

Ayla had never seen the Royal Consort's chambers. She hadn't realized such rooms existed. They were not as large as the Queene's rooms, but they were no less grand. Though they had never been used, they were well maintained, with fine furniture from the Upworld that did not accommodate

Faery bodies. In the antechamber, things were arranged as neatly as if Mabb had overseen the preparations herself.

They continued through the room, into another chamber, led by one of Garret's guards.

"Stay close to me," Cedric whispered to her, and she nodded, though she feared she would appear weak, relying on the strength of the Guild Master.

The next room was not so fine as the first. It was not fine at all. The walls were not covered in tapestries, and there was no furniture. Slumped in a corner, shackled by his ankles to a thick iron loop on the concrete floor, Malachi lay motionless. And Garret stood beside him, his head held high and proud, his triumph barely concealed in his expression.

Close, but not too close, Ayla noted, judging the gap between Garret and his prisoner. That meant Malachi was still alive, at least, enough to frighten Garret.

"I have come, as you have summoned me," Ayla spat. Her fingers clutched into fists and she hid her hands at her side, in the folds of her robe, so that Garret would not see how the sight affected her. "What was so important that it could not wait until my morning audience."

"Ayla." Garret said her name as though he were

speaking to a child. The way he used to speak to her when she'd grown frustrated with training or the lack of assignments. Now, he did it with such pleasure that she imagined reaching out and snapping his neck. He walked slowly closer, a grin splitting his smug face. "Would you really have wanted the Court to have seen proof of your little indiscretion?"

"I see no proof of anything," Cedric said calmly. "Only a Darkling you've smuggled over our border and tortured nearly to death."

Garret's rage was sudden, and as violent as the storms of the Upworld. "I did not address you! You will not speak to your King as though you are equals!"

"He will speak any way he pleases!" Ayla fixed Garret with her most angry stare. "You will remember that you are not a King. You are the Queene's Royal Consort, in the presence of the Queene, and you will hold your temper."

"The presence of the Queene?" Garret laughed, looked about as if expecting his guards to laugh with him. They dared not. "You are only Queene because I made you so! You were nothing but a half-breed Assassin until I made the mistake of aligning myself with you.

"And you." He turned his ruthless gaze to Cedric. "You would never have gotten so far in the

Court if you hadn't been my sister's little pet. Do you really think you would have ended up the Master of the Assassins' Guild without her intervention?"

Cedric nodded. "Yes. I do."

"Then you are a fool."

Ayla interrupted their argument. There was a more important task at hand: removing Malachi from Garret's custody. "Guards," she called, then, "My guards," she clarified. "Take the prisoner to the dungeon. And find the healers."

"Halt." Garret motioned to his guards. "Do not let them near him."

For a moment, panic rose in Ayla's chest. If Garret wished to prevent them from taking Malachi, he would succeed. They had only the two guards who'd accompanied them. She knew well the advantage an opponent had in their own domain.

"You cannot hold a prisoner the Queene wishes freed," Cedric said, sounding almost bored. "Your guard must stand down or you will be charged with treason."

In the tense moment that Garret's face colored, his eyes and nostrils flared wide, his antennae quivered with his rage, Ayla felt relief such as she'd never known. Garret would not risk an open display of defiance, not of this magnitude.

"Guards," Cedric said coolly, then with a nod of his head in deference, "Unless Your Majesty objects?"

"No, I do not." Her voice did not shake. She showed not a sliver of the emotions she felt. And she was proud and grateful for that.

When the guards lifted Malachi off the floor, he seemed to rouse. He lifted his head for a moment, matched his gaze to Ayla's with the one eye that was not swollen shut, but there was no recognition there. Then his head lolled on his neck and his body sagged between the two guards supporting him. They staggered under his weight, but they did not drop him as they moved for the door.

"Your Majesty," Cedric said with a bow to Garret.

He did not respond, but turned to Ayla and bowed stiffly. "Your Majesty."

Ayla turned her back on him and followed the guards from the room.

When they had left the antechamber, when she was sure that Garret's servants could not hear, Ayla halted the guards holding Malachi.

"You will not take him to the dungeon. I wish for him to be kept in comfort, in my private rooms." She turned to Cedric. "There are spaces in my private rooms where this can be achieved discreetly?"

"Yes, Your Majesty." Cedric gestured to the guards. "I will show them the way myself."

"Thank you." The tears in her eyes and voice surprised her, and she forced them away. "Come to me after you've seen that the healers have tended him."

Cedric bowed to her, and she watched them leave, bearing Malachi with them. She ached to run to him, to rouse him from his stupor and assure him that she would not let him be harmed further, to take away the despair that hung around him in a thick fog. She could not do it now, as she could not have shown him affection before she had become Queene. Never in her life would she be free to love Malachi openly.

She had gone from one prison to another.

Twenty

━━◦◦◦━━

They had moved him again. He'd thought it all a dream, but when Malachi woke he was still surrounded by the sights of the night before. The bleak, bare walls, stained black from smoke and the tattered canopy above him were as they had appeared when they'd first brought him here. In the center of the room was a fire, built under a huge, square metal opening in the ceiling that lead into darkness. The smoke from the fire escaped through this chimney, but not all. It thickened the air, made it hot and dirty.

The sights of the night before were the same, but not the sensations. The pain was mostly gone. His eye was not swollen shut. If he moved too quickly or breathed too deeply there was a twinge of pain, but somehow, in the night, he had improved.

If it had been only one night. He'd drifted in and out of sleep, woken at times by a droning hum that seemed to be made of voices and color all at once, lulled back into the depths by the same sound.

At the edge of the fire, a shadow moved. Slim and slow moving, the shadow straightened, the firelight casting orange through her garments. She was at once frightening and familiar. She was the healer he had visited with Keller.

"That was the sound of the Faery healers," she said, in that way she had of speaking as though she could read his mind as Keller had been able to. "They sing to heal. They put on quite the concert to fix you."

She sat beside him on the bed, fussing the blankets with her withered hands. "Are you thirsty?"

He nodded, and she reached past the edge of his vision for a cup of water. He ached all over when he sat up, and she helped him with a surprising, gentle strength.

When he had finished, gasping from exertion, he asked, "Where am I?"

The old Human set the cup aside and eased him down on the pillows. "You are in the Lightworld still. In a cell, in the Queene's private chambers."

"The Queene?" Something pricked at his memory, but he was tired, so tired.

The woman nodded and smoothed his hair away

from his brow, humming softly. "She was here, you know. In the night."

He recalled seeing someone in the midst of his pain, someone who'd looked like Ayla, but far too fine to be her. She had been clean and shining, like a beacon from another world. She had looked like a Faery. It could not have been Ayla.

"It was her." The woman sounded sure. "She struggled under the weight of great suffering to see you. She is as lost and afraid in this world as you are."

"She is Queene?" He closed his eyes, trying to remember perfectly. "I thought I remembered that she was. But I am not certain of anything that happened before this."

"This was a trial," the woman said in sympathy. Strangely she could give him that without sounding as though she pitied him. "You will face further trials, if you choose the fate that will keep you at her side."

"I do not believe in fate. I believe in will." He winced and adjusted his wings beneath him. "To believe in fate is to believe that God has taken away free will."

"Yes, to your kind the idea of fate would seem perverse." She chuckled, as though she knew all there was to know of his kind. "But there are many fates for a single person. They are chosen through action and deed, not by the random whim of the universe. And one of your fates lies here. But you would have to be strong."

He opened his mouth to protest. He was injured. He was in pain. He had endured nothing but strife since becoming mortal, and she would ask him to submit to more.

But her wise smile stopped him. He had survived great suffering in his time as a mortal, but he had also experienced pain of another kind, the ache of love for a creature he could not imagine being parted from, even as he had lain dying. He had felt the joy of her flesh, had felt the sting of uncertainty as she had slept in his arms, fearing that she might be taken from him, that there would someday be a place where he could not protect her.

How could this healer see other fates for him, without Ayla? They could not exist because without her, he would not exist.

The healer nodded and rose. "You are strong. Now, you must be strong for Ayla. And for your child."

Child? The word struck him like the fall of the spectral lash that had cleaved his wings from him. "My child?"

The woman did not answer. She nodded to the fire as she passed it, then slipped out a door that revealed itself as an appearance of light in the darkness.

He lay back on the bed, uneasy in this room that seemed at once a prison and a comfort. His child? What could she possibly mean? He had been aware of mortal coupling before he'd experienced it with Ayla. He knew it as the way mortals created more mortals. But Ayla was a Faery. Was it possible that their joining could have resulted in a child?

The door opened again, and he sat up, ready to demand the healer give him answers. But as the slender figure passed the fire, he saw glints of orange wreathing her that rivaled the flames, and his breath froze in his chest.

Ayla appeared to him slowly, revealed more and more as the darkness between them evaporated. Her hair was loose, slithering around her shoulders and arms, seeming brighter against her shining skin and the filmy white of her gown. Her antennae twitched a nervous blue against her forehead, and the jewels at her head and neck and wrists echoed the changing light of the fire, capturing and dispersing it at their whim.

She looked nothing like the way he remembered her.

"You are…better?" She shaped the words carefully, halting as she approached his bedside.

He nodded, unable to find his voice for anything other than, "You have a child?"

Her eyes flared wide, and she spoke something in her own language. Then, carefully again, she said, "I do."

She reached for his hand, and he drew it away. He did not know why, and when he moved it back she gripped it tightly and pulled it to her stomach.

There was nothing there, no proof for him but the action. It was proof enough.

Slowly he withdrew his hand, the feel of her skin still hot on his palm.

"You are better?" she repeated earnestly, her eyes shining wet in the firelight.

As stunned as he felt, he would not prolong her worry further. "I am. They sent healers."

She nodded. "I saw them. I was…" She gestured toward the fire. "All night. You did not wake."

"The healer told me about the child." He looked down, where her hands still touched her stomach.

Ayla shook her head. "That is not possible. No one knows."

"She knew," Malachi insisted. "The Human healer."

"There were no Humans here in the Light-world." She laughed at him then. "They are not allowed here."

The troubling feeling that there was an important misunderstanding between them vanished in his sudden anger at her. "Is that why I am in this cell?"

"This room is in my private apartments." She appeared stung by his tone. "I do not want you in the dungeon."

"Did you know I was here?" He grabbed her by the arms and jerked her forward. "Did you know what they were doing to me?"

She shook her head frantically, eyes wide in... fear? She had never feared him before. It was at once gratifying and horrible. He did not wish for her to fear him.

"I was a prisoner, as you were." She tore away from him, her chest heaving, tears streaming down her face. "I would not let them..."

"Prisoner? You are Queene." How could she not have known? "You did not care."

"I did!" She fell to her knees beside the bed, hands clutching the mattress. "I wanted to find you. I asked..."

Her words dissolved into her own language, and in her grief they became the sound of mournful wind.

He reached for her. She didn't resist him when he lifted her to sit beside him on the bed. His injured mortal body screamed in protest, but he needed to have her near, hoping she could feel his remorse so that he would not have to speak it.

"You are tired. You stayed by my side all night." Her hair was soft against his face, and smelled of something clean and pleasant. "Do not cry."

It took her some time, but she calmed, wiping her eyes on her sleeve. "I did not want to leave you."

"I am glad you did not." He held her close to him, tried to be used to the feeling of so much separating them.

She turned in his arms to face him. "I am Queene. But my position is not secure. There is still much danger from Garret."

It did not make sense to him, but he did not care. She was with him, finally, even if she was different, somehow broken, in the time that had passed since he'd held her last.

She stayed with him for a long time, long after the fire had died and they lay in the cold of the room, not sleeping, but not speaking, either. She seemed content enough to stay there, so he did not move her, even when his neck was stiff from keeping still and his arms ached under her weight.

Better that they ached from holding her than from not.

When the healers arrived the next morning, Ayla reluctantly left Malachi's side. "You will be safe," she had reassured him. "I will return to you."

In truth, she had to leave him before she told him all that had happened and all that must be done. The less he knew, the safer he would be, she had decided.

Cedric awaited her in her private meeting room with her council. Garret was not present, she noted with some relief. Had he already told them of Malachi and what she had done to keep him?

Although Cedric had stayed awake with her much of the night that Malachi was with the healers, he appeared to have gotten enough rest since then. He smiled at her when she entered, and bowed in deference, but something about his manner seemed strange.

"There is some news, then, if you are all here." She tried to sound unconcerned. "Some rumbling from Garret?"

The despicable Faery who had shown preference for Garret during their first meeting made a noise of disgust. She glared at him and continued. "Best to be out with it. What has he done?"

Cedric stepped forward and held out a bit of paper rolled as though it were parchment. "This came from the Royal Consort today."

She did not take the paper. "I will not touch anything from his hand. What does it say?"

Two of the council members exchanged knowing glances, and Ayla drew herself up taller.

"He has left the Palace, seeking sanctuary with the Trolls. He has taken a number of guards with him, and several valuables belonging to the treasury." Cedric paused for a moment, tapping the parchment against his palm.

"Let him take what he wishes, as long as I'm free of him," Ayla said with a laugh, and at once wished she had not. It sounded foolish, as though she did understand the tenuousness of her position. "There is more?"

Cedric nodded. "He has issued a challenge, stating that you killed his sister, the Queene, and expressing his wish to settle the matter outside of a legal proceeding."

"A duel?" This time, Ayla was not ashamed of her laugh. "Garret has not wielded a weapon in years. Not in actual combat."

"He managed well enough against your Darkling pet," the unpleasant Faery muttered, his face turning red.

It was enough that no one at Court would believe her innocence without jewels and pretty words. She did not need to hear doubts and aspersions against her from the people who had been entrusted with guiding her reign.

She did not shrink from the Faery's cold stare. "You may leave."

"Forgive me, Your Majesty," another of the

council members spoke. "But perhaps it is not wise, considering your current position, to dismiss your council."

"I am not dismissing my council. I am dismissing the members of Mabb's council who prefer to remain allied with my mate." Her gaze flicked briefly to Cedric, but he showed neither pride nor displeasure. She continued. "If you believe that I am a murderer, then go now. If you believe that Garret is more fit to lead the Lightworld, then you may also go. If you believe that I am incapable of making decisions on my own without your wisdom and guidance, go. I am not merely the King's contrary mate, nor do I plan to rule under that distinction. I am Queene. If you disagree, I can do very well without you."

There was a shared, withheld breath in the room. Though the desire to say something else, it did not matter what so long as it broke the silence, was overwhelming, Ayla held her tongue and her stony pose before them.

Finally, as she had expected, chairs began to scrape back. The Faery who'd most vocally supported Garret turned red from antennae to throat. "In all of my years on the royal council, no Queene has ever been so disrespectful."

There was no response she could make to him that would not sound petty, so she said nothing at all. She watched in silence, feeling Cedric's stare on her as all but one member of the council filed from the room.

When the door closed behind the last of them, Ayla turned to the one who stayed. It was the small Faery, the one with the shrewd, piercing blue eyes. She looked back, unblinking. "I do not agree with them."

"We can see that." Cedric walked around the table to stand beside Ayla. Low, for only her to hear, he said, "They will join up with Garret. Before, he would have collapsed under his own lack of intelligence. Now, he will have greater minds working for him."

Ayla nodded. "And I would worry, truly, if I knew Garret less and thought he might listen to them."

With a smile, Cedric said, "You are wiser than I imagined."

"Not wise." A hitch of sadness caught in her voice. "If I had been wise, I would never have gotten to this place."

She wiped her eyes. If she crumbled in front of her last remaining council member, she would be truly on her own.

Not quite on your own, she reminded herself. Cedric had been so helpful. He had defied Garret, risked his life. If she failed and Garret became the ruler of the Faery Court, Cedric would lose his life for treason, just as she would lose hers.

As if sensing her change in mood, Cedric addressed the remaining council member. "The Queene is still tired from her unfortunate imprisonment. I will meet with you later, to discuss how we will handle the formation of a new royal council and an official announcement of the original council's disbanding."

The Faery nodded her head, her yellow hair gleaming under the Human electricity. "Yes, Guild Master."

Ayla put her hand up to stop Cedric from ushering her from the room. "You are from the Assassins' Guild?"

The Faery nodded, but let Cedric speak for her. "Flidais kept the records for the Faery wars on the Astral, before the rift opened between our former world and this one."

"Many council positions for worthy Faeries opened then," Flidais interjected. "And I was one of those Faeries."

"I am glad you were." The deceptively small creature disturbed Ayla. She seemed so young, even for an eternally youthful race, and yet she was old, perhaps as old as Cedric.

Flidais rose from her seat and bowed to Ayla before Cedric led her from the room. "She is trustworthy," he assured her. "And far more intelligent than the rest of the council was."

"You think I am foolish for dismissing them." Ayla nodded to a passing servant. It was something Cedric had taught her, to always acknowledge even the lowest ranking Faeries in the Palace. It showed a respect for them that Mabb had not had, he'd told her.

"I would never go so far as to call Her Majesty foolish," he said, a note of reproach in his voice. "I do worry that news of this will upset the Court."

"Then I will have to pile on more jewels to blind them with my wealth," she snickered.

Cedric stopped and put a hand on her shoulder to turn her. It was a moment between teacher and student, not a subject and his Queene. "You must not believe that you are safely installed as Queene. The coronation has not taken place, and cannot until Garret no longer opposes you. And the courtiers are fickle. Once you lose their support, you will not be able to get it back."

"I know that. I do," Ayla reassured him. "Why are helping me? The risks are just as great for you as they are for me, if not greater."

He patted her arm, and they resumed their walking. "That is a story for another time. For now, it should be enough that I do not wish to see Garret as King."

"For now, it is." Ayla meant it.

* * *

With a twinge of regret, Garret watched his guards load the last of his royal belongings into the cart. After all the time he'd spent, all the plans he'd made and revised and acted on, to leave the Palace seemed an abandonment of his goal. And when it was so close.

"Your Majesty?" a voice said, and Garret turned. Bran, formerly of the royal council—no, not quite formerly—stood waiting beside the cart. "We should go now, before we are noticed further."

"Yes. Thank you." He climbed up to sit on the back of the cart, and motioned the guards at the front who would pull it away from the Palace.

"It is only for a little while." Bran was shrewd. He'd seen the reason for Garret's strain without needing more than few moments of observation. "Soon, the false Queene will be deposed, and you will be restored to your throne."

"Of course I will be," Garret responded, a bit more sharply than he'd intended. To keep from appearing too tense, too unsure, he added, "I have great faith in all that my loyal subjects have done, and will do, to help me in this matter."

The cart lurched forward, and again the pain of being separated from his birthright stung him.

I will return, he repeated silently. *I will return.*

Twenty-One

❧

The healers' art was masterful. Within the few hours they had attended Malachi, Ayla had watched him progress from broken wretch to recovering invalid, all the way to the state he stood in before her now.

"You can walk." She felt the grin that spread across her face and knew she must be beaming like the moon.

He smiled, too, and it felt like the time they had shared in the strange Human's workshop. She remembered the Human and wondered if he would look for Malachi. "Does Keller know where you are?"

Malachi's smile faded, the happiness drained from his eyes with a flinch. "He is dead. The guards that captured me killed him."

The thought of the Human, so fragile and unprotected, dying at the hands of Garret's soldiers brought tears of anger to her eyes. She did not let them fall. "But you are alive. That is what matters."

"Does it?" Malachi shook his head. "He helped you as he helped me. Do you have no feelings?"

This stung. "I have…feelings. I feel for you."

He did not answer. Instead he went to his bed and sat in the tangle of bedclothes there. "You seem uneasy."

She did not wish to speak to him further, but unreasonably, words came from her. "I am concerned."

"What are your concerns?" Malachi patted the place beside himself, a gesture so Human and startling that Ayla froze in shock. She willed her legs to carry her forward and sat stiffly beside him.

How could she possibly communicate to him all the fears in her heart? That she would do nothing, and Garret would return to the throne. And, in that event, she would lose her life, and Malachi would lose his, as well.

Or, should she tell him that she might be forced to fight, possibly die, and he would be doomed then, as well?

It was better not to tell him anything at all, not until it was decided, so she shook her head and said, "It is nothing," and laid her head in his lap and kept all of that fear inside, hoping he would not see it.

He put his hand on her hair, stroking the tresses before stilling his palm at the back of her neck, where it remained like a weight. "You do not care for me, or you would tell me."

"I do not tell you because I wish to protect you." Was that the correct word for it? It was so much more than a need to shield him from harm. She wanted to keep him from any fear of harm that could come.

More than anything, she regretted that Malachi had ever come into the Lightworld. It was strange and unsettling to have him with her, though it was the thing she'd wanted terribly before. He was the bridge between her life before and her life now that made the past so painful, and the present so unbearable.

Still, the thought of not having him tore at her heart in such a way that she could not bear to think of it at all.

"I do not need your protection." He resumed his gentle stroking of her hair. "If it were not for you, I would never have come here. It is too late for you to protect me."

She could not disagree with him. "Garret has challenged me. He wishes to kill me and take the throne."

Malachi said nothing at first, but his body stilled. After a long silence, he asked, "Garret is the one who captured me?"

"Yes." She twisted on his lap to look up at his face. "What do you remember from when he took you?"

A line creased Malachi's forehead as he thought, and when his features relaxed, the ghost of it stayed behind. How strange mortals' bodies were.

"We were approaching the Strip. That was when the soldiers took me. They wanted nothing with Keller, but they killed him. I do not understand why they killed him."

"Garret is cruel." It was the only explanation that she could give him, though it would not be satisfactory to him. It didn't satisfy her, either. "You were not in the Lightworld when he took you?"

Malachi shook his head. "We were still in the Darkworld. I thought we were safe. Keller said the Strip was a neutral area, and that your soldiers did not enter the Darkworld."

"They do not, under normal circumstances." Such as when they had been ordered to go on a revenge mission by a power-crazed Faery who wished to be King. She closed her eyes and made a noise of frustration. "I must bring this information to my council. Will you be awake long tonight?"

Now, Malachi sounded frustrated. "You leave me in this room, I am not free to wander, there is nothing to occupy my time except for your visits and now you will leave again?"

She sat up and put both of her hands on the sides of his face. Though he tried to turn away, she held him there. "I keep you here for your safety. I still have enemies within the Palace, and my position is not secure."

With a roar, he pushed her off of him and growled, "You keep me here for yourself!"

"I keep you here to protect you!" She rose onto her knees on the bed and watched him stalk across the room. "You could not survive in the Darkworld on your own!"

"I could make my own way!" He pounded his chest, so hard it must have hurt him. "I could have lived in Keller's workshop, done what I had to do to survive! It would be preferable to being kept as your pet!"

She wished she could tell him that he was not just a possession to her, that she could not let him go because she feared what would happen to him, feared she would never see him again. But the words would not come. "You could not survive in the Darkworld, even when you were an immortal! It is only through my mercy that you lived, not just on our first meeting, but when I rescued you from that Demon. You owe your life to me, and I wish you to stay, so you will stay!"

She climbed to her feet, heart pounding, and left him in that lonely, bare room. She did not look back at him.

Life in exile was not as horrible as Garret had imagined it. It was worse.

The rooms that he'd secured in the Troll Quarter were barely sufficient. Dirty and covered with rock dust—the foodstuff of choice for the cave-dwellers—the fetid, disgusting chambers still reeked of the mortals aboveground.

All the more reason to mount a quick offensive and reclaim his place. But as his loyal council worked to maintain allies, he had nothing to do but wait. The waiting would drive him crazy.

"Bran!" He did not bother to wait and see if the Faery would respond. Though it was the middle of the night, and though his advisor would stumble, sleepy, from his makeshift bed, he would come. The hunger in his council to be restored to their places, as well, inspired the most disgusting loyalty.

"Your Majesty?" His hair was mussed from sleep, his face lined from too little of it. He looked almost…mortal. The exile took its toll on everyone.

Garret waited for the man to complete his bow. "I have something to ask of you. In the morning, seek help from the Dragons. Take as many of my guards with you as needed to appear impressive before them. They are fond of such displays. And take them something valuable, as a token of my friendship."

"The Dragons, Your Majesty?" Bran repeated in a sleep-choked voice. "They will not be easy to win over. They have rarely allowed any of their number to become involved in the affairs of the Faery Court, or any other business of the Lightworld, for that matter."

"And that is why it would be so beneficial to my cause if I had them." Could none of the council think properly on their own? "Ayla will not have the sense to garner allies from such a venerable camp. And were the Dragons to side with me, the Court, the whole Lightworld, would fall in line. Out of respect for their ancient wisdom or fear for what they might do if angered."

Bran hedged further. "The Faery Court does owe a hefty sum in gold and jewels to the Dragon King, Your Majesty. A debt run up by your sister, while still on the other side of the veil."

Of course. Mabb would still muddle things for him, even in death. "Do not avoid the subject when meeting with the Dragon ambassador. Be sure to let them know exactly who has possession of those treasures, and assure them that once she is removed from the throne, the debt will be repaid. Stress that I wish only good for the Lightworld, and that cooperation between all races within it is my solemn goal. This should appeal to their pacifist nature."

"Yes, Your Majesty." Bran bowed again and took a few steps back. Clearly he needed his bed as badly as Garret needed his own.

"One last thing, Bran." Garret turned away and made for his own bed, not a thin tangle of blankets on the concrete, but the bed from his royal chamber, disassembled for the journey and reassembled at the farthest end of the cave. "If they are adamant in their refusal, remind them that a Darkling gained admittance to the Lightworld disguised as one of their Human servants. They do owe us something, in that respect."

"So, Garret ordered his guard into the Darkworld?" Cedric paced the length of the long table in the council room, talking to himself as though two other Faeries did not sit in the room with him.

"He must have understood that this could be seen as an act of war." Flidais was similarly lost in her own thoughts, and Ayla struggled to follow both meandering paths of thought at once.

Cedric's pacing distracted her, as well. She

ached to stand and mirror his movements, but forced herself to keep calm. Three minds in a room thinking independently of each other would not help as much as three working together. "Who would declare war? The Darkworld is disorganized and ungoverned. Isn't it?" She looked to Flidais for confirmation, and her stomach tightened when the Faery shook her head.

"The Darkworld is largely ungoverned when compared to the Lightworld, it is true." The antennae on Flidais's head twitched as though accessing the knowledge themselves. "While each race here governs itself, there are factions running rampant in the Darkworld with no real government. The Gypsies have their own primitive codes of law, but no real leader, and there are some Humans living there who answer to no one. Only the Demons and the Calli have organized courts, but the Elves have an army."

"Will they strike at us?" Ayla looked to Cedric. "And if they did, would we have anything to fear?"

Cedric stopped his pacing. "The Demon King has no interest in us. He wishes only to be away from mortals."

"And the Calli? What is their King like?" In truth, Ayla knew little about their race, but she would not show her ignorance before Flidais. She did not know her enough to trust her fully, yet.

"Blind," Cedric answered, resuming his pacing. "Like all of them, though some of them have regained their sight here in the Underground. He is old, losing his mind from captivity. The leader of the Elves, though, hates us. His son has taken on many of his responsibilities and is said to be a revolutionary. He circulated a pamphlet not long ago, calling for war against the Lightworld, but he has few supporters. Should word of Garret's venture past their borders reach them, they might be able to rouse more interest in a war."

"The Gypsies will never fight," Flidais assured her calmly. "They will flee the Underground first, as likely will most of the Humans."

"Then all we have to fear are the Elves, and any allies they might have." Ayla tapped her fingers against her lips. "And Garret. I have heard rumors that he intends to rally the Dragons against me, that he has already sent an envoy."

Flidais paled and turned to Cedric. "If he succeeds, all is lost."

Raising his hand to silence Flidais, Cedric said calmly, "Remember, Your Majesty, that the Dragons are far wiser than Garret. He will appear to them as the arrogant, ineffectual schemer that he is, and they will remain neutral."

"There is no chance of winning them to my side of the cause, then?" Though she had only now imagined the possibility, the loss of that hope stung her. Was she truly on her own, then?

"I would caution Your Majesty against it. The Dragons are, by nature, treasure hunters, and Mabb relieved them of a great deal of it during her reign. I am sure it would dishearten you as it would me to see the Fae Court added to their hoard to repay an old debt. They do not fight, and are content to stay Underground, so long as they can extort tributes from the rest of us."

"Then there is no hope." She covered her face with her hands, rubbing her tired skin. Resting her chin on her hands, she looked up at the mass of broken pipes clinging to the ceiling. "As long as Garret lives, he will try to raise up enemies against me. As the true and legitimate heir, he will find a way to curry favor, regardless of his crimes. I am Queene on borrowed time. When I lose favor with the Court, when my newness wears off, I will be back in the dungeon while Garret sits on the throne."

"If Your Majesty will forgive my unsolicited advice, there is another way." Flidais paused, as if unsure of whether or not to continue. "You could answer the King's challenge."

Cedric drew in a breath, while Ayla was unable to breathe at all.

Flidais continued. "You said before that he was your mentor, but that he has not fought in earnest in quite some time. If you are confident that you could best him, this might be the only way to safely secure your throne."

"It is impossible," Cedric said, his voice low. "The Queene is with child."

"Ah." It was all Flidais seemed able to manage.

"This must, of course, be kept confidential. It is known only to the three of us and Garret." Cedric cast a sideways glance at Ayla. "Which is what makes his challenge all the more despicable."

Ayla saw Flidais working the story out in her mind. The Faery was far too clever to believe that Garret would risk killing his own heir, especially one from a legitimate Queene, but she was also too clever to voice her suspicions. Instead she said, "If we are the only ones to know about the child, then what is to prevent her from fighting him?"

What was? She closed her eyes and laid a hand on her stomach where the babe grew, though the evidence could not be seen yet. Could she risk the life of her child in fighting Garret? Could she risk its life by not fighting, by not taking the only chance that had presented itself thus far?

She had believed it when she'd said her time was limited. As long as Garret was available to the Court as another alternative, a new, exciting change, they would consider him whenever she made a mistake or unpopular decision.

But could she kill her mentor? Though Garret had proved himself despicable, deceitful, a part of her still ached for her trusted friend and advisor. He had disappeared that night that she had agreed to become his mate, though, and even if she had never challenged his rule, even if they had received the throne of the Lightworld together, her teacher and friend would never have returned. The kindness Garret had shown her had been the lie, while the truth had lurked in him, waiting until he could take what he wanted.

"Flidais, will you excuse Cedric and I?" Ayla asked, and the Faery made her bow and left. When the door had closed behind her, Ayla turned to Cedric. "I will fight him."

Cedric shook his head. "It is not possible. I cannot, in good conscience, let you endanger an heir to the throne."

"The heir to the throne is no more royal than you or I." She looked him in the eye, so he could see she was not ashamed. "You know that the child I carry was fathered by the Darkling."

It took Cedric a long time to speak. From the agitated twitching of his antennae, she could see that he tried to work out what to say to argue with her. She could see, too, that he knew he would.

"And what about the babe's father? Would you have him stand by while his child is put into danger? While you are put into danger?"

Now was the moment Ayla had dreaded since being with Malachi that morning. Something in her went dark, without her willing it to do so, something closed off in her as though it knew to protect her. "I will send him away."

"Send him away?" Cedric's voice was a hollow echo from him.

She did not need to try to keep her voice level, emotionless. It happened without effort. "He never needs to know what has happened here, and he has already made it plain that he wishes to return to his world. It will be better for him, and for us, if he goes."

Cedric's voice told of his disbelief, his anger. "You risked your life by letting him come into the Lightworld. You were imprisoned for your…involvement with him. And now you act as though none of that matters."

"Because it does not." All that mattered now was that this silly game come to an end, that the waiting for death ceased, as it would whether she was victorious or not. "It hurts our cause more than helps it to have a Darkling kept in the Palace. If I were to bow to his will in this matter, I would end both of our lives."

"And what is Your Majesty going to do? Throw him onto the Strip while he is injured?" To hear Cedric defend Malachi was too touching to bear. "If he tries to return, will you have him killed?"

Now, the rising anger in her threatened to upset her calm, and she forced it aside. "He is no longer injured to the point of incapacity. You will escort him to his lodgings in the Darkworld. Occasionally I might see fit to send him a small gift of coin for trade, but he has assured me that he can live on his own quite well. In the future, if he changes his mind, I will not keep him from returning. For now, until Garret is dead, it is best that he remain at a distance."

"And you will keep him from his child." Cedric spit the words at her as though she were not a Queene. Though she enjoyed being spoken to as an equal most of the time, this rankled her.

She drew up straighter in her chair. "I will do what I feel I must as Queene. And you will do what I order you to do."

Mocking her with a bow, Cedric intoned, "As Your Majesty wishes," before turning on his heel and leaving her alone in the council room.

Only when she was sure he would not return did she lay her head on her arms and weep.

Twenty-Two

Dragons.

Bran checked his reflection once more and decided to add another ring. The Dragons respected wealth and beauty. He smoothed his dark hair behind his ears and brushed rock dust from the shoulders of his tunic.

He had assembled six of the King's guards. More would have seemed a threat, less would have implied that the King had no support. Six would be the perfect number, he hoped.

They had a guide who would lead them. A Troll, the same hulking, gray mass that had lumbered into the Dragon territory and set up the meeting for them. He tromped up the tunnel, and Bran took his place ahead of the guards to follow him.

The King had not risen to see them off.

The tunnels in the Troll Quarter might have once been the varying shapes of the Human structures left over in the Faery Court, but years of Troll appetite had rounded them, huge bite marks carving the walls away far more effectively than any drill. The cavernous space dwarfed them, though it was a tight fit for their guide who stooped down and occasionally swiped bits of hanging rock from the ceiling.

Bran did not duck the falling debris. Fear was undignified.

The walk seemed never ending. At the border to the Dragon Quarter, the Troll carved a niche for himself from the wall to turn around in. "I go no farther."

He wouldn't have been able to fit. The tunnel that led into the Dragons' territory was substantially smaller. They left their guide behind, where he waited, crushing cement between his huge, yellow teeth, and proceeded into the Dragon Quarter.

Bran spotted the Dragon envoy awaiting them at the first fork in the tunnels. He did not raise his head or show his face beneath his hood. "Follow," he commanded, crooking his finger.

The Human wore the same deep red cloak as all of the other Humans in Dragon service. The protective symbol, embroidered in gold on the back of their cloaks, kept them safe in the Lightworld where other Humans would not be. It disgusted Bran. No matter how loyal the animals might be, to keep a mortal in your dwelling…

He forced a neutral expression and held his breath as he walked behind the mortal. Humans stank of sweat and grime, no matter how clean they appeared.

In their home, the Dragons displayed their wealth on every surface. Tapestries covered bits of the walls that were not embedded with glittering gems, and coins of gold and silver littered the floor. They flaunted a wealth of another kind in small holes hollowed from the cavern walls: skulls of every race in the Underground, displayed for their visitors as a warning.

Bran smoothed his hair down and adjusted the cuffs of his robe.

Their guide took them silently through twists and turns so numerous and seemingly random that soon Bran had no idea which way would lead him out of the Dragon Quarter. This was, no doubt, the intention.

All he needed to do was keep his cool, remember his purpose, and soon he would be away from this despicable place. Once the Dragons were allied with the King's cause, the ridiculous exile would be over, and they would all be safely back in their own Quarter with their own race.

The next turn brought them abruptly to a stop. In the dim light of the fires burning on the ground, larger piles of coins gleamed. They bled from a huge pile of coins, jewels and other assorted valuables, atop of which perched a coiled, yellow-green mass of scales.

"An ambassador from the Faery Court," the guide said in a low voice, and two orange, slit orbs flickered in the darkness as the Dragon woke.

The Human envoy seated himself beside the Dragon and said, "It has been a long time since the Faery Court has contacted us."

Bran stared at the Human, unable to believe that he would so freely join a conversation between two of his superiors. Then, the slit pupil in the glowing orange eye narrowed, and Bran understood. The creature spoke through his Human.

Bran bowed. "Too long, by my master's account."

"And who is your master? We had heard that the Queene of Thieves had met an unfortunate end." A great cloud of sulfurous smoke emitted from the Dragon on a sound that would have seemed a laugh from any other creature.

"Yes, my master, King Garret, mourns the loss of his sister." Bran motioned to the guard who bore the casket of jewelry Garret had sent. "However, he looks forward to creating a lasting alliance with you."

The Human assistant rose and came for the box the guard offered. He brought them before those impossibly large eyes, and the bulk of the scales shifted. A tail uncoiled and brushed a wave of coins from the pile beneath it. It was long, studded with sharp, boney spines. A claw, larger than the Human's head, but still small in comparison to the rest of the creature, emerged, one gleaming black talon sifting through the box with surprising delicacy.

The Human returned to his place beside the Dragon and spoke. "This is a paltry offering, compared to what was taken from us."

"King Garret recognizes that our race owes you much, much more. However, at the moment he is unable to return to you the objects you desire." Bran cleared his throat, pretended to be ashamed of what he would say next. "He is, unfortunately, in exile."

"Exile?" Another smoke-accented laugh. "How can a King be forced from his own Court? How can a male be the leader of your kind?"

The creature was taking things far too lightly. He did not show the respect owed to an ambassador of the King. Bran swallowed his irritation before speaking. "Treachery. His mate, a devious Faery with no royal blood nor claim to the throne, forced him out by gaining the fickle attentions of a few key persons in the Court."

The Dragon's eyes slid closed and open a few times, slowly as the Human voiced its thoughts. "You bore us. Your politics are no concern of ours."

"If I might be so bold," Bran began, trying harder to keep his irritation from his voice, "it does concern you. The usurper has your treasures. She flaunts them before the Court, mocking you."

With a roar that shook the cavern and sent the coins at Bran's feet vibrating, the Dragon straightened. It was an awesome sight, all of the towering, green-tinged creature unfurled in space much too small for it. Its head and neck, though stooped, still touched the ceiling, and its wings curled around the back of the cavern.

Over the noise, the Human shouted, "Do you believe that we can be mocked? We, who are older than any Fae to ever walk the Earth, any Troll to tunnel beneath it? Do you believe we are threatened by the foolish actions of one insignificant Faery?"

"We believe that you deserve more respect than that!" Bran shouted back. This was where he would prove himself. Surely a creature like a Dragon, always feared, often venerated, would appreciate being spoken to so honestly, as if he were an equal.

The Dragon paused in its wrath and settled into its earlier pose. "We listen," the Human said.

"My master, the King, wishes to restore what his sister stole, but he cannot unless he himself is restored. If you were to join in his cause, the Queene would have no choice but to back down, and he could reclaim his throne. At that point, he would be in a position to restore your lost treasures." Bran nodded to the casket of jewels lying on its side, contents spilling to the concrete floor. "And more."

The Dragon puffed out a breath so hot that Bran had to will himself from covering his face. "You will hold our property ransom, then? Until we give you what you desire?"

That was a take that Bran had not foreseen, but it seemed that the Dragon was now appropriately broken down to negotiate with. "I would not call it ransom. Merely a gesture of friendship."

"We give our friendship to those who earn our respect, and we repay those who hold a debt against us." The large eyes slid closed. "Not to those who seek to bargain for it with trinkets."

With a deep breath, Bran called out, "You do owe us something!"

The eyes snapped open, wide.

Bran stepped forward. "The Faery Quarter is closest to the border with the Strip. Your Human envoys cross through our territory every day. Recently an enemy from the Darkworld infiltrated our

Quarter disguised as one of your Humans. Perhaps, to repay us for the irresponsible actions of your Human servant who supplied the Darkling with his Dragon cloak, you could pledge your support to my King."

The Dragon's lids closed, leaving slits of orange in the darkness of the cavern.

The envoy who returned Bran's head left Garret with little hope of support from the Dragons.

"We do not respond to threats," the man had intoned from behind his hood, before disappearing into the inky darkness of the Troll tunnels.

So, the Dragons would not side with him.

With an inarticulate roar, he pushed the box of returned jewels—and Bran's head—from the table they rested on.

"Am I interrupting?"

He turned at the sound, his skin prickling with irritation before he even saw the intruder. "What do you want?"

Flidais, his sister's traitorous handmaiden, stood at the opening of the cavern. She lifted her robes to step delicately over the discarded head. "I am not sorry to see him go. He smelled of lavender water. Too much lavender water."

Suddenly too aware of his own scent, Garret sniffed the air. Damn Flidais. She had a way about

her, with her shrewd, piercing eyes and her quiet
nature, that could cause even a confident Faery to
question himself in her presence. Some Fae could
do such a trick with their beauty. Flidais was not
beautiful. It was merely her way of staring, unblinking, as though she had nothing to hide, when
he must hide everything.

No, she must have something to hide. Something to bargain with.

"My mate sent you, no doubt." He motioned to
a guard to clean up after Bran, and extended his
hand to Flidais. "Come in. My household is greatly
reduced, but you are welcome in it all the same."

"Even after I did not follow you to your self-
imposed exile." She did not take his hand. "I come
to you as a wartime messenger under the code put
forth during the war of the Tuatha. No harm can
come to me while I am in your enemy camp. Do
you accept these terms?"

"Flidais, please." He smiled and went to find
some of the Human wine they had unearthed in the
walls. "I would not harm you, even if you came
with the intent to assassinate me."

She made a small laugh, a snorting, unfeminine
sound. "I could not assassinate you. Your guards
would have taken my weapons."

"Ah, so she has considered it?" He poured out
some of the wine into one of his fine wooden cups

and offered it to her. "It hurts my heart to hear of such treason from my mate whom I once loved dearly."

"Treason?" She waved the wine away. "I will not stay that long. But tell me, how could it be treason, when she is Queene? You are merely her consort."

"She has no royal blood!" He slammed the cup down on the table, spilling the remains of the bottle in his anger. "Am I the only Fae left with a care for our bloodline?"

Flidais squinted her eyes. "Did you not realize that by making her your mate, you would give her royal blood? That by mating yourself to her, you gave up any hope of your throne?"

He took a swallow of the bitter Human wine and looked away.

"You knew. Just as you knew that your sister had powerful enemies." She snorted again at this. "You would have killed Queene Ayla. You've already proven with your challenge that you would be willing now. But why her? Because she was no one? Because she was something you might keep, if you found her easily manipulated?"

Garret whirled to face her. "You said you came with a message. Give it to me and get out!"

With a nod and an acquiescing smile, she reached into her robe and withdrew a folded parchment. Garret recognized his own seal, broken, at once.

"It seems you will have your chance to kill the Queene after all." She tossed the parchment to the ground, where Bran's blood stained the dirt. "I am sure you have had plenty of practice."

He tossed the bottle after her, but it landed short of her calm, measured retreat.

It had been a long time since Ayla had held a weapon, and yet it felt like no time at all. She moved through her forms with care, the broadsword swinging arcs overhead, swooping at her side, slicing the air effortlessly and felling whole fields of imaginary enemies.

But it was only one enemy she feared.

Garret would fight with an ax. He'd always fought with one, brought one to the front lines of the wars against the Humans and the wars among their own race. It was the first weapon he'd trained her on.

The only one she'd never been able to defend herself against when he wielded it.

The door to the Assassins' training room scraped open, and she quickly sheathed her weapon, out of habit. It was Cedric who entered, and his eyes, so troubled lately, flashed amusement beneath their fair brows. "It is refreshing to see a Queene remember where she came from."

In no mood for levity, she hoisted the sword once more. "You have seen him fight."

"Yes." Cedric slowly walked the circle on the floor. "He is very skilled."

"If you remember those skills, take up an ax and assist me." She wiped a sweat-damp lock of hair from her forehead.

Cedric bowed and shrugged off his robes, standing before her clad only in his brown leather pants. For a moment, she saw him as a Faery, and not as her superior who had become her friend. He was handsome, with the long, lean musculature of a well-trained warrior. If she had not lived so long presuming herself unworthy, she might have thought of him as a possible mate one day.

But now, she cared only for her Darkling.

She pushed her thoughts of Malachi from her mind. They twisted in her chest, where her tree of life spread its branches. If she went to this fight with Malachi in her mind and heart, she would fail. Her sorrow would cripple her.

Cedric lifted the ax and dropped into a stance that mirrored Garret's fighting posture. Cedric did know Garret's fighting skills well.

Without Ayla asking, Cedric said, "I have not remained alive as long as I have by ignoring the more ambitious Fae around me."

He swung out in a wide sweep, keeping her far out of range. Just as Garret would do.

She leaped back and opened her wings, pushing

off the ground with the sword high over her head, ready to strike a death blow. "You knew he might someday be a threat to you?"

Cedric easily rolled away from her strike. "Good, good. You are not fighting to prolong the fight, you are fighting to end it."

"It is what Garret taught me," she huffed, somersaulting over her wings and landing on her feet, ducking in time to dodge Cedric's next swing. "You feared him?"

"I do not fear anyone, Ayla." Cedric stepped back, creating another protective space between them. "Drop your elbow, you leave your left side unprotected."

"If you saw it, and everyone at Court saw it—" Ayla dropped into a crouch and jabbed at Cedric's legs "—why did I not see it?"

Now was where Garret would have taken his chance and wicked the arms from her body, but Cedric took a different path. He sprang over her head and caught her before she could face him, bringing the ax to a halt just before it buried in her spine.

Puffing and sweating, she turned and collapsed to the floor. "Why did I not see it? Why did I not see him for what he was?"

Throwing the ax aside, Cedric sat beside her. His arm was strong and comforting around her shoulders. Exactly the way a friend's would have been. And it struck Ayla then that she had never had a friend. Garret had been the only Fae she could have truly considered a friend and now that she knew his true nature, she could not believe she'd been so foolish.

He leaned his head against hers. "You did not see it because you are better than most of us. If you had the capacity for treachery, you would see it coming at you from every angle."

"I see it now." She was suddenly much more tired than a simple training session should have made her. "Does that mean I am becoming like him?"

"It means that you are being cautious." Cedric rose and offered her his hand. When she got on her feet, he swept up her sword and tossed it to her. "Again."

This time, she struck out before Cedric was ready. It was dishonorable, but Garret would not fight with honor. Her swing caught Cedric off guard, and he nodded his approval as he blocked it. "Now, you are thinking as you must to protect yourself."

Thinking as I must. It was such a coldhearted way of living. "After Garret, there will be other enemies." She grunted the last words as she lunged at him.

Cedric stepped aside and brought the ax down to prevent her raising her blade again. "There will always be enemies. You are the Queene."

"So I must live in fear for the rest of my days?" She opened her wings and propelled herself forward to kick Cedric off his feet. With her blade free, she brought it down, aiming for his throat and stopping its ascent at the very last. "If that is what it means to be Queene, I do not want it."

She pulled her blade back and Cedric rolled to his feet smoothly. "Then let Garret kill you. Or surrender the throne to him, and he will kill you then. But you will not live so long as you are not Queene."

With a cry of frustration, Ayla hurled her sword into a nearby rack of weapons. When the clatter of the falling arms subsided, she had calmed some, at least outwardly. Inside, desperation swirled in her in torrents. "I could leave here. I could take Malachi and hide in the Darkworld."

"Garret would find you." Cedric did not allow her even the illusion of escape. "You would be hunted for the rest of your life, as long as you are his legitimate mate and you carry the heir to the throne."

"How legitimate can our union be?" She heard the petulant note in her voice, like the creak of grapevines twisting the wind. "He wishes me dead."

"And you left him the night of your mating to go to a Darkling. He has as much right to wish you dead as you to wish him dead." Cedric went to his discarded tunic and picked it up. "Have you spoken to Malachi yet?"

She began to right the weapons she'd knocked down. She might be Queene, but that was no excuse to destroy Guild property. Also, it helped her avoid looking at Cedric as she answered. "I have not."

He did not say anything for a long while, taking the time to straighten his robes and smooth his hair. When he finally did speak, he did not sound angry or disappointed, as Ayla expected. "I will not speak for you. If he does not know that I am to return him to the Darkworld, I will not take him, and you will have to deal with the consequences."

For a moment, she was tempted to reprimand him for talking so to his Queene, but it would have been ridiculous, when that was what she relied on him to do. "I will go to him tonight. I will try to prepare him." Pain lanced through her heart. "He will be angry."

"He will have cause to be angry," Cedric said quietly, and then, in the silence that hung between them, "I am sorry, Your Majesty, it was not my place."

"It was not," Ayla agreed, but in her heart she

knew he was right. "Do not apologize. I have made my choice, and I will, as you say, have to deal with the consequences on my own."

She only wished those consequences did not include sending Malachi away from her forever.

Twenty-Three

The fire had nearly gone out when she came to him.

"I had almost given up hope," he said in the darkness, watching her move through the shadows in her bare feet. She was dressed for bed, had probably already gone through the ritual of climbing in and being covered by her handmaidens. She'd described to him the ridiculous lengths the servants of the Queene went to in order to care for her. Ayla could only sneak away when they were certain she was unconscious and would have no further needs until morning.

"But you did not," she said softly, coming to kneel beside the bed in the cloud of her white nightgown. "I am sorry. I returned late from a training session."

"Training? Learning to be Queene?" He reached to touch the soft tendrils of her hair, brushed to gleaming by the patient hands of her servants. "You would let someone teach you?"

She looked down at her hands, twisting in her lap, and a sinking began deep in his guts. He pushed it aside to concentrate on her words. "It was not…it was training for combat."

"Fighting?" He laughed despite the trepidation he felt and tucked some of the fiery length behind her ear. "Do you still have use for that as a Queene? Do you not have guards to fight for you?"

"Of course I do." She pushed his hand away. She would say something now, something he did not want to hear. His stomach clenched when she looked up at him. "I must tell you something, and you must listen to me and obey me as Queene, no matter how you might think of me after."

There was no denying it, no matter how he might try to keep the conversation between them light, no matter how he might playfully touch her. He nodded, his tongue too thick for words.

"You must go back to the Darkworld."

He found his voice then, and in good time, for there were many things in his brain clamoring to get free. "You will go with me."

She shook her head. "I cannot. I am…banishing you. For your own safety."

"You are the Queene! Who poses a threat to me so long as you desire to have me with you?" The anger rose in him far too quickly. Mortals were too quick to feel everything, like the panic in his chest, the pain that burned his lungs. "I will not leave here without you."

"You must. Cedric, my advisor, will accompany you back to Keller's workshop. You may live there, or go somewhere else." Her voice broke, and though she recovered it, her bottom lip trembled. "It does not make a difference to me where you will go."

"It does not make a difference," he repeated, disbelieving. "You risked your life to come to me. You risked your life again to save me from your Garret."

"And I am saving your life now, sending you away." She took a deep breath and looked back to her hands, worrying the hem of her gown. "Garret will meet me tomorrow morning, in Sanctuary. That is a place that we have, a sacred place. He will meet me, and we will fight."

She said they would fight, but the word held so much more, such a sinister connotation. "He is coming to kill you."

She nodded. "He is a stronger fighter than I am. Centuries older. He trained me. It is likely I will fall."

"Then do not fight!" He pounded his fists on his bent knees. "Come with me, tonight. We will leave here and you can forget that you were ever Queene."

"I cannot." A tear slid down her face, and he knew at once that it was not her vanity that kept her in the Lightworld. "I am Garret's mate. I will always be the Queene, and he will hunt me until he finds me and kills me. I must face him."

"So, you would die now, instead of later? What if he never found you?" What if Malachi found him, first? He would destroy the Faery. The torture he'd inflicted on Malachi would seem slight compared to the pain he would endure.

She shook her head. "He will find me. Vengeance seems to be his lifeblood."

"And yet you laid down with this creature? You professed love for him?" It was a cruel thing to taunt her with. It did not ease the hurt in Malachi, but it did satisfy him, somehow.

"I did not know!" Her tears came freely now. "I did not know that I could love until I woke to find that you had followed me here!"

His frustration overwhelmed him. "You did not know that you could love, but you loved Garret!"

"I did not love him! He represented to me all that I could have asked for with my low birth." Her eyes searched the darkness, as though something there would make him understand. "You do not understand because you do not know what life I lived before you!"

"You killed the creatures of the Darkworld, I know that. I do not believe that whatever your life might have been, Garret was the answer to your happiness!"

"I was not happy!" She screamed this, and the scream died on a sob. "I never sought happiness with him. I only wished for safety, for a life better than what I could achieve on my own!"

She tore at her nightgown until she could pull it free from her body, to pool at her feet. Her wings unfurled behind her. "Do you see this? I am a monster among my own kind! I am half-Human! I did not know that I could feel the things a Human can feel. I did not know that I would not be as cold and unfeeling as a Faery. I wish to the Gods that I were! It would not hurt half as much to turn you away if I did not have love for you in my heart."

To see her stripped bare, chest hitching under the force of her tears, her small body shivering in the cold of the room, killed his anger. His arms ached to hold her, to offer her the comfort Garret could not have. But he stayed where he was, hands clenched in fists. "Why do you not let me stay and fight for you? For our…" His voice caught. "For our child?"

The word hung between them. Ayla looked away, ashamed, though it was clear she did not wish to show it. She pulled her gown back up, held it together in front of her as though it were a shield.

"You would fight and die with our child inside of you?" If the child were a reality, if she showed any outward sign of carrying it within her, it would be more terrible.

She made no excuses. "If I do not fight him and he overthrows me, the babe will die with me then."

His mind made terrible grasps at anything that might stop her, but it did not take long to realize it was useless. "And so you will send me away where I cannot protect you."

"Where you cannot be hurt," she corrected, her voice dripping ice.

"The very act of sending me away hurts me!" He stood, unable to remain still any longer, and paced to the dying embers of the fire. If he lifted one in his bare hand, he would not be scorched half as badly as her words burned him. "You have kept me here, a prisoner despite your intention, for my safety. And now, you send me away for my safety. At least here, in this horrible, lonely place, I can see you and touch you and know that you are alive! To send me to the Darkworld… How will I know if you survive this fight? How will I know if I can return to your side?"

"You cannot return." She met his eyes now, and hers shone with tears. "Even if I survive. You cannot return to me."

This was, perhaps, the worst blow of all. She did not wish for him to return to her? "You risked your life to save me."

"It was a mistake," she said, her voice trembling so that she could not have really believed what she said to him. "I broke my geis. I broke my vow to my race. It is terrible enough that I have mortal blood in me. But even if I kill Garret and keep my throne, I will not be safe to keep you. You are an enemy of my world, accidental or not. And you will never be accepted by the Court as my consort."

"I do not wish to be accepted by your Court. I wish to be accepted by you!" He'd believed she felt for him the way he felt for her, the same desperate need to be with him the way he needed her. That she clearly did not wounded far more than his heart. He'd been foolish in believing she loved him, and now he wished he had not.

"You cannot be with me, Malachi!" She stood, moving faster than any creature he'd ever seen. In the blink of an eye, she was at the door.

"Wait!" He ran at her, caught the hem of her gown as she slipped into the hallway. She halted and turned, then gripped the fabric and jerked it back.

"Do not leave," he begged, knowing he sounded as foolish as he felt. "You will banish me. I can do nothing but obey. You are the Queene. But stay until morning. Do not leave me like this."

"How should I leave you?" Her voice sounded thick and painful as it bent around her words. "If I could, I would keep you here with me. You do not believe that it is impossible. No matter how or when I leave you, you will hate me."

She feared he would hate her? The very thought of it was absurd. Certainly he felt anger toward her. So much anger that he did not trust himself to touch her. But no matter how her decision pained him, he could not hate her.

Perhaps that was reason enough to begin hating her. The very fact that for the rest of his days, short though they might be in his mortal form, he would be unable to stop feeling the love that crushed his chest with each breath.

Without another word, she turned and left him. He let her go. She was right. Even if he held her there with him, even if he swore never to let her go, he would have to. And when he did, it would pain him more than anything he'd felt in his mortal life.

Ayla returned to her chambers through the secret passage, careful not to be observed. She worried at Garret's commitment to the morning's fight. It would be easy enough to send an Assassin after her in the night. She would not lead one to her bed.

Once inside her chambers, she climbed onto the bed and pulled the blankets up. Why her servants thought she was incapable of doing this herself, she did not know. It seemed that the more powerful one became, the more one's ability to do simple things was doubted.

Simple things like killing the one person who'd helped her become what she was.

Though she knew she needed rest to face Garret, sleep would not come. Over and over, she played out every memory of sparring with him in the training room, working out his weaknesses. There were none. He'd been fighting for centuries. What could her meager five years in the Guild have taught her that would help her now?

She tossed and turned in her bed until she could no longer stand it, then rose and went to Mabb's dressing table. Her things still lay exactly as she had left them. It was a like a tomb, and Ayla felt the ghost of the former Queene as though she stood over her shoulder.

And then, seated before the mirror, Mabb's shade did appear behind Ayla's reflection.

Ayla did not turn. If she had, the image would

disappear, for no immortal's shade would tolerate being looked at directly.

In death, Mabb's entire being was as icy-blue as her eyes had been in life, the twisted stumps where her body's branches had withered fading into nothing. Her expression was not kind, nor was it cruel. She did not blame the new Queene.

There was nothing Ayla could say to Mabb now. There had been no love in her heart for the Queene, and her death changed little. But she would not show her disrespect by ignoring her presence or banishing her from the room that had so recently belonged to her. The room that she had lived in in the hopes of being restored to her rightful kingdom aboveground. The room where she had died, beneath the cold ground. Her Palace had become her burial cairn.

"I will kill your brother tomorrow." She said it simply. Whether Mabb feared for her flesh and blood beyond the grave was to be seen. Whether she believed Ayla would succeed, she did not say. But the shade motioned, as if it still had a hand with which to point, to an urn on the dressing table. Hair ornaments, the sort that Mabb had worn the night Ayla had come to see her in her chambers, jutted from the top. Ayla reached for one and withdrew it. The handle, two coiled serpents, each swallowing the tail of the other, flashed bronze with emerald eyes above two long dagger blades. As it gleamed in the darkness, a drop fell from the blade and hissed against the top of the vanity.

"Poison," Ayla whispered.

Mabb's ghost nodded, then withdrew into the shadows.

When Ayla turned, the shade was gone.

Hands trembling, Ayla returned the dripping knife to its urn. She lifted the vessel carefully, and the sound of liquid movement testified to the fullness of its contents.

Pulling on her robe, she hurried to her chamber door. At the other end of the hall on the opposite side, two maidservants slept, propped up against each others' wings.

"Wake up," Ayla called, and the two startled to alertness. "Summon Flidais. And bring me my sword."

The hour had not come that would assure her victory, but a hopeful moment, at least, had arrived.

Twenty-Four

⟡

A Faery came in the early hours to rouse Malachi. Not one of Ayla's guards, nor Ayla herself. A Faery taller than any of the others Malachi had seen, though still not as tall as himself, with pale hair and eyes, who looked substantially stronger than the others of his race.

When he had stepped through the door, Malachi had woken from a fitful sleep, certain for a moment that it was Ayla returning to him, to recant all that she'd told him the night before. The disappointment he'd felt was not as terrible, in hindsight, as it should have been. Perhaps he had truly accepted their separation.

"So, you are here to take me away," he'd said as he'd begun dressing.

Though he'd not expected the creature to understand, the Faery had responded in Malachi's language, so convincingly that he'd not betrayed even a hint of the strange accent that colored Ayla's speech. "She has sent you this," he said, slinging a pack off of his back. "It has clothes, some money and a weapon."

"I do not know how to use weapons." He pulled on his tattered shirt. "And the clothes I have are fine." But he took the pack, anyway, and put it over his back. "You speak like a mortal."

"As do you." It was the only reply the Faery seemed inclined to give him. "We must go now."

They moved out of the Palace quickly. The halls were deserted.

"Where is everyone?" Malachi remembered throngs of people gathered to watch a Darkling dragged into prison by Garret's guards.

"Run off. They do not wish to be seen as traitors should Garret win the fight." The Faery did not look at him as he spoke, but kept his gaze straight ahead.

Malachi made a noise of disgust. "I thought they would assemble to watch. Your kind seem far too interested in the blood and death of others. Why are you not running?"

The statement was intended to insult the Faery, but instead, he threw back his head and laughed. "You have a far higher opinion of our race than I."

Then the mirth disappeared from his expression. "I will not abandon the Queene when she needs my support."

They walked on for some time, the Faery's words echoing through Malachi's head. Did he believe that Malachi abandoned Ayla? That was unbearable, to be seen as a coward as he suffered for the loss of her.

As if he'd read his thoughts as Keller would have, the Faery spoke. "I know you do not wish to leave her, but she will have it no other way. It is a tragedy, the kind a bard could not craft half so convincingly, that she cannot accept the love of her people to forgive her such a slight sin as keeping a Darkling hidden in her chambers."

"I am not just a Darkling." For the first time, this term bristled Malachi. Perhaps because Ayla always referred to him that way, that it stung him now to hear it used so casually by another. "Your kind labels all who dwell outside of your world as evil or inferior. I have made the acquaintance of a Human who was twice as good as any I've met in your world. Possibly even your Queene."

Again, the Faery took his words mildly. "Well, you will be free to return to this Human, once you are quit of our kind."

"Your kind killed him," Malachi spat back, his hand fisting around the strap of the pack.

The Faery nodded. "I am sorry."

They were out of the Palace, into the tunnels of the Lightworld before the Faery spoke again. "I, too, have known the Humans, long before we found ourselves below the ground. They were a good people, lawful. But you must understand that the ways of the Fae cannot be judged by man. They are too foreign, too ancient for a mortal mind to understand."

"I understand that Ayla loves me, that she grieves for me, but that she wishes never to see me," Malachi said quietly. "But I cannot understand why. Perhaps your ways are not so strange because they are ancient, but because they are wrong."

The Faery seemed to think on this for a while, his antennae twitching the way Ayla's did when she thought. When he spoke, it was not in defense of his race's incomprehensible ways. "She does love you. Of that I am certain. And it is that love that drives her away from you."

"Because she wishes to protect me," Malachi said wearily, the phrase repeated so often by Ayla that it had burned a groove into his mind. "She has already told me so."

The Faery shook his head. "No. That is only a fraction of it."

The mouth of the tunnel to the Strip loomed

ahead; already the sounds and smells of the busy area reached them. Instead of continuing on, the Faery stopped and faced Malachi for the first time since they'd left his glorified prison cell.

"You do not know all of Ayla's history. If you asked her, she would not tell it to you. I know it only through what Garret told me, when he was her mentor in the Assassins' Guild. She has led a hard life, Malachi. And she is young still. She does not understand that love is not only loss." The Faery motioned for Malachi to sit. It was impossible, on the bare ground, though the Faery was able to fold up his wings comfortably. Malachi bent his knees, squatting down until the tips of his wings dragged in the sand on the tunnel floor.

"Ayla came to the Lightworld only five years ago. She is barely twenty full years old, practically a child by our race's standards, an infant compared to the ages of many of us. But she is half-Human, and was not born to our Court.

"Her mother was a lower ranking member of Queene Mabb's Court. She became infatuated with the Humans on the Strip, then with one in particular, and she stayed with him until she bore Ayla. But once the babe was delivered, she returned to the Lightworld. I am not certain anyone knows who she is now. She fell out of favor with Mabb, but so many do that it would be impossible to tell which of Mabb's enemies was Ayla's mother.

"So, for her childhood, Ayla lived as a mortal on the Strip. Stealing food, money. Her father was a Human, and so few of them have any desire to make their lives bearable. When she was old enough, she came to us and begged admittance to our world, to our race."

"But she is of your race. Her mother was one of you." Malachi pulled the pack off his shoulder and let it rest on the ground. "Why would she beg you?"

"Because we do not accept all of the spawn of Faeries who have gone beyond the boundaries of our world to couple. I am sure there are those among us perverse enough to lie down with De-mons, and we would not allow such a sullied blood to mix with ours." Cedric did not appear sorry for his blunt statement, but continued on. "Ayla would not have been accepted, but that Garret loved her from the moment he laid eyes on her, and as the Queene's brother he was in a position to impose his opinion on the rest of the Court."

Malachi's jaw tensed with anger. "He did not love her. If he did, he would not wish to kill her."

Cedric shrugged. "Garret loved her as much as he could. The blood in him is pure Fae—love is not an emotion that comes with a selfless face to that kind. And he was never taught otherwise."

"How would you teach a creature like that to love?" The very thought disgusted Malachi, the picture of Garret in his mind like the taste of something rotten on his tongue. "How could he learn?"

"It is possible." Was there a note of sadness in the Faery's voice? "We can learn to love, and quite well. But it was Garret's ambition that he gave to Ayla, and not love. It is all she knows."

"She knows she has hurt me. And she sends me away without another thought." Though he suspected it was not true, Malachi would not let himself admit it just yet.

"Perhaps, when this has passed," the Faery began, then paused. "And if, by the will of the Gods, she succeeds against Garret, you could return."

"She does not wish for me to return." He stood and moved on, trusting that his companion would follow. No doubt he was as eager to see a stranger leave his precious home world as Ayla was.

"What someone wishes and what they need are often not the same." The Faery followed him, almost reluctantly. "I have the authority to tell you that if you wished to return, I could make it so."

It was such a strange thing to say that Malachi could not simply ignore it. He turned to face his companion, to protest, but the Faery continued to walk, as if not noticing that his charge had stopped.

"And who are you, to make this claim?" Malachi called to the Faery's back. "She is Queene!"

"And I am her friend," he responded. "Keep up, or I will not return in time to be at her side when she needs me."

Garret's return to the Lightworld was not received with as much enthusiasm as he had expected. It was true that in times of strife, the weaker of the species fled to safer ground, but never had he seen the Faery Quarter so barren.

"The ingratitude they show me is appalling," Garret grumbled, wishing, for just a moment, that he still had Bran to agree with him. Served the fool right, though, for treading so incautiously with a Dragon.

From the head of his caravan, someone sounded an order to halt. The cart bearing him, empty of his belongings, for it would look presumptuous of him to bring them back as though he had already won the duel, tossed to the side as the guards pulling it settled it to the ground. Garret struggled to remain upright, then climbed down from the cart altogether. The delay stung him like an insect that must be swatted away, the urgency and irritation growing with every step he made toward the front of the line.

"What is this?" he snapped, his anger nearly overflowing at the sight of the armed guards blocking their way.

"You are not to pass," one of the guards intoned blandly. "The Palace will not receive you. You are to go to Sanctuary and establish your camp in an out-of-the-way location in the tunnels surrounding it, to wait until the official time of the duel."

"The Palace will not receive me?" He threw his head back and laughed, as if he truly found the idea absurd. Inwardly, he boiled. "I am the King. Never has there been a circumstance in which the King has been prevented from entering the Palace."

"Never has there been a situation so grave as this," the guard said, seemingly unimpressed that his monarch stood before him.

So, they were on her side, then? Garret took a deep breath that flared his nostrils. He looked imposing when he did this, he knew. Regal. Far more royal than the creature who sat on the throne now.

He would have all of the Palace guards executed and replaced with his loyal subjects once he killed Ayla. For now, though, to dispatch this one would be enough. "A sword," he called to the guards behind him.

The traitor before him held up a hand. "We are also charged with informing you that an attack on the royal guard is an attack on the Queene herself. An act of war will negate the validity of your request for a duel, and you will be banished from the Light-world."

"If I do not cut down all of you first!"

A guard pressed a sword into Garret's hand, and he tossed it aside. He turned to his party. "We will go to Sanctuary. A bit of extra time spent there will not harm me in the least. In fact, it will give me a greater advantage." He addressed the rest of the disloyal soldiers blocking the tunnel. "Perhaps that will be your Queene's final mistake."

They dressed her in armor. She had never worn armor, never needed it. All of her fighting had been done without rules, without the niceties afforded to a warrior. It had been raw and cruel, and only her skill had protected her from harm.

"It is not an insult to you," Cedric said when she had questioned it. "And it will not protect you from a death blow, should Garret land one. It is a ruse, a costume. You must look like a Queene, not an Assassin."

"If I went before him in rags, I would not look a Queene, but I would not die in the fight, either." She plucked the edge of the light metal covering her shoulders. "I cannot fight if I cannot move."

"You will be able to move. It is no heavier than

the gowns you have been wearing." Cedric stepped aside as a serving maid bustled through. Two maids took it upon themselves to coil up Ayla's hair, so tight that her skin felt stretched, into two large rolls at the base of her skull.

"I did not fight in gowns." It was not the thought of the weight that truly disturbed her, but the thought of what Garret would have said, when he was her mentor, if she had thought to protect herself in such a way.

His voice, which had always seemed gently mocking, though now she knew it to be true mockery, came to her through her memory. *Do you doubt your skill so much, Ayla, that you would need armor to shield you from your own mistakes?*

Perhaps it was because it was true, that she did feel somehow safer, that it stung all the more. She had no illusions about her skill when compared to Garret's, and the armor did, shamefully, seem as though it might save her.

Cedric did not answer her. Perhaps he realized all of these things as well, or perhaps he simply did not wish to argue with his Queene. Instead he answered the knock at the door, and took a box from the guard waiting outside.

"What is that?" The impatience in her voice was that of a child awaiting a present, and she turned her attention to the puffs of her gossamer sleeves protruding from the open joints of the armor to appear disinterested.

Her servants bowed to her, and she realized without looking up that Cedric had motioned for them to leave. When they had gone, and the door had shut behind them, he lifted the top of the box and removed something from within, his back to her.

"I had this brought up from the treasury. I told them it was on your orders. I hope you do not mind that I pretended to have your authority." He turned, and in his hands he held a crown. A twisted, arching thing of fragile hawthorne branches twined with silver spikes like blades of daggers. The spikes rose up from a glittering silver band, from which sparkled bloodred garnets. Garnets dripped down from the base on chains so slender they appeared to be spiderwebs.

"What is this?" Ayla had not spent much time at Court, but she had never seen Mabb wear something like this. No, she had preferred delicate ornaments, things that would not outshine her own beauty and majesty.

Cedric's voice held a note of sadness, one that Ayla had come to recognize in his voice whenever he spoke of the dead Queene. "This is the crown Mabb wore in the first battle with the Humans. They say that as she rode into the Human city, she looked like a Goddess of war."

"The first battle, and not the second?" Ayla pondered the wicked-looking thing in Cedric's hands. Would Garret remember the sight of his sister, whom he had fought beside in two such battles, and whom he had killed without remorse?

A smile quirked the corner of Cedric's mouth. "Not the second."

She did not need an ill omen riding on her head when she faced Garret.

Cedric lifted the crown over Ayla, and she braced herself for a heavy weight that did not come when he settled it on her head. The front of the band was pointed down, dipping onto her forehead like a diadem, with one large garnet settled between her antennae. They twitched at the cold touch of the stone, and Ayla smoothed them back.

"Now, Your Majesty, I think it is time."

They walked through the empty Palace, encountering only a few random and isolated guards who did not look at her, but stared straight ahead. *As if I am already a ghost.*

The corridors outside of the Palace were equally deserted. The Faeries that would normally clog the path to the Palace gates, begging for money and food and favors, had fled in anticipation of the coming unpleasantness. Unpleasantness, Ayla knew from experience, was as undesirable as hunger to the poor and wretched of the Underground.

She thought for a moment about the other Quarters of the Lightworld. There, they might not know, and probably would not care, that a Queene might die today. The title still struck her as absurd; she was no more a Queene than she was a scholar. Surely Garret assumed she fought for her crown, when all she sought to preserve in this duel was her life.

They trooped through the bends in the tunnel, just herself at the lead, Cedric but a step behind her, and a small retinue of guards that she had not noticed until they had cleared the Palace walls and their footsteps had stirred up a ringing echo in the vast, open tunnels of the Quarter at large. She wondered how Garret would look after his days in exile, how he would try to approach her. Would he play upon her sympathy, appeal to her that they were once mates, once friends? Would his days away from the Faery Quarter show on his face and clothing? Would he appear haggard?

They came now to the mouth of Sanctuary, the high, round arch of crumbling bricks framing a beacon of white-green light. A bird chirped from somewhere, perhaps the Upworld, and Ayla's heart thrilled as it always did at the prospect of fresh air and clean nature. Her heart was half-Human and half-Faery, and both creatures in her longed for the world above.

At the top of the stairs she paused. Of course,

Garret would not try to win her affection again, nor would he let his time in exile show on his person at so critical a time. He stood within a crescent of guards, traitors pulled from the Palace ranks, his ax in hand. He did not wear the robes of a mentor or courtier, but the clothing he had worn as an Assassin. Leather trousers and vest, as all Assassins equipped themselves with, but black instead of the brown Ayla had worn. Black laces wound around his arms, binding two daggers there, in case he was unarmed. Like Ayla, he'd left his wings free. He bowed to her in mocking, and laughed, and an uneasy response went up from the guards behind him. *"Your Majesty,"* he said, the laughter still present on his face. "I did not realize that I was so fearsome a foe as to warrant all of this." He indicated her armor and crown, and laughed again.

"I did not wish for your blood to stain any of my garments," Ayla called in response, hoping the quaver in her voice would not be perceptible from so far away. She moved down the steps, opening her wings to light from one broken piece to another.

"Ah, the Queene of the Faeries has come to grace us with her beauty," Garret said to his soldiers, loud enough for all to hear.

Ayla had heard enough insults over her Human appearance, though, and his words did not have the desired effect.

Finally they faced each other, a sword's length between them. "Are you finished playacting for them now?" Ayla asked, drawing her sword. "Shall we fight?"

Garret lifted his ax and nodded.

And then, without ceremony, they took to the sky.

Twenty-Five

~~~⤳⤳⤳~~~

For a long moment, it seemed Garret would never strike, and Ayla would not allow him the satisfaction of doing it herself. So, they circled each other, twisting to stay aloft and still keep the other's movements in focus.

"Could you really stand to kill me?" Garret taunted, darting toward her, but never raising his weapon. "Without me, you have no one. Everyone at Court thinks of you exactly as you are—a disgusting Human. You would still be eating rotting food from the floor of the Strip if it weren't for me."

Ayla nodded. She would not argue. His words were his only defense, and they betrayed his nervousness at the fight. She flew closer, as though she would make an attack. He lifted his ax and swung, but she had already retreated, and he spun wildly with the force of his movements.

Furious, he righted himself and charged at her, swooping down at the last minute to attempt a strike from below. She dove past him, toward the blinding green of the ground, and knocked his blade cleanly aside. While he recovered and attempted another swing, she struck out with her sword and pierced his torso, just below the ribs. He hissed and darted back, the wound leaving thick, saplike blood on Ayla's blade.

It was not a killing blow. Ayla cursed herself for that. Like a wounded animal, Garret would fight harder now, more dangerous than he was before.

With a roar of disbelief, he lunged at her, wild and careless. She easily avoided him, and dared to strike out on her own, leaving her body open as she did. It would not matter; he would not have time to swing at her.

He did manage to clash blades with her, and threw off her sword. It took more strength than she expected to keep the weapon under her control. By the time she pulled it back, tightly into her defensive space, he was ready to strike again.

She let him take the swings he wished, fending him off with both hands gripping the hilt of her sword. Her weapon would not falter, and his frenzy would do nothing but tire him.

As if he'd realized this in conjunction with her thought, he used his next swing to push himself away, somersaulting backward through the air, far out of her reach. For a long while, he simply watched her. This was something Ayla had seen him do many times when sparring against an opponent in the training circle. He would wait until the other fighter seemed to relax, then he would make his move.

She let her shoulders slip, an almost imperceptible movement. But he'd spent so many long hours training her. Days, weeks, months of experience working together in the Guild Hall. This would be his downfall.

He flew forward, and she pretended to fumble, as though she would not pull her sword up in time. She braced herself for the moment when he would swing, a calculated blow aimed for her neck. Closer, closer. She gripped the hilt of her sword tighter, preparing for the counter swing that would sever his hands from his arms.

At the critical moment, she saw her error unfold before it happened. He would not try for her neck. He brought his ax up, over his head. If she'd kept her sword down, she might have had a chance to strike. Now, the closeness, the angle of her arms and the position of his body, prevented her from doing anything but ducking and turning to dodge him. And she could not turn fast enough.

The blade of the ax struck her at the juncture of a wing and her back, and stuck fast. She pulled forward as he wrenched the weapon free, sending an arc of crimson through the blinding white of the sun through the grates. In her pain, she saw the droplets fall past her and mistook them for the garnets of her crown.

Though it was agony, she forced herself to move, trying to distance herself from Garret's next swing. With one injured wing, she could not stay aloft. The pain shot like arrows through her, and her vision flickered between red-black nothingness and the harsh green of the trees rushing at her as she fell. She twisted and turned her back to them. Above her, Garret watched her fall, and she did not have to see his face to know that he would look pleased.

The branches assailed her as she broke through them, ripping at her already wounded back and poking through her hair. It slowed her fall, but she was beyond caring about anything but the agony that slowly crept around to steal the breath from her chest.

Then, as if in mutual agreement with each other, the trees let her suddenly go, and she plunged to the rock pool. Once her body broke through the surface, she saw no more.

When Ayla opened her eyes, it seemed hours had passed. She wondered where the time had gone, and then wondered why she'd woken at all. The soft, crashing sound of water came through then, and the feel of it brushing her side. She pulled herself up, expecting to ache from the wound in her back, but there was no pain. The sand below her was stained pink from the mixed blood and surf, but she felt nothing. Across the endless expanse of beach was a figure, staring out at the waves, and she pulled herself up to walk to it.

Was this what the other plane was, then? she wondered as she walked. The sand moved beneath her feet, the wind slapped her hair into her face, but if she had not remembered how mortally wounded she was, she would not have been able tell.

"This place should not exist," she said aloud.

Though the figure was far away, it answered her as clearly as if it stood beside her. "And why should it not? Because you believe it should not be here? Because others have told you it is not?"

And then the figure was before her, squatting down beside a shallow pan of seawater boiling over a fire built on the sand.

"You…" Ayla's voice deserted her momentarily in the face of recognition. "You are the healer."

The old Human woman nodded, and the realization that she was not Human, not at all, broke over Ayla. "You know me in other faces, as well." The woman's appearance changed to the young woman on the beach, belly swollen with child. "And your mother knew me, and your father. All of you know me, whether you have heard my name or seen my face."

Ayla opened her mouth to question her, and was overcome by images that passed before her eyes. Moss, creeping across a forest floor, taking longer than a lifetime but rushing like water in her vision. Fire, raging from a mountaintop to scourge the earth around it, heading to the sea to form new land. Forest animals birthing young, the young maturing, the mature animals being eaten, nourishing other creatures. The whole of nature, the whole of creation and destruction, unfolding before her eyes in the time it took to blink.

When the visions cleared, the old woman was back, stirring the water in the pan. "When the Humans began to search for me, when they called on me and sought a return to me, I welcomed them. But it became something else. They stopped looking for a piece of me inside of them for answers, began demanding them. Stopped appreciating what was around them, on their plane, and wanted more. Power. Magic they could see. Creatures that dazzled them.

"They did not see that I was all around them, and they sought me here. That is what caused the rift. That is why I hide away."

"But what about us?" Ayla asked, and realized that in her anger, she had slighted a Goddess. She was half-Human. She should not have sought her here, either.

"You did not seek me. You were summoned." The Goddess stopped her stirring and looked up at Ayla.

And then she remembered where the wound had come from, and what had happened. "I died."

"No." The Goddess amended quickly, "Not yet."

Her eyes filled with sadness as she looked out across the waves. "They did not want what I had given them. I gave them more. I gave them the other world they sought, and they rejected it."

"Then take it back! Let us come back here!" To her ears, Ayla sounded like a child demanding her will. "We do not wish for this separation. Every day, we become more like them!"

"You do," the Goddess agreed. "You are more power hungry than ever you were on this plane. You wish to have the comforts of Humanity, and still maintain the honor of your race."

"There were courts and Queenes in the Astral long before the veil tore!" Ayla wished she could remember all of the history that she'd been taught when she'd come into the Lightworld. And then she realized it would not matter. All of that history…that was the reason. "You gave the Humans what they wanted. And you gave our races…"

"Faeries modeled themselves after the Humans. Dragons coveted the Human wealth. Trolls and Elves sought to make war, as the Humans do. They all wished for Humanity. I gave Humanity what they wanted, and I gave your race, and the others like it, what they wanted." She did not seem sad. She did not seem disturbed that things had not worked out for either side. She simply stated things as they were.

"How do we fix it?" Ayla asked, though she was not sure she would ever be able to tell anyone. Her back still bled, and the tree of life within her flickered and lost its autumn leaves. "How do we make things the way they were?"

"You cannot." The Goddess continued her stirring. "But she can."

"She?"

The Goddess reached one hand out and touched Ayla's stomach, and the fingertips disappeared through the armor, delved through her skin, touched the child in her very womb. "She can."

"She cannot. I am dead." Ayla wondered if the child within her still lived, and found that the answer must be yes, for she felt no pain or sorrow in answer. "She cannot live if I am dead."

"You are not dead. And you will not die." The

Goddess lifted the stick she stirred with. Seawater clung to it, dripped from the jagged end in fat, twinkling drops. The Goddess took one droplet onto her finger and held it up before Ayla. "You must protect her from all who would do her harm. There will be many. She has a great destiny, and there are those who will sense it without knowing it and wish to destroy her because of it, without ever seeing that her power could benefit them."

"If I am not dead now, I will be. Garret will kill me. I am broken, I will not be able to defend myself." If she could stay here, just a while, and rest… But the rest would do her no good, for now she could feel the pain, and knew her end was not far.

The Goddess did not speak. She grasped Ayla's chin, and forced her mouth open, then smeared the drop on her tongue.

Like lightning striking a tree in the forest—or so Ayla had heard, for she'd never seen such a thing with her own eyes—something in her ignited. She fell back, onto the sand, still burning, and the ground closed over her. She fell down, through the sand, into water and into darkness.

She opened her eyes, saw Sanctuary's green above the silver mirror of the water's skin, wavering and flashing. She swam toward it, the seawater still burning her, her wings pulling against the currents in a bloody cloud.

When her head broke the surface, she took what should have been her final breath. Above her the trees still rustled from her fall through them; it was as if she had never left this place.

She moved to the edge of the pool. Though the fire still burned in her, strengthening her, she felt that fire weaken. If she would kill Garret, as the Goddess had said, then she must do it soon.

The branches above rustled again. Something else fell through them, a more controlled fall. Garret emerged, headfirst, wings folded tight against his back to protect them. He righted himself in the air once he'd cleared the trees and opened his wings to slow his fall. He landed as Ayla clawed her way up from the water, to stand dripping on the bank.

"I thought you would have hit the ground and dashed your brains out," he said with sniff. "Not much good they would do you."

She limped toward him, dragging her nearly severed wing behind her.

"It is a shame it had to end this way. When I killed my sister, I truly meant for you to become Queene. To sit at my side, as my second." He shook his head and tossed his ax from hand to hand. "But your damned honor. You take yourself far too seriously."

She dropped to her knees on the moss-covered ground, lowered her head in defeat.

Now, he sounded truly regretful. "I meant for you to be so much more."

The blade of the ax disturbed the air, parted it like water as it neared her head. She lifted her hands, as if to feebly shield herself from the blow. Instead she gripped the bejeweled pin that held her coiled hair in place, and pulled it free.

The blade still fell, but it fell onto empty earth. Ayla sprang up, gripping Mabb's poisoned ornament in her fist, and plunged it through Garret's throat.

He clawed at the dagger through his neck, never touching it in his death struggles as his hands shriveled to bare branches. He staggered backward on legs that twisted into gnarled, barren roots, and when he fell to the ground, his eyes staring in shock and horror at the canopy of green above him, his mouth opened wide and a wind of winter chill blew dry, dead leaves from his throat.

Ayla stumbled and fell. Her task was finished, and the spell of the Goddess had deserted her. She lay her head against the cool, mossy floor and turned her face away from the sight of Garret's twisted corpse. His eyes were still open, and she could not bear to see into them.

Above her, a raven sounded a warning call,

then flew deeper into Sanctuary. She watched its black wings spreading and wondered if it had come for her or for Garret. The foliage rustled; someone approached.

If it were Garret's men, she would be dead for sure. She did not have the strength to fight them. If it were her people…she might still die.

Cedric broke into the clearing first, his face ashen, as though he'd taken a death blow. His frantic gaze moved from Garret's body to Ayla. There was relief, then pain, as he gazed at her. "Guards!" he shouted, even as he ran to kneel at her side. "We must get you to the healer. Hold on to me if you can," he told her, and lifted her in his arms.

As he ran from the clearing, bearing her like a bag of stolen jewels, one of the raven's black feathers drifted down to Garret's unseeing eyes.

Then, Ayla knew no more.

Twenty-Six

The morning of the coronation dawned, and still Ayla did not feel like the Queene.

Her maids helped her dress. Not because she was a Queene with servants to attend her, but because, though the healers had visited often, every day in the weeks between the duel and the coronation, she still moved stiffly, and held herself too straight.

"It is only a ceremony," Cedric had told her the night before. "You are not being put on display to be judged. You are already the Queene."

It did not help her now, with only her maids surrounding her. Cedric had gone off to attend to the business of the coronation, and she had no other advisors to comfort her. No matter what Cedric had assured her, she would still feel like a condemned prisoner marching to her trial when the throne room doors opened.

They dressed her in robes that were not inherited from Mabb, but sewn for her from materials stolen from the Upworld. Golden silk, floating around her from neck to toes and well past her fingertips. She supposed she was meant to appear as a Goddess, but she felt a fraud.

"Your Majesty," one of the maids said somberly, setting a mirror before her. "Do you approve?"

She looked over her reflection, at her hair, unbound against the silk, and the high collar of the robes obscuring her Guild mark. She folded the collar down and pushed her hair over her shoulders. "This mark is not a shame to me," she said, trying to sound queenly, trying to make it as important to the servants around her as it was to her. "In the future, I will not wear garments that cover it."

"Yes, Your Majesty," the servants dutifully replied. And that gave her a bit more confidence.

She walked at the head of a two-abreast line of ladies-in-waiting, all turned out in their best robes for the occasion. Two guards marched ahead of her, and guards flanked the procession on both sides. The halls of the Palace were once again deserted, but not for the same reason. All of the courtiers would be crowded into the throne room, along with all the highest ranking Guild members.

Finally she stood before the throne room doors. They opened from within, painfully slowly, revealing curious faces as the opening grew wider. All assembled craned to see their new Queene, and she could not back down now. She walked through the doors and kept her eyes straight ahead on the throne.

A murmur ran through the crowd, following her as she passed, like a wake in a pool of water. Her wings were covered, so they would not see the scars of her injury. There had been enough speculation about her duel with Garret to last a lifetime, and she would feed no more.

From the dais, as she settled onto the throne, she surveyed the crowd. The nameless courtiers, the Healer Guild, the Bardic Guild, and finally, the Assassin Guild. At the head of the latter sat Cedric, looking pleased, but serious. Perhaps he'd been wrong when he'd said she would not be judged this day, for he looked as though he awaited a grim decision.

Now, seeing her Court in front of her, she was much at ease. Let them judge her. They would find her wanting. They would find anyone who came to the throne unfit for the job, for the job itself was unfit for their race.

She was a pretender, and would always be, now that she knew that power she wielded was the power sought by those who had succeeded only in banishing their race from their true home. She would keep the traditions, do as she was expected, to protect their future. But she would not encourage them in their lust for Humanity. She would protect her child, their future, while protecting them from themselves.

A priestess sang a chant, encouraging the assembly to follow along. Ayla looked out at them, chanting in unison, clinging to their Human-like traditions.

And at the back of the throne room, beside the door, where she should have seen him, but had somehow overlooked him, stood Malachi. Malachi, in the throne room of the Faery Court. In the Lightworld.

He had come back. Though she'd threatened him, though she'd begged him not to, he had come back. And she had never been so happy at someone's complete disregard for her wishes.

She smiled at him, over the crowd. And she knew he was meant to be there.

* * * * *

LIGHTWORLD/DARKWORLD

ACKNOWLEDGMENTS

To me, this book symbolizes a beautiful flower that grew out of the rotting rib cage of a murder victim abandoned in a shallow grave. Thank you to everyone who made that weekend such a horrible experience and forced me to retreat into a fantasy world where a sewer full of monsters offered more hospitable company than yours.

Nice people and objects that made this book possible were the Friday Night Mudslingers, my supportive family, Diet Coke and Emmy Rossum's "Inside Out" album.

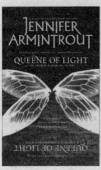
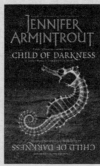
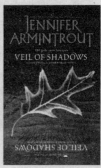

REQUEST YOUR FREE BOOKS!

2 FREE NOVELS
FROM THE ROMANCE/SUSPENSE
COLLECTION PLUS 2 FREE GIFTS!

YES! Please send me 2 FREE novels from the Romance/Suspense Collection and my 2 FREE gifts (gifts are worth about $10). After receiving them, if I don't wish to receive any more books, I can return the shipping statement marked "cancel." If I don't cancel, I will receive 4 brand-new novels every month and be billed just $5.74 per book in the U.S. or $6.24 per book in Canada. That's a savings of at least 28% off the cover price. It's quite a bargain! Shipping and handling is just 50¢ per book.* I understand that accepting the 2 free books and gifts places me under no obligation to buy anything. I can always return a shipment and cancel at any time. Even if I never buy another book from the Reader Service, the two free books and gifts are mine to keep forever.

185 MDN EYNQ   385 MDN EYN2

Name _____ (PLEASE PRINT) _____

Address _____ Apt. # _____

City _____ State/Prov. _____ Zip/Postal Code _____

Signature (if under 18, a parent or guardian must sign)

Mail to The Reader Service:
IN U.S.A.: P.O. Box 1867, Buffalo, NY 14240-1867
IN CANADA: P.O. Box 609, Fort Erie, Ontario L2A 5X3

Not valid to current subscribers of the Romance Collection,
the Suspense Collection or the Romance/Suspense Collection.

Want to try two free books from another line?
Call 1-800-873-8635 or visit www.morefreebooks.com.

* Terms and prices subject to change without notice. Prices do not include applicable taxes. Sales tax applicable in N.Y. Canadian residents will be charged applicable provincial taxes and GST. Offer not valid in Quebec. This offer is limited to one order per household. All orders subject to approval. Credit or debit balances in a customer's account(s) may be offset by any other outstanding balance owed by or to the customer. Please allow 4 to 6 weeks for delivery. Offer available while quantities last.

Your Privacy: Harlequin is committed to protecting your privacy. Our Privacy Policy is available online at www.eHarlequin.com or upon request from the Reader Service. From time to time we make our lists of customers available to reputable third parties who may have a product or service of interest to you. If you would prefer we not share your name and address, please check here. ☐

BOB09

JENNIFER ARMINTROUT

32537	BLOOD TIES BOOK FOUR: ALL SOULS' NIGHT	___ $6.99 U.S.	___ $6.99 CAN.
32494	BLOOD TIES BOOK THREE: ASHES TO ASHES	___ $6.99 U.S.	___ $8.50 CAN.
32418	BLOOD TIES BOOK TWO: POSSESSION	___ $6.99 U.S.	___ $8.50 CAN.
32298	BLOOD TIES BOOK ONE: THE TURNING	___ $6.99 U.S.	___ $8.50 CAN.

(limited quantities available)

TOTAL AMOUNT	$ _____
POSTAGE & HANDLING	$ _____
($1.00 for 1 book, 50¢ for each additional)	
APPLICABLE TAXES*	$ _____
TOTAL PAYABLE	$ _____

(check or money order—please do not send cash)

To order, complete this form and send it, along with a check or money order for the total above, payable to MIRA Books, to: **In the U.S.:** 3010 Walden Avenue, P.O. Box 9077, Buffalo, NY 14269-9077; **In Canada:** P.O. Box 636, Fort Erie, Ontario, L2A 5X3.

Name: _____
Address: _____ City: _____
State/Prov.: _____ Zip/Postal Code: _____
Account Number (if applicable): _____

075 CSAS

*New York residents remit applicable sales taxes.
*Canadian residents remit applicable GST and provincial taxes.

MIRA®

www.MIRABooks.com
MJA1009BL